LUKE READER
blind detective

Also by Sean Dennis Cashman

BOOKS

*America Ascendant: From Theodore Roosevelt to FDR
in the Century of American Power, 1901–1945* (1998)

*America in the Gilded Age: From the Death of Lincoln to the Rise of
Theodore Roosevelt* (1984, 1988, 1993)

African-Americans and the Quest for Civil Rights 1900–1990 (1991)

America, Roosevelt, and World War II (1989)

*America in the Twenties and Thirties:
The Olympian Age of Franklin Delano Roosevelt* (1989)

*America in the Age of the Titans:
The Progressive Era and World War I* (1988)

Prohibition, the Lie of the Land (1981)

*Healing the Heart of the Cities:
Young Voices Speak Out* (Editor: Ford Foundation, 1994)

MUSICAL

Next Year in Jerusalem, Mark My Word
Musical by David Brown; music and lyrics by David Brown;
additional music by Matthew Brown; book by Sean Dennis Cashman
(2003)

ARTICLES include:
"African-Americans and the Quest for Civil Rights"
First chapter of 1992 book republished by Houghton Mifflin 2007 as
Chapter 11 in *Portrait of America, Volume 2: From Reconstruction to the
Present*, edited by Stephen B. Oates and Charles J. Errico

"Born to Dance: Scott Wise." *Spokesman-Review* (April 1999)

"Kurt Masur: London versus New York." *Musical America*:
Internet. December 15, 1998

"Act of Revenge: Bodybuilders at War." *Connecticut Magazine*
(January 1996)

Articles on Lauren Bacall, James Baldwin, Bela Bartok, Miles Davis,
Ralph Ellison, Leontyne Price, in *Encyclopaedia of New York City*
(Yale University Press, 1995)

97 Articles on US History, in *Oxford Illustrated Encyclopaedia: 4: World
History from 1800 to the Present Day* (Oxford University Press, 1988)

LUKE READER
blind detective

How New Yorker Luke Reader overcame going blind,
resisted the advances of his rehabilitation officer,
exposed the dark secret of a police chief,
and won a disability discrimination suit

Sean Dennis Cashman

First published in the United Kingdom in 2012
by Sixth Avenue Books

ISBN 978-0-9571281-0-1

Produced by
The Choir Press, Gloucester

Contents

For
Stephen Harrison,
loyal friend of many years,
whose support made possible the
publication of this book

Every day people discover that they are losing their eyesight. In addition to the physical and psychological shock, society sets them on paths of classification and rehabilitation—of "learning to be blind." Disabled people are also challenged by society's conventional expectations of beauty, whether in classic paintings, Hollywood movie star ideals, or glossy fashion plates. This novel is drawn from such experiences. Set in the late 1990s, the action of *Luke Reader* moves between New York as many might remember it and the fictional town of Norse Hoven that shares characteristics with various towns in New England, New Jersey, and Long Island. Any resemblance between characters in the novel and any persons living or dead is coincidental and unintended.

I thank Miles Bailey, director of The Choir Press, his colleagues Rachel Woodman and Adrian Sysum, and the copyeditor Fiona Thornton, for their care, diligence, and courtesy preparing this book for printing and publication. I also thank Spencer Pearce of the University of Manchester for supplying the Italian dialogue in the scene in Rome Airport.

Fall

---

1 New York Sunset

It was like a red tornado, a mini-atomic belch of red explosion in an abstract painting—and it was growing inside his head. Blaze! Boom! When Luke Reader saw what looked like a tomato growing in his eye, he knew what was happening. He had been there before.

It was 11:30 PM. The street outside McSorley's bar downtown glistened in the mellow October rain days before bitter wind would sweep through the open tunnels of Manhattan's streets. Outside, tiny yellow streetlights sparkled like tiny bulbs on premature Christmas trees, blinking in Luke's vision as if controlled by an on-off mechanism.

Spread out on the aged table were his precious grainy and well-thumbed photocopies of yesteryear beauties, film stars and fashion models among them, and his favorite, an unknown print model from Pennsylvania, honey blonde, amply shaped but slender with delicate features.

He had been collecting them for book illustrations.

There were just two of them in the bar.

Luke was finishing a side plate of potato chips when he caught sight of his reflection in the outsize fine-edged mirror behind the bar—a shady silhouette lit up in purple and green. He stood up. He was thinking, "I didn't know I had put on so much weight." He looked twice and saw himself twisted and thin and then shaky and undulating. But he knew he was perfectly still.

The bartender came into view, polishing glasses, ready to close.

"This guy really thinks a lot of himself," thought Luke as the bartender started to juggle the glasses, tossing them behind his back with his right hand and catching them with his left in front of his preening figure. For no apparent reason, Luke thought of Alice in Wonderland peering into the baby carriage and watching the tiny infant's face change into a pig's head. Then he realized that the bartender's face was also changing. His neat aquiline nose grew bulbous—a real W.C. Fields-schnozzle. His tight lips curled into a pucker like a melon about to burst, then twisted. His head swelled but also seemed to wobble.

When Luke steadied himself by looking down at the table, his precious beauties were starting to distort, the elfin Virginia Mayo seemed to be acquiring pendulous breasts, and Elizabeth Taylor was becoming skeletal, although he could still focus on her precious outsize pearl, la Peregrina. The pearl seemed to twinkle as if the photo was in 3D. Yes, it was true; everything was shimmering as if the earth moved.

Luke knew he was in the first movement of a macular hemorrhage, something that happened to very short-sighted people when an overstretched retina fractured at the focal point.

On that late night in downtown Manhattan, when the bartender came over to collect Luke's empty plate, he said, "Anything wrong, my friend? Seen a ghost?"

Luke could feel a tear rising. He gripped the uneven table.

"Been here before," added the bartender, helpfully. "Like the baseball player said, 'Déjà vu, all over again.'"

Luke could hardly say he *had* seen it all before because the point was not seeing.

"Better go," was all he could manage. He faltered as he rose and gripped the table again.

"That's right, my friend. Sleep on it."

Then, to the glass: "Half empty or half full?" asked the bartender, holding up the leftover Bloody Mary. "This dead?" he added inconsequentially.

"As a doornail."

Luke wanted to grope to the door. He knew if he did it would look as if he had had too much liquor and was trying to walk a straight line to seem sober. When he got outside, he gave a sigh of relief. It was raining heavily and Luke did not bother to brush aside his tears of frustration. Fumbling to fasten his coat collar and pulling his woolen hat down over his head gave him something to do besides walking ahead. The wobble in his eyes, the pelting rain, his slithering along glistening sidewalks—everything was a blur. There he was, bewildered—in some sort of psychological limbo between the inside of his head and the outside reality as the rain stormed around him while he edged forward.

For safety, he practically clung to the shop fronts along West 4th Street upwards to the point where 7th Avenue and 7th Avenue South met. As he neared the confusion of streets by the diminutive park, he gave out an audible sigh of relief that he did not have to cross the avenue but only grope his way across side streets.

Back in his apartment, he threw off his clothes and fell into bed. But he could not stay down. He put out the light and sat bolt upright, staring into the shadows. For something, anything, to occupy his mind till morning, he reviewed the past week, like flickering frames of an old movie, full of vibrant color. Luke's world was intensely visual. He knew that had already changed—as had his career as an assistant editor at the publishing house of the great and the good.

He stood five foot eleven, all freckled, preppy eagerness. Within himself, Luke was embarrassed by his unruly hair and the way his cheeks could blush vivid scarlet at jokes with innuendo and occasional praise from colleagues. He had already lost much of the sight in one eye in an accident. A bus on which he was traveling had swerved and made an emergency stop to avoid two kids with a ball. Someone had fallen onto Luke, her arm and hand thrust into his left eye, causing internal bleeding and leaving his sight distorted and reduced. But he kept quiet about that.

Very short-sighted anyway, he had long ago exchanged his coke-bottle eye glasses for Boston gas permeable contact lenses that he wore despite discomfort because his pigmentation made him intolerant of soft lenses and that discomfort made him frequently on edge. There were always drops to counteract conjunctivitis, other drops to keep his eyes moist, and to control glaucoma—a wearing round of dependency.

Along East 42nd Street, around Grand Central he used to gaze longingly at enticing opticians' adverts for disposable contact lenses you could wear for a week, and for laser treatment—all at apparently peppercorn prices. At one time, when he was an undergraduate, Luke had been enticed into enquiries inside the opticians—but no longer. For sales staff's dire response was uniform: "Sorry, not in your prescription" or "Not in your case; you have too many other optical issues."

Ironically, at college, professors had praised Luke's unerring eye for distinctive images. But his art classes taught him that, as a painter, he was in the third division. But he was good at those interfaces where art, social history, and literature collide. Indeed, Luke Reader breathed and almost tasted images in paintings, photos, and movies.

Luke's first brief in the publishing house of the great and the good on 3rd Avenue had been to locate prints and photographs, help manage publicity, and check copy-editing. For a front-of-house display for Professor Theo Cardenza's book on Stalin, Luke arranged pictures in playful apposition: a cartoon Stalin as a bird of prey aside Ivan the Terrible from

Sergei Eisenstein's film. The tsar's hulking shape and the pattern of his gown were echoed by the slither of rock in which he stood and the trailing snake of the abject crowd below. Luke enhanced this deft interplay by setting it against a parrot-like Long John Silver cartoon of Stalin. His display caught the eye of ambitious editor Mickey Garnier.

"See here, kid, your work for Professor Cardenza is interesting. You're motivated in a task many people dislike doing. What drives you?"

"Well," Luke took the risk of appearing childish. He did not say that the very thought of Ivan Grozny filled him with shame. Instead, he said, "Like Alice in Wonderland I always ask, 'What is the use of a book without pictures?'"

That was the start of his rise through the ranks. In the publishing world bursting with words and still more words cascading upon editors and their drones, Luke was the gofer who could find the perfect picture for every chapter, every book, every title. He soon found his way round the various collections of all sorts of illustrations, the Bettmann Archive, archives of New York museums, the Prints and Photographs Collection of the Library of Congress in Washington, and even the little store on the south side of 14th Street in Manhattan between 7th and 8th Avenues that sold movie stills over the counter.

Luke loved what he did and could never decide which cliché best summed up his hitherto charmed existence in New York. Was it the blue sky over Manhattan that tasted like fine champagne or that every time he went to work he seemed to smell the whiff of ever greater success ahead? With his boundless enthusiasm and yuppie optimism, Luke Reader was riding the crest of a wave. The 1990s were drawing to an end. He looked forward to the dawning of the new millennium, imagining that the start of the twenty-first century would be his golden period. Luke was the man, whether it was to redress faulty copy-editing or rearrange illustrations so that clever juxtaposition enhanced images uninteresting in themselves. That was why he had been fast-tracked to assistant editor for books on art, and history, ancient and modern. Yet, underneath the skein of compliments and prophecies of future potential, Luke harbored a disturbing fear about his eyesight.

That morning he moved along Midtown, his head brimming with ideas and images from his current assignment from Mickey Garnier.

"The writer is an ardent feminist," Mickey had told him two days earlier. Her book is about male eroticization of the female figure. It's thorough but it needs some pizzazz."

"What's it called?"

"'Viragos, Virgins, and Vamps: Showpieces of Women as Victims.'"

Intrigued, Luke could not resist peeking into parts of the text that detailed the commercial transformation of Marilyn Monroe and Audrey Hepburn into mass-produced icons in the 1960s. However, he was stumped when it came to finding anything other than dowdy images in the film stills of the 1920s. He decided to call Hermione, his mother's best friend. Luke knew that they had both been in love with his brother and, when they lost him, somehow this had made them firm friends. Hermione lived in Norse Hoven, seventy-plus miles from New York

Courteous but to the point, she said, "Women discarding corsets and bustles eighty years ago were not followed by a boyish figure in the 1920s—whatever historians say. The abrupt sheath dress and bobbed hair were ultra-feminine. They carried men's eyes upward along plastic limbs of arms and legs. This was ultra-provocative in a society steeped in covered-up women and their amplified bustles that dared to rustle."

Luke considered Hermione's words and went back to books in the NYU Bobst Library in Washington Square.

There he threw himself into finding full-length Hollywood images of stars with flesh impact to prove his point: mannish lapels with firm lines on Marlene Dietrich and wasp-waist dresses on Bette Davis.

"That'll show 'em," he thought.

Hermione had also recommended that he consider a collection of Vogue and Vanity Fair-type models from the 1960s. Their photos were reproduced in a coffee-table book aimed at the nostalgia market. He might—just possibly— locate this in a second-hand bookstore in Greenwich Village. Finding just such a book on a street vendor's stall, he thought it might be worth a try. Ignoring Jean Shrimpton and Twiggy, two pictures leaped out at him.

The first was interesting because of the caption that said that Juno Foster, a fetching brunette in a Dior gown, was from Norse Hoven. The other model was the honey blonde from Pennsylvania with a magnetic smile and a body that, as photographed, was special. It conformed to the *de rigueur* conditions of emaciation yet the model palpitated with three-dimensional enticing curves. Luke made photocopies and wrote down the references.

In his cowl-like cell, Mickey Garnier, the editor, had been more than a little impressed by Luke's findings, especially the unknown beauty from Pennsylvania.

"I don't know that the author will appreciate your eyes being keener than hers but I sure do. You've saved this book. As always, kiddo, one thing's crystal clear: you live for, you practically exude, visual images. Your name says it all: Luke Reader: you look and you read—none better."

Happy with success early that afternoon, Luke walked down 3rd Avenue. Then a punch landed in the face as he turned a corner gave him other priorities than finding more portraits.

He heard the sound of a scuffle round the corner of East 44th Street immediately before he turned into it. As he did so, a huge hard guy in a blue T-shirt hit him fair and square in the face. It floored him as the guy fairly jumped across the avenue, wending his way like a streaking pro in and out of the path of stationary and moving cars at the lights.

Another man, older, grayer, dapper, was at Luke's side, helping him to his feet.

"You hurt, guy? He got you fair and square. Boy, were you in the wrong place at the wrong time. The guy had ripped a gold chain off of the neck of this young lady in the bar down the street."

"Thanks," sputtered Luke. "Just a shock."

A bottle blonde, tears streaming away her eyeliner, was at his side.

"Thank you, young man, for trying to stop him, the damn thief."

"I did nothing—just got in the way."

She was not listening.

"I was sitting with my girl friend, having a cocktail in our neighborhood bar when this—this brute—tore my necklace off."

She caressed her neck and Luke could see where the tearing away had strained her skin sore till it was bleeding a little. Suddenly, she was off with her new, older protector. Luke stood and winced. His cheek hurt real badly. When he looked around, the victim and her new protector had gone, lost in the flotsam and jetsam of New York's passenger traffic as the bustling people of the city that never sleeps moved like automatons on their sleepwalking way.

Luke got back to his apartment. He phoned Hermione and gave her the bad news.

"Are you sure, really sure?" she asked.

"No doubt."

"Call me tomorrow."

Then Luke braced himself for the inevitable by going out again and reaching for the bottle in his favorite watering spot on the nearby East Side. When it came in McSorley's bar—the effects of the punch to his face—it was, indeed, like the spattered explosion of red in a Mark Rothko abstract painting.

2 Diagnoses

The next morning, as soon as it started to get light, Luke rose, poured himself some milk to cushion the aching pit of his stomach, washed and dressed as if by rote. On the back of an envelope, he scrawled a note for his roommate to explain where he was going and went out.

Inside the Manhattan Eye, Ear and Throat Hospital on East 64th Street, Luke felt so uptight he wanted to wrap himself in the jaundice-green color of the walls. While he waited in the emergency section, from a side consulting room, he heard, but could not see, a doctor arguing with a nurse.

"They've no right to treat us like that. I completed all the forms on time, had them counter-signed, and made sure all the receipts were in order. Now, I'm summoned like some high-school dropout."

"I know, Ira," replied the offstage nurse. "Try and calm down. You've got four patients waiting."

"Christ, they get here earlier and earlier."

"It is a hospital."

"One running out of money and, maybe, next week we'll all be out on our ass."

Then the doctor poked his head out of the door. His red hair, as flaming as his flushed face and anger, struck Luke.

"This won't do your blood pressure any good," went on the nurse from inside the consulting room. "Or mine."

"The doctor looks worse than I feel," Luke thought.

"Hi!" opened the doctor, with an assumption of instant-aneously acquired decorum. "I'm Dr. Ira."

Luke jolted himself. He had his own reciprocal mask of composure. "Ira—is that because you're irate?"

Uncomfortable that he had allowed his invective against the hospital to be overheard, the young doctor's face went redder than his hair. Anxious to reassert his authority, he snapped back with a glare, "It's because I rate with the best. I'm Dr. Ira Haile."

Luke sensed his unease, first the unexpected contretemps over expenses and now over a more unexpected diagnosis.

"What's up, then, doc since you seem to know?" sneered Dr. Haile.

"I'm having a macular hemorrhage—in my right eye."

"How do you know that?" asked Dr. Haile with disbelief. "Self-diagnosis?"

"I had one about ten years ago in the left eye—someone crashed into me on a bus when it jolted: it's a very distinc-tive experience—not one you're likely to forget."

"What are the symptoms?"

"It's like watching a tomato grow in your eye—the blood you know."

"When did this start to happen?"

"About eleven last night."

"We'll take a look. First, we'll need to dilate your eyes."

"Shall I take out my contact lenses?"

"Sure." The doctor had obviously suppressed a smart aleck remark about pearls and swine. For that Luke was grateful.

Sure thing it was. Luke's eyes dilated quickly.

Like many contact-wearers, Luke was a pliant patient, amenable to the inspection, to following instructions for the magnifying lens. Yellow dye stung his eyes as he nudged his head forward in a metal frame for the doctor to examine them while he was perfectly still.

"So," remarked Luke during the examination and trying to lighten the situation by ceding ground graciously to the still-angry young man, "Dr. Haile, you come highly recommended."

"Correct."

It had worked. Dr. I-rate-with-the-best soon got excited. The accounts were forgotten.

"It *is* a macular hemorrhage. And it's in full bloom. You know at present, there's no treatment. You were right to come in. You must avoid all contact sports—football, ice hockey, basketball, and so on. Be careful about bumping into things, no knocks to the head that can jolt the retina again, make it snap from its moorings and get detached."

"Yes, sir!" said as if Luke was standing to attention.

"You've been here before so you also know that the blood will drain. Your condition is pathological myopia—the retina is overstretched because the eye is too long and you get all sorts of adverse side effects—floaters, tears—you've got more than your fair share of those—glaucoma. I can see where there's been a repair to your right retina."

"Yes, it was detaching when they caught it—also about ten years ago."

"But the eye's still scarred—and now you have this hemorrhage. Had a blow to the head?"

Luke gave a telegram version of his story about being knocked down. The doctor nodded. Luke concluded, "And, where the retina heals, my sight will remain distorted at this focal point."

"When you say you see things distorted, what do you mean?"

"When I look at things with my left eye, they're all curvy and twisted. So, if I look at the floor of the Bobst Library at NYU with its vivid patterns of black and white—"

"A jolting visual experience, anyway—"

"I'll say. The different tile panels of black and white merge into one another; it's like they're dancing in a macabre way and not all on the same level. Still objects come right up at you."

"Your left eye is weaker than your right eye and so you're developing a lazy eye so you will begin to see double."

Luke knew the doctor was ahead of him.

"You won't go blind in the sense of total eclipse—darkness—but your sight will remain distorted. For years you've managed everything with just one good eye—well, lots of people do that. But now both eyes are damaged.

"Where do you work?" asked Dr. Haile.

Luke told him.

"What exactly does your job in publishing involve?"

"Reading manuscripts, selecting illustrations, tidying up copy-editing. Here's the thing, it needs heaps of reading and scrutinizing. It has to be done at speed and with razor-like precision."

"That sort of work involving details your eyes can't manage is out of the question, I'm sorry to say. You won't be able to sort things, compare pictures, and check details. Your other eye has only a limited field and what there is, is distorted. This latest accident has damaged your better eye in the same place. At present it's all blood and wobbly distortion. There's no question of you working in publishing at the same sort of job—at least for six months, maybe longer."

Although there was now a little warmth between them, Luke felt that the doctor enjoyed taking the high ground of professional supremacy, and that he was twisting and turning his medical expertise to undermine Luke's sense of worth. It was almost as if he was trying to make Luke feel ashamed of his eyes.

"Hmm. Now, we'd like to ask you a favor."

Luke was all ears.

"Can we photo your eye? Usually when people come to

the hospital and something is wrong with their eyes, the process is well under way, maybe it's over, but, since you came almost immediately, the hemorrhage is on full course. You don't have to agree, but, if you do, the photo will help doctors and their patients in future. If you agree, we'll have to inject a dye into your veins for the retinal photo to work; it's painless."

"Yes."

While they took the photo, the running injection hurt damn bad.

After it was over, Dr. Haile said, "Make an appointment at the desk to come back in ten days' time."

That was his farewell.

Luke felt relief—even though all that had happened was that he had had his suspicions confirmed. Then he realized that he needed to pee. He had not been all morning. He went to the men's room and started to urinate in one of the bowls. He could not believe it. His urine was a psychedelic orange glow. He thought he had finished. Then he realized he could not stop. It went on and on.

"Jeez, s'pse someone comes in and sees all this day-glow color," he thought as his water cascaded over the white enamel and down the shoot. He felt dizzy again. When he was done, he groped his way to an empty chair outside behind a line of people in reception. When he stumbled out of the hospital, the rain had stopped. The sun was in high heaven beaming down on him. The light was so intense into his dilated eyes that he trembled.

Luke knew that all his learning could not save his career. He recognized that all the wit and wisdom in his beloved books had really been as much a shield from the world as a sword in the battles of life. Luke had fully grasped the doctor's message that his time with the publishing house of the great and the good might be numbered in minutes rather than hours, let alone days.

When he knocked on Mickey Garnier's open door, Mickey was ready for him. He even stopped chewing his lunchtime sandwich.

"Where the hell have you been, kiddo? We've been calling you all morning. When your roommate answered, he said you'd gone to a hospital. We needed the Viragos and Virgins job done like yesterday. What's going on?"

"Mind if I close the door?" asked Luke.

He took another grunt from Mickey as permission. When Luke had finished his story and told him he could not see well enough to get the pictures ready for the book, Mickey threw the remains of his lunch into the trash bin.

"Guess I lost my appetite. Cheer up, kid. What was it Greta Garbo said to Laurence Olivier just after she got him fired? 'Life's a bitch.' Give yourself four weeks. Give me four weeks. Then we'll talk. I'll be sure to call you. I'm on my way to our accountants uptown. I'll come down with you in the elevator."

When they left the gleaming rose-marble-clad lobby, hardened editor and no-longer-rising picture assistant editor went their separate ways into bustling streets, moving through sunshine speckled with shade from buildings and trees. Both were too discomfited to heed the noise of cars and trucks and take stock of the folk hurrying along the streets of Manhattan Island, nestling between three rivers and the mighty sea.

However, at the corner of the block, Luke glanced back and noticed Mickey Garnier having a last furtive puff along with other cigarette smokers—the usual motley collection of New York workers all the way from CEOs to cleaners and janitors, ostracized from their workplace while they took their nicotine fix. In his new eyesight, they seemed to undulate and quiver like some post-modern art installation, although Luke knew they were standing still.

Mickey Garnier had now lost his prize tool. Luke was

without a job and, because he was so junior, he had no rights as regards compensation apart from temporary sick pay. He had lost his career, his identity.

He called Hermione again.

"I have to face the fact that my career—every prospect I had—they've all been eliminated in an instant—along with the faculties that enabled them."

Hermione was as welcoming as ever.

"Luke, I know you're not asking, but we've been here before with your brother's eye condition years ago. I know the score. You've come to the end of your funds. Your publishing job in the city is out of the question for the time being. You'd better come and stay here. There's plenty of room. Once you've adjusted, you can think things out—whatever it is you want to do. Money's always tight but, if you need cash, there are plenty of temp jobs available."

And that was what Luke Reader did. He made arrangements to move to the twin New England towns of Norse Hoven and Babel City. He was able to cede his apartment completely to his roommate because the roommate's girlfriend wanted to move in. And he traveled light.

On the Metro North train journey to New England, once so familiar when Luke had been a regular weekend visitor to Hermione, he felt strangely comforted by familiar sights. The train was treading ground he knew. His newer sight could still recognize, albeit in a distorted way, the American landscape.

At South Norwalk, the train cut into the streets of the town at an acute diagonal angle as if it were about to hurtle into the black windows of the terracotta-colored office buildings and lodge itself on a ledge of their ochre-colored setbacks, leaving everyone stranded on high, awaiting rescue by the fire department. That image seemed even sharper in Luke's eyesight with the distortion at the macular center. Now the sharp, cutting, dividing lines were twisted into undulating curves.

There was the same old Stamford to dazzle travelers with its panorama of glass-wall skyscrapers of billion-dollar corporations just hinting at shanty poverty behind. And Bridgeport, with its profusion of shoddy clapboard houses just peeking at the train behind token attempts of urban renewal, was still thrusting its decline into the gaze of passers-through.

Then they were at the final stop, Norse Hoven, once the supposed arrival point of Norsemen who had come to the Americas before Columbus. Now it was better known as host town to the great Milhous College. Luke came through the tunnel under the tracks to the main railroad station, a turn-of-the-twentieth-century building with a spacious atrium and sky-high upper windows, plus a collection of bijouterie retail outlets. Everything was now prematurely decorated with outsize Christmas garlands and wreaths.

From the commotion, Luke soon realized that the station had been turned into a temporary film set, host to a Bollywood movie. Troupes of chorines in saris were awaiting their cue.

Luke thought he would be blinded by the outsize arc lights. Security guards led him and other passengers to the main entrance where, by the taxi rank, many cars and drivers were awaiting their expected guests.

Among the passengers waiting for a taxi ride into the town was a young African-American man with stick-insect legs, already rigged out in black vampire costume with a cape for Halloween that had something written on the back in silver speckles. Through the open window of his cab, Luke heard him tell the taxi driver, "Remedial Recuperation Services, Brook Street, and sharp about it."

Then Luke heard to his side, "Hi! I'm Steve Sharp, Hermione's neighbor."

This came from a man with abundant sandy hair, button nose, and designer casual clothes.

"Hermione asked me to meet you and I recognized you straightaway."

Steve chatted enthusiastically while his flash car sped along the longer, more scenic route that, because there was less traffic, was a quicker route to Hermione's suburban home. They skirted the desert of downtown urban renewal; juggled left and right through gentrified streets with their yuppie cafes and bars. They sped past arboretum neighborhoods and aside a craggy hillside park to descend to Hermione's house from Rigid Street that ran along the hillcrest.

"Where the rich live; this way, we avoid the hoi polloi," explained Steve Sharp.

Luke was not used to such enthusiasm over nothing. Steve Sharp sensed Luke's unease and had an explanation ready.

"Hermione's my opposite neighbor. We help one another out. My wife died two years ago and I work for the Network News Norse Hoven TV station as a news editor: long hours. Hermione's good enough to take care of my nine-year-old, Dennis."

Indeed, Hermione was ready with young Dennis who opened the door and fairly leaped with joy onto his father when he and Luke got out of the car. It was all very doting, very picket-fence contentment, without any fence in sight.

Hermione's several cats were looking at this interloper through, Luke suspected, gritted teeth as if to say, "This is kitty heaven; don't even think about disturbing us."

Hermione interrupted her reading of the *Norse Hoven Courier* to reheat Luke's dinner in the microwave. Luke caught sight of the articles she had set aside. She started to read while she waited for the microwave to ping.

"It says that 'Zack Flower, 24, a young father of three, was shot dead in broad daylight at the junction of Olive and Pearl Streets. Someone pulled up at the intersection in a

Ford and showered his pizza delivery van with 9mm bullets from a Russian Baikal pistol. Police believe that the delivery boy was killed because Louvre Ville drug gang leaders thought he was a member of a rival gang, the Hill Crew.'"

Hermione turned again to the newspaper.

"Hmm. Here's an interesting detail: 'Police Chief Leo Guerra, known for his flamboyant sense of dress with power ties, metal-studded belts, expensive gold cufflinks, and his assertive comments, said, "This case has necessitated an extraordinary amount of work for the police".'"

"That's it, Luke, my dear. Welcome to the university city of spires in the air and dreams spiraling down as another one bites the dust.

"However you see your life—in five acts like classical theater or three like Broadway plays—if you live in this city the backdrop is drug dealing, drug wars, killings, police raids. Be wise. Beware. Be wary."

Luke steeled himself for whatever lay ahead. He knew the curtain was slowly descending on his eyesight yet he sensed a different curtain was rising on the darkness of Norse Hoven.

3 Speedy the Vampire

Halloween was a bomb, all right. It was not yet October 31st but Speedy the Vampire was in for a big surprise when he took his cab from the downtown railroad station where they were filming the Bollywood movie.

He had come to wreak havoc in downtown Norse Hoven but his reign of terror did not go according to plan. Yet he had prepared everything meticulously: his spooky makeup, his tight, figure-hugging black jeans and slashed leather jacket, his name displayed in sequins pasted onto his cape, and, most importantly, his balloon pouches filled with baboon blood for spraying around, and, not least, the card for his agreed appointment at the Bureau of Remedial Recuperation Services.

Once inside the converted redbrick factory building, he walked gingerly up the sixty steps to the reception office on the third floor—not taking the elevator so as to avoid attention. Once there, pausing for breath, he gave his bog-standard US name to the sullen receptionist. He looked her over as she asked him to sit and wait for remedial officer Marie Louise Garden.

Speedy the Vampire sat down. He took precautionary notice of the other guy waiting—a thickset dark-haired man with jutting chin, huge arms, and the washed-out look of a habitual druggie.

"Easy-peasy," said Speedy the Vampire to himself.

Yet Speedy was distracted by the silent guy's sudden bursts of hand movements; first, he flapped his hands and, then, his whole body seemed to shake. Then he dived in and out of his paper carton of chicken nuggets, like a fox sniffing about.

"Ms. Marie Louise Garden will see you now," said the sullen receptionist. "Here she is."

With that, Speedy got a jolt and no mistake.

First, he wondered if he was looking through a telescope the wrong way round. He stared in utter astonishment.

To say Marie Louise was small would exaggerate the dimensions that "small" implies. She was tiny and deformed. It looked as if her body and frame had not grown properly but disjointed and as if her bones were about to shatter the slender covering of skin.

As he moved forward, Speedy could see she had a lopsided gait because of a disjointed hip. Her diminutive body extended to scrawny but muscular arms peeping out of her smock like pipe cleaners. Speedy sensed that the other guy waiting on the nearby pretend leather sofa was also staring in astonishment.

Speedy pulled himself together when this diminutive, lame creature hobbled towards him.

She said, "Come this way."

Her tone was guttural, baritonal, and unfeminine.

He accompanied her along an open corridor.

"Listen, honey," he purred as they proceeded, "in my pocket"—he patted his jacket—"I have a balloon filled with HIV-infected blood. I'm going to spray your fucking walls with it. Just run between the drops, honey. When I splatter everything everywhere, you'll sure want to miss the speckles."

But meeting this strange dwarf had thrown Speedy off-balance.

For her part, Marie Louise started for a moment but steadied herself momentarily against the white corridor wall. As they walked what, after all, was only a short distance but that day seemed to last forever, Marie Louise realized what Speedy the Vampire's problem was. He was afraid of her and other disabled people. His hatred was rooted in his anxiety. This gave her flickering courage on the slender thread of this realization that, whatever her physical frailty, she was emotionally stronger than he was. That was her reasoning. Without a glance, she pressed a button low down the wall.

Carmine, the receptionist, was at her side in a trice. Carmine had an awkward manner so gauche as to seem truculent. But, as a former police receptionist, she had hidden skills. Carmine touched the vampire's elbow. Then she took his lower arm. Her grip was like a vice but her tone was all Oprah Winfrey at her most winning:

"Let's talk this through, sir."

Speedy's dead red eyes narrowed with more surprise.

"I'm ready to shoot my load," he sneered, sticking to his script but with much less conviction.

By then Carmine had somehow steered him around. He found himself in the middle of a trio as they retraced their steps to the elevator.

Marie Louise was visibly shaking. Pro that she was, she set her face grimly. The elevator was already at their floor and opened to Carmine's touch.

For Speedy, it was now or never.

"I'm not suffering from insanity if that's what you're thinking. I'm enjoying every minute of this. Is it good for you? Catch this, ladies of the night," he called out exultantly.

But before he could "shoot his load," he had fallen to the floor, whacked in the back of the knees. The other guy from the couch had felled him sure enough.

Next, Speedy found he was trapped in the elevator with this bizarre, mismatched trio, a leering dwarf, a lady bull, and a thicko with bad breath. When the elevator opened on the lobby floor, two policemen were waiting.

"Come this way," said the uglier cop.

"How butch!" stuttered Speedy.

"We'll give you butch!"

Speedy found himself dragged out of the elevator, frog-marched to the car lot, turned around, and spread-eagled over the front of the police car.

"You can't do this to me, I've done nothing wrong," spluttered Speedy.

"Face the car, punk, and keep your arms and hands stretched over the body while we search you."

"You can't search me. I ain't got no drugs. I ain't done nothin'. I know my rights."

"You ain't got rights, punk."

"What are you, punk? Shitty in yourself and the cause of shit in others."

21

Speedy was getting increasingly hysterical.

"You can't make a whore of my sister and shut me up."

"We can do whatever we want, punk. We make the law. Now you shut it."

As the cops forced Speedy forward over the cop car, a little photo fluttered away from him.

Speedy heard the other cop say to the Remedial staff, "Thank you, Carmine. You, too, Ms. Garden. We'll take your statements later. You, too, sir."

This last was said to the new client, who bent down to pick up the photo.

"Real pr-pr-pretty," he said, eying the portrait of a teenage girl with tiny white imitation flowers dotted in her braided hair.

The cops were not interested and he pocketed the print.

One of the cops took a handkerchief from his pocket and partly wiped off Speedy's makeup.

"Just as I thought: it's our old friend Rayard Quint. Well, who'd've thunk it?"

"See, Mac, look what's here—little balloons filled with black stuff."

"Ink, d'ye think?"

The last thing Marie Louise heard Speedy say was, "Call yourselves rehab officers when you won't help my disabled sister and leave her in the gutter to be grabbed by the fuzz?"

Marie Louise could not suppress a sigh of relief that he was gone.

And this tragicomic incident was Marie Louise's introduction to Louis Cans, whom she had expected to meet at eleven, ahead of the introductory group meeting at noon. Already he was her savior.

"Thank you," she said.

Louis answered, "You're we-we-welcome."

4 Louis Cans

The two of them stared at one another.

To Louis Cans, to think this remedial officer was a grown-up, and yet someone who also looked like a child of six—as he discovered later the age of children's clothes Marie Louise Garden bought—might give an impression that she was like a grave little girl. But her outsize head with beaky nose, wizened features, and over-cherried lips was crowned with a flame of gaudily dyed, refulgent hair, decked out with girlie, cutie bows. The effect made her look part ever-watchful American eagle, part Cupie Doll.

Marie Louise was scrutinizing Louis. He seemed to be about five foot ten, had broad shoulders, and naturally powerful arms. He had tight curly dark brown hair cropped close and a small dark mustache above his generous lips. She thought Louis might have Mexican parents. His nondescript clothes suggested charity shop re-sales, chosen at random, apart from a stylish black leather jacket he had hung carefully over the back of the chair in her office.

As Louis listened glumly, Marie Louise glanced at some of his notes from the psychological study—all written by a psychiatrist to show that Louis was a classic Asperger Syndrome guy. She noted the phrases "miscomprehension of nuance" and "abrupt transitions," and "excellent auditory and visual perception."

Marie Louise tried to get down to business. She had read in the file that Louis was twenty-seven but he seemed so washed-up he looked nearer forty.

"Years of self-destructive behavior," she told herself thinking of the formulaic summaries in her training. Against the chances of Louis being able to hold down a job were ranged a whole raft of conventional social and ideological barriers.

As surprised as he was by her, Louis was equally startled by Marie Louise's office. The desk and high chair were adapted for her to mount a scaffold to the desk for the day's work. Then, some other details on her desk caught his eye: a family photo of a strikingly lovely woman, two little brown bags, and a toy fox.

Marie Louise read his mind and thought it might lighten him if she said, "Yes, that's my mom. Very beautiful—especially in her heyday as a honey-brunette. She worked as a print model, you know—for clothes catalogs and magazines."

Louis did not take this as an overture to speak about his own mother. He said simply, as if Marie Louise's opening overture was for him to present to her another photo of a beautiful woman, "The guy dropped this. The cops weren't bo-bo-bothered."

Louis handed Marie Louise the shabby photo and she put it on her desk among the piles of papers.

From the first moment she heard Louis's drawling voice in her office with its disarming, raspy inflections, Marie Louise knew this former construction worker would become her current obsession—although she hated to use that word, even privately to herself. But he was not marriageable material.

Louis's file summary also told her that, when he was sixteen, his stepfather had turned him out of his home for smoking pot. He had been in and out of trouble for petty crimes of shoplifting, even joyriding, but there was nothing of truly serious consequence, except that his crimes were always drug-related. The implication was that his brain was addled.

Liberal Marie Louise saw Louis's drug problems as a token of his feeling worthless. Louis had too much time on his hands because he was not working and he was not working because he could never stick to anything. It was as if his mind's response to his descent into a toxic round of poverty and petty crime, of loneliness and drugs, was inner moaning.

"I thought we should talk and get to know one another before the main introductory meeting at noon."

Silence.

"At Remedial Recuperation, our aim is to get clients, people who are recently disabled mentally or physically by some accident—industrial, domestic, or automobile—or long-term ill-health, back into the world of work. Once there, we're here to protect them against adverse, discriminatory office politics."

With this spiel, Marie Louise knew she had already lost Louis. Yet, it was so simple. Her disabled clients needed education to acquire benefits and master the mysteries of complex forms, and, through the contacts of Remedial Recuperation Services, to get them placed in some simpatico organization.

As the conversation continued, Louis noted more about Marie Louise. As she moved papers around her desk, he realized that, without her puce-coated hearing aids, she was deaf. As she hesitated in reading his file documents, he recognized magnifying glasses, an auditory loop, targeted lights, and two faded beanbags among the physical stock-in-trade of the office. Marie Louise used her many appliances with double dexterity.

Marie Louise started playing with one of the beanbags, molding it in her hands, as she started to think things out. She started softly.

"How's where you live?"

Louis knew it was now or never. He wasn't used to speaking to strangers but something in his core told him this little woman could help him open doors. It would be better to make a show of cooperation.

"It's funny, in a way. I'm gr-gr-grown up. It's a halfway house, I know that. But I'm supposed to get p-p-permission for such everyday things that they turn into pr-pr-privileges like going out alone or bringing a girl back."

"It's named Lancaster House, after one of the towns in the north of England where they started the cooperative movement during the Industrial Revolution.

"We're trying to get you back on your feet and in places like Lancaster House, there are house rules to help you get better organized so that you can re-enter the world of work."

Then came his alcohol-aged voice again. Marie Louise found herself both aroused by it and wanting to imitate it as Louis answered back, "It's meant to be about rewards but it's about p-p-punishments. There's a cu-cu-curfew and I'm twenty-seven years old—not a little child."

In her mind, Marie Louise went back to her training instructions about organizing disabled people. She decided that Louis's response was just the standard response of a disabled resident to the discipline of halfway houses: conversion and colonization, or withdrawal and intransigence.

When Marie Louise started to question him further, it became clear that Louis did not know what he was doing—except that he was trying to avoid reprisals. He was staring at her toy fox. She would set up some training sessions for him—remedial Math and English lessons. They agreed to meet in a week.

Marie Louise heard her co-worker, Rod Fortune, start his seamless speech at the group session.

"Welcome, you guys, to Remedial Recuperation Services. You're here because you need help—primarily financial because bills travel through the mail twice as fast as your pay checks. We know. We empathize. But we are a state-run, non-profit organization—that is 'profit' with an 'f' and 'prophet' with a 'ph': we can't predict your future. We can't wipe the slate clean."

Rod went on to summarize categories of disabled people whom RRS could help and categories whom RRS could not help, either because the level of impairment was not serious enough or because another state organization was responsible, as was the case of VIPs: visually impaired people.

Marie Louise witnessed the gathering glide seamlessly into the distribution of application forms for completion. The whole process rattled along with the sort of clickety-click precision Marie Louise identified with railway journeys. She glanced at her co-workers, John Cash and Jimmy Carey. They were the office's well-known Cash and Carry.

Marie Louise thought co-workers Cash and Carry, despite their professions of support, regarded her as a deviant—that she was just there to boost their statistics of disabled employees and make the state's portfolio of disabled workers look better. She was quick to determine office politics of promotion, demotion, and hypocrisy.

She thought it was so odd that here they were in this loft renovation of a former factory building, all red brick and dark iron supporting beams aside one of the world's supposed great universities whose older stone buildings were being unsheathed from industrial grime to reveal dark-pink rose-colored stone. It was as if the great university cast a pall by the spread of its Colonial presence from the heart of the old quadrangle with its eighteenth-century buildings and white Georgian window frames and green side shutters, in a style repeated across the city from banks to bars. Yet there was such a division between town and gown that the great mind of the one, protected from giving by its charitable status, never supported the stomach of the other, the town of Norse Hoven that remained physically impoverished, as if its very soul was being starved.

That must certainly be the way these clients saw it.

Back in her office, Marie Louise began a campaign for Louis Cans's career rehabilitation, starting with a modicum of social security payments until he was back in work.

Her colleague and ally, Rod, went to the little onsite library and brought back a red box file with photocopies of articles.

"It says, here, and we know this: that 'Autism Spectrum Disorder, or Asperger Syndrome, is characterized by difficulties in social interaction and communication and restricted interests and repetitive behavior. ASD begins in infancy and has a steady course without remission. There is intense preoccupation with a narrow subject, physical clumsiness.'"

Having started to imitate the way Louis Cans spoke her name, "Marie Louise," she seemed to find some sexual satisfaction from his croaky modulation. That was to herself. To her co-worker, she simply said, "Rod, we can never rehabilitate him while he's confined to a hand-to-mouth existence."

"Like living on bu-bu-burgers?"

Marie Louise gave him a sharp look as if to tell him not to mock her new darling.

"Another thing," added Rod with all the hindsight benefit of a psychology graduate who had written a much-praised thesis on alienation in dysfunctional families, "Remember, this young guy has been passed around from foster family to foster family since he was six. Friendships presented, then withdrawn. It is not possible for him to forge lasting ties with other people.

"This has increased his AS problems. All children want companionship. AS children are more at risk of failed social encounters and this failure numbs their innate needs. It's not his fault. You always go the extra mile. I don't want you to get hurt. He cannot reciprocate. Remember."

But Louis Cans was not ready to fall into Marie Louise's web. Not yet.

5 Fireworks at Halloween

That same night, after a soulless dinner and an early evening sleep in which Louis Cans dreamed of the two women in the photos, the teenage girl in the hood's lost picture and the beauty on Marie Louise's desk, he planned to get high, as he always told himself, just one last time. He waited at the side of a late-night downtown bar for the johns to come out, hoping they would give him some change before they tumbled their ways home. He noted the working girl, Della, with the amazing legs and the flashing smile get into a car with a john. She signaled "Hi!" with a miniscule wave. Although it was late October, they were having an Indian summer and to Louis the night seemed alive with mosquitoes. He hated mosquitoes.

From time to time fireworks went off, as if this was just as much a way of celebrating Halloween as trick or treat.

First, Louis took a hit in the shadowy recesses of a closed shop front, and then staggered onto a slip road leading to a thruway. An auto knocked him down and sped carelessly away into the night. When Louis came to, his head was ringing.

Crying out, "Jeez!" he clambered up the grassy bank of the slip road only to fall down into the main road again.

Then, all of a sudden, things went wrong once more. It was as if someone had lit a firework that seemed to explode above the raw confusion of the city streets. All Louis could do was to crouch down, hoping no one would find him. This time a truck hit him fair and square.

High, desperate, and paranoid though he was, Louis realized his right leg had been hit damned sore. In the midst of all the blaring noise, the pain in his leg whined as if it was singing tenor above the automobile drums. It was like a never-ending scream. Louis sensed his leg lay at an awkward angle to his body. Leaning against a slope, he bent forward to touch it. He knew what it was. He felt he was in a swamp and his body was perforated with cavities, all sorts of pools being trampled by the tiny feet of little animals. He slipped into unconsciousness.

During Louis's coma, it was as if the outside world was just beyond his paper-thin skin. When it was bright, it was like an opaque summer day and he was lying supine by a pool, surrounded by dragonflies. He thought of beer and dozed off. Once he imagined a passing mosquito landing on his cheek. He thought that, to the tiny mosquito, it must be like an airplane landing on a runway. Beyond the runway of his cheek he had a funny sense of there being an angel protecting him. She looked like a picture he had seen on a desk, smiling and beckoning to him.

But sometimes it was pitch dark.

He felt hungry and there seemed to be a picnic basket nearby with chicken nuggets. When Louis tugged at it to open it, he upset it and pulled out the fried poultry pieces. There was some sort of shot that distracted him. He looked around, found nothing and came back to the basket. It was on the cold ground. The remains of the chicken nuggets were scattered all about for some little animals had also tugged at the basket and then scattered at his approach.

Stealthily, Louis made his way back to the basket. Big mistake. For some sharpshooter was hiding behind a tree. He raised his rifle, took aim, and shot Louis.

Instead of dying straight away, light peeled away the darkness. Louis could not stop it happening, no matter how much he willed it not to. It was glaring, ultra-bright. It seemed to blare in Louis's head.

He had been unconscious for a week. The doctor in the hospital told him, "Stay still. Your right leg and arm are broken. You've been badly concussed. I'm sorry—that's the good news because in time we can fix that, if you are compliant."

The doctor tried to tell him his brain was damaged. He could not understand. Louis could see the bandages on his arm and leg. Using his left hand, he felt the bandages around his head and face. To begin with, he could not speak properly because his jaw was wired.

Louis's prolonged period of recuperation and extended stay in hospital—apart from medical scrutiny and now legitimate drug intake—seemed to revolve around managing his daily bodily actions: eating and washing, urinating and defecating. All these entailed close assistance from hospital staff that Louis found embarrassing. In particular, he found toilet assistance mortifying. It was as if his body were no better than a naked, belching, farting, excreting tube.

To improve his chances of walking again, the doctors took a muscle from his inner right thigh and implanted it in his lower leg, where they had had to remove a muscle damaged beyond repair.

But he was not as good as new.

The police notified Remedial Recuperation Services, after they found Marie Louise's card in Louis's wallet.

6 I, Candy

Across the city of Norse Hoven, in a rickety clapboard house in Louvre Ville, a dark blue-collar dormitory area, Candy lay on her bed waiting for him, the big guy with the sweet breath. His supple, wandering hands excited her when he touched her nipples. It was almost as if he was flicking on a light switch.

"You make me feel like fire and ice," he had told her, using a flip line from one of his trophy wife's novels—

although he did not tell little Candice that: "All fire and ice."

Candy waited as patiently as her half sister had told her. But she was raging inside, expecting his slippery, cold fingers to draw off her top, unloosen her bra, and then let him begin to work his mouth and tongue down her torso. The light was switched off but, though her room was dark, there was light from the hall below. It cast a filter light that forgave the ugly wallpaper and shabby furniture and increased Candy's sense of sexual glow.

Candy heard him enter downstairs silently enough but the old stair boards creaked as he tiptoed up to her room.

"You came, jes like you said, Mister," said Candy as his hulking figure stood for a moment in the doorway before he advanced to the bed. In a swift second, he was on her, inviting her to unzip his trousers. As she fondled him, he said, "Your fingers are cold but your mouth is hot," and kissed her eager, open lips.

The big guy noticed a book on the bedside table: *The Color Purple*.

The baby began whimpering in the next room. Candy started to rise.

"Let her be," the man told her. "It's just the terrible twos. She'll come out of it. Give her time."

Candy hesitated and drew back.

"She'll be all right. I promise," he added. "Like I always do."

"You always deliver. That's for sure."

He took her silence as more than enough invitation for him to continue their occasional nighttime ritual until they both fell back perspiring heavily. They lay interlocked for some time—maybe fifteen minutes, maybe half an hour— Candy did not know. She was happy to be possessed.

"You're my one special girl," he murmured in her ear: "Little Lamb."

He noticed another book, a child's book, gaily decorated.

"It's my diary."

He flicked through the pages: empty, blank.

"But, somehow, you never get round to it. Gotta go," he announced abruptly. "Put fifty dollars under the pillow. Make sure you keep twenty."

With that, he was up and dressed, tottering down the creaky stairs. He left so fast he forgot his power tie—red silk with a crest.

Candy heard the front door close, then a car engine start up. She knew he was away like a thief in the night. That's what Carrie had always told her. When she put the light back on she noticed brown makeup stains on the pillow and she knew they weren't hers.

Two days later, Candy took an evening shower and anointed herself with some leftover perfume of her sister's. Then, she dressed in her sister's underclothes. The shift was loose on her teenage figure but it made her feel provocative.

She opened the drawer of her cabinet, took out two little plastic vials with blue caps. Then she took out a slender glass tube, open at both ends, and put some metal mesh in one end. She stubbed it in with an old pencil. She opened a vial and tipped grainy powder into the glass tube above the wire mesh screen at the end of the tube. She breathed out. Then she held the tube to her lips and began to turn it as she lit her cigarette lighter underneath it to start smoking. When she exhaled, the smoke from her lips seemed to fill the room. She gasped for breath. When she fell back on the bed, she felt dizzy, then nauseous, then glowing, then nauseous again.

"Start gently. Don't get too high too fast. Take your time."

CJ was standing by the side of the bed. He continued. "Make sure he gets his share before or after sex. It don't make much difference. There'll be more in the drawer. And keep the baby quiet."

CJ left the room and went along the corridor.

When the big guy with the little bald patch entered, she

was ready. She heard CJ say from downstairs, "She's ready for you—if you know what I mean."

He suppressed a guffaw.

Candice was up and prepared for the big guy when he entered her room. She drew him close. He found her feverishness exciting. There was the same vitality, the same endless pleasuring but the big guy sensed some other urgency in Candy.

When they had finished, she followed her script. She took out a cigarette from a packet on the bedside table and drew a puff before handing it to him. Then, still in the dark, she took out her glass pipe, opened another phial, lit it, and drew a breath. The air was heavy with smoke.

"It's crack. Whatever next?" said the big guy.

"It's freebase, big guy. That's what CJ says. You'll feel comfortable and we can go on and on."

She put the pipe in his mouth, lit it, turned it, and said, "Breath in gently."

In the twilight he could see her lovely pert breasts gleaming with sweat. He knew she would let him continue. If only the damn baby would stop crying.

After he had had two more blasts, Candy said, "Let's do it again, Mister."

With that, she pulled him to her, adding, "My, you're big tonight. Ready to satisfy me."

It was not a question. Sex was not as good as before to the big man but he was too fascinated by Candy's body to care.

A car horn hooted in the street below. He knew it was his car, his signal.

"Gotta go. Love you, Little Lamb."

"Leavin' me?"

It was back on with underwear, shirt, trousers, socks, and shoes and lastly he covered his paunch with his jacket.

"I knew you needed to be quick," said CJ coming into the room. "But this is, like, Speedy Gonzalez."

34

CJ smiled and his perfect teeth clicked as he crunched them, spitting out some flakes of tobacco.

The big guy almost tumbled downstairs.

"Back soon?" asked CJ after him.

There was no need to ask.

"I thought he was coming; but he was going," added CJ.

When the big guy got into his car, his driver put his foot on the accelerator. It seemed they sped across Norse Hoven with such a whoosh it was like flying.

"Had fun, boss?" asked the driver laconically, not expecting any answer.

The big guy slumped more comfortably in his seat, and fastened the seat belt. For no reason, except some sixth sense, he felt inside his jacket pocket. There was something small, hard, and round inside. He knew what it was. He did not show it to the driver—such a klutz.

Winter

7 Unnatural Selections

Hermione was the most comfortable person Luke had ever known, comfortable in herself, her Goyaesque figure, her Matisse clothes, her Titian hair, and her liberal attitudes. For the first week, she acted as Luke's guide around downtown Norse Hoven and Milhous College.

Bursting forth in its melange of Ivy League architecture were the 1930's Gothic ensemble of colleges and central university showpieces, such as the Law School based on the perpendicular Gothic of chapels at Cambridge, and the Gymnasium, a towering cathedral of physical fitness. As Luke knew from one of his architectural history professors, most of this was superior in execution to its English models, thanks to the superior contribution of Italian stonemasons' quality work.

The outsize yellow-and-brown, cream-and-saffron stone tower of the Great Library rose like a giant swelling of organ pipes against the azure blue sky, commanding the scene. It was like an elongated and widened new Gothic, as if Walt Disney's animated film version of medieval palaces had come to roost, a Disneyfication of the great university.

This particular all-purpose Gothic style seemed to chime in with Luke's most individual eyesight, the double macular hemorrhages twisting all regular building shapes into tapering spires and curling blocks of vermilion and ochre.

Luke could not help comparing the desert of downtown Norse Hoven with its closed shops, its two outsize, derelict, and blocked-up department store buildings and empty streets with its punctuation here and there by tiny oases: jazzed-up shop fronts or chi-chi restaurants with exotic cuisines— Turkish, Ethiopian—amid regular Italian American and all-American bars with deli fare.

Then, Luke and Hermione set aside the guided tour to concentrate on Luke's need to find work and a new identity while keeping his secret safe. After filling in temp agency forms with Hermione's help and passing various typing and IT tests, it seemed his life was on a moving walkway, as he proceeded from a first visit as a temp to Filter's Bank, processing letters and acknowledging bank receipts, to a foray as a temp in an insurance office that required an educated-sounding voice to answer phones, and then a second visit to Filter's Bank, this time sending off letters reminding borrowers they had not paid their monthly deposits.

Lurking in all his dealings from office chit-chat to office politics to maneuvers with editors and writers lay Luke's unresolved dilemma: to tell or not to tell anyone about his eyesight; how much to admit and with what consequences. He knew he could appear normal throughout an interview. But would his secret be discovered later?

In the past he had been so aware of his difficulties seeing that, to protect himself from any social fallout in office politics, in his jobs in college and grad school, he had always chosen the drip-drip of passing limited information to people: first, that he wore contact lenses—nothing unusual about that; then, that he wore those contacts with some discomfort—again nothing unusual; then, that he had very poor eyesight; and, finally, that he had already had eye surgery. Thus he tried to minimize the possible severity of adverse office politics by passing information a morsel at a time.

But everywhere he went to temp work he always had the suspicion that his co-workers had rumbled him and thought that those who resented his educated manner would take mean advantage of his problems by altering computer settings in his breaks to double his problems.

After a week of expecting something good and another week of expecting just anything, a temp agency called to say there was some sorting job at Fast Track Sports.

"Starting at eight first day, finish at 4:30pm. Thirty minutes for lunch; two fifteen-minute comfort breaks."

"Sorting what?" Luke asked the agency assistant.

"Dunno. The rate is $7 per hour—good for starters. Yes or no?"

"Yeah."

"Be there seven forty-five first day tomorrow."

When recruits arrived in reception in Fast Track Sports, Security and Human Resources processed them. Human Resources gave them marching orders that could be summed up in words emblazoned on three giant wall placards: "No Shirkers," "No Time-Wasters," "No Trouble-Makers"—just in case anyone failed to get the message.

This was underlined by the security guard's scowl when he finished: "This way, take the right. The boss is Mistress. She'll show you what to do."

The recruits were left by themselves—a middle-aged woman, a college girl, and Luke. In his button-down-collar shirt, Luke felt like a preppy misfit. The three of them stared at one another without speaking a word. They moved from reception into a large warehouse. Luke soon realized this warehouse was one half of an even larger U-shaped room that bent its way round an inner tower that housed the central staircase, elevators, toilets, plumbing, and electric cables for the entire building, and ended in a second connected warehouse.

The first warehouse had piles of clothes spilling over several huge hampers at one side. At the other side were empty hampers and outsize rails with coat hangers dangling from square frames that could be moved on castors. In the middle were two elongated trestle tables with benches at each side.

As yet, there were no people in this first warehouse. From within the second warehouse round the bend they heard an unmistakable sound. The young girl, evidently accustomed to her surroundings, led the way. In the inner chamber were three large women, one white and two black, all asleep, one in an old tattered armchair, the other two slumped on the bench over the trestle table. They were snoring.

"Mistress," called the young girl gently.

The woman in the armchair started, rubbed her eyes, and sat bolt upright and said, "Why it's Ellie."

"Yes, I'm back part-time."

"Must be a junior by now?" asked Mistress.

"That's right; a senior next Labor Day, ya'know."

"How's your daddy doin'?'"

"Dad's keeping fine. I see you're well."

"Guess I'll have to get up early in the morning to stop the police chief's daughter catching me out."

The trio of women workers laughed. Ellie winced.

"No worries on that score, ya'know," she said.

"Hey, you guys, here," started Mistress.

Luke was not sure if she meant the new temps or the other workers who had started to sort out clothes as if that was all they had been doing before the temps arrived.

"Ellie, you know what to do—can't teach you anything— so you can get started with April."

After moving back into the first warehouse, Ellie settled down with April, a comfortably dressed woman with a ruby acacia flower in her hair and lipstick to match.

What looked like a random pile of less-than-charity clothes must have some unfathomable logical order. What that was, Luke was about to discover. Mistress led Luke and his other co-worker down to the front warehouse and, with other supervisors in tow, began the much-practiced lesson of the day:

"This, here, is the Recycling Center of Fast Track Sports. Fast Track Sports make sports apparel for wear on and off the pitch. Not the tops and bottoms and trainers and track-suits that footballers, basketball players, and other athletes wear when they're playing. This, here, is sports apparel for fans, for kids of all ages, to don in their search for the fast lane of the American Dream. Fast suits for fat cats. We sell it but China and other countries in this, here, Asia make it. Sometimes, after it's sold, there's a problem and we get the problems. Heaps!"

Mistress rummaged around clothes on a trestle table. Seemingly out of nowhere, she plucked two manuals. Holding them up, she said, "One's a book of rules; the other's the style book. Here we sort and check. People return our clothes for three sorts of reasons. One, they got damaged in some way—got ripped, dirtied, colors ran in the wash. The damage may be wear, it may be tear, or soiled, or a hole, or a button that's broke—that's not our concern.

"Two, the fit is wrong—mistakes in labeling or cut; an extra large size waist with a small collar; a zip that won't fasten—that sort of thing. Three—and this is tricky—which is why we have the style book—the design is wrong: it's meant for one particular sports team and there's been a mistake. Perhaps the colors are wrong; perhaps the colors are right but the logo is wrong. Red Sox fans don't want to look like damn Yankees.

"That's where the catalog comes in. You have to be real careful here because a design fault can be small, kinda invisible to the naked eye of the general market but it comes out in 3D to the genuine sports fanatic."

While Mistress took them through her instructions, one of the other workers called out gaily, half singing: "In olden days, a glimpse of stocking was looked upon as something

40

shocking but now, in hose, cross-dressing goes."

Luke looked sideways at a curvaceous woman in ultra-tight jeans and a revealing red halter-top sporting outsize gold hoop earrings who had come into the workplace.

"Take no notice," interrupted April. "That's Sister. Carrie Behan is her real name. Because her granddaddy was Irish and her mommy's from the West Indies, she thinks she's licensed to wit."

April and Carrie cackled audibly together at this private joke, as if singing in stereo. Mistress carried on regardless.

"In each of these three cases we have to categorize in one of three ways. First, there's not really much wrong and we can recycle them internally as a Second in the Fast Track Sports store. Sometimes, the garment has worse problems but it's still good enough to wear if you're not particular and so it can be recycled for charity stores. Third, the damage is so bad or the design fault so gross that the garment is unusable."

Mistress huffed and puffed with good humor.

"Each garment in these piles will end up in one of these clearly marked hampers: rejects, charity, seconds. When we categorize a reject based on a design fault, we write a note on one of these, here, yellow cards and attach it with a safety pin—that is, if it's going to Seconds or to Charity. If it's an outright reject, don't bother with the note."

Luke groaned inwardly. He still did not yet know if in the workplace he should explain or not explain, tell or not tell others about his condition. Whether he chose revelation or concealment, there would be consequences. One thing was for sure: he knew he would need his eyesight more than ever. He simply did not know where to begin. Mistress could tell that Luke and the older woman, Sylvie, felt overwhelmed.

"Don't fret. You'll soon get the hang of it. This morning, one of us will work with you and show you how it's done."

In Luke's individual eyesight not only the clothes for recycling but also the walls and the bend between the two sections of the U-shaped room swelled and rippled. He had to move between the two. He soon learned which was his own area of the trestle table, his workstation. But he was never sure where he was in the two airport-style warehouses, the outer one for the drones or the inner one for the supervisors.

The various workers were a chance mixture of older pros trying to train the new arrivals with their ideas and make them copies of themselves. No one had any obvious sense of whither they were heading or enough education to get out of their present fix.

While they worked methodically but negligently, they fantasized over male film stars. Luke heard them roll out the names Mel Gibson, Brad Pitt, and Denzel Washington, all with flesh-rating approval, personal estimations of intimate quality time together with oysters and champagne for starters before dinner, followed by physical exhaustion for dessert.

"Here we are, working for a company that makes and sells clothes," observed Sylvie, "and what they want is a procession of Hollywood's most photogenic male stars, wearing next to nothing."

"Why not?" asked April beside Ellie. "Any moment of pleasure or love has to be seized gratefully—and in secret. There are obstacles in the way of anything any of us wants—you'll soon learn. Everything is stolen from us."

Luke stared at an outsize bundle, grabbed a full, two-arms' worth of clothes and moved to a vacant part of the table. He felt all eyes were on him. But, despite Mistress's offer, he worked alone. The first individual garment he picked up was a tousled red top. He pored over it. Staring closely, he thought it was probably complete but he sensed it was dirty and decided Charity Case.

The second garment was a pair of blue pantaloon trousers. Drawing them carefully from left to right in front of his eyes, he sensed that the stripes down the legs were uneven. They seemed to undulate yet there did not seem to be anything else wrong, so he thought, "Seconds—Fast Track Sports store."

Thus, he proceeded on to a third garment and then a fourth, making his allocations like a professor giving dismissive grades to freshmen essays. But, after twenty minutes, the garments and colors, more and more, began to merge with one another. When he looked up and across at the trestle table, strewn with sports apparel, he felt he was inside the confusion of some cubist painting. However, instead of sharp lines and cascading angles, it was as if all the geometric shapes had lost their hard edges and become floppy, waving flannel. Each and every garment swirled into every other one. He tried to carry on even though he had a blinding headache. When he looked up, his co-workers seemed to be swaying like mango trees in a tropical storm.

Later, he went to see Mistress in the second chamber to seek her approval. As he approached, instantaneously she started from her sleep. He took her over to his hampers with their piles of neatly folded clothes. She gave him his first tutorial.

"Now, here, honey, these bottoms have a tear at the hem. It's not obvious but some know-all in a charity shop would object. Let's put them out of their misery."

Mistress tugged at the hem of the bottoms, expanding the tear. Then, she said, matter-of-factly, "Now it's a definite reject."

With that, she tossed it aside into the reject hamper.

"Now, here, honey, this here top is meant to be a Red Sox top—that's the logo—but the colors are Blue Cardinals. We can't sell it as a second—even though it's in good condition.

But it's all right to wear for doing the laundry, honey, so it'll go in the charity hamper.

"Now, with this, hone, the buttons don't fasten; and, with this, the zipper won't pull. Don't fret, hone. You're a beginner here. This ain't supposed to be skilled work but it does take experience. It's all a matter of practice and routine. Keep your eyes peeled and stick to an order: general condition, then attachments working or not, then design accuracy. Keep to that order of inspection and make your judgment calls in the same order."

From the side, April added, "Mixed up here are some very strange objects, not just combs and buttons but also money—dollar bills—sometimes a ten. Then, there are relics of old love affairs: fairground rings, handkerchiefs with lipstick smudges, dried-up condoms."

"Here, like you said—a brand new pink comb," said Luke.

As Mistress rose, she patted his shoulder. He smelled her perfume and stared at her cleavage. She heaved a sigh and moved back into the inner chamber and her armchair to resume her sleep. Soon, she was snoring.

Over sandwiches in a drab room designated for lunch, one temp passed around a copy of the day's *Norse Hoven Courier* with yet another story about the Louvre Ville Gang's murders. The paper solicited readers' comments in its mail section, published as a special Op Ed feature: "It's a simple matter of fact that, if the thugs in these horrific episodes had ever done a stroke of real hard work, instead of living off of state benefits and fathering children across the slums, these crimes would never have happened."

Towards the end of the little group's tut-tutting, Sylvie said with some self-satisfaction, "When I read horror stories like this, I just count my blessings that I live on the coast well away from downtown slums where animals like these practice their deadly traffic."

Luke hardly heard her. He kept thinking: are they scrutinizing me? Have they rumbled me? Are they talking about me behind my back? On and on he asked himself these troubling questions till he was sick with worry.

The second day, Luke ached for a rest. He knew there was a wall clock opposite high up but he could not see the figures. As unobtrusively as possible, he pressed the side button of his digital watch. When the piping Japanese voice began, it seemed to reverberate and ricochet around the hangar: "Eleven ten AM; eleven ten AM," again and again. Luke realized everyone was looking.

"Stomach rumbling?" asked April, followed by a belly laugh.

Luke muttered, "Something like that."

He turned away, feeling his cheeks flush.

"Go for your break now," said Mistress, suddenly back in the room.

"You, too, Ellie and Sylvie."

As they sipped sodas in the lunch room, Luke took an interest in his co-workers.

Sylvie had curly cropped gray hair and could have been any age. To Luke, her reserved manner implied she hated the job but, like everyone else, she needed the money. It was as if she had gauged what she was in for and would endure almost any toil, any humiliation, until her work at Fast Track Sports got her out of whatever was her present financial pickle.

His chance to appraise Ellie came two afternoons later. Mistress asked Luke and Ellie to go together to the third floor via the huge service elevator and return with eight outsize hangers for extra clothes. While they were up there in a dingy, cavernous car park lot, Ellie suddenly became like a liberated tourist just over the border into Mexico, swinging on the outsize hangers almost as if they were trolley cars in San Francisco and whooping for joy as she propelled them to the elevator, resting one foot on the bottom rails as she swished them forward with the other.

Her sudden impulsive behavior made Luke realize that Ellie was something else. This vivacious girl seemed to be playing several parts. For, in the brief time Luke had known her, she was always changing her name from her original Ellie or Ella to a longer version, Magdalena, then Lena. To Luke, she was not entirely sincere and, as he had learnt, also the police chief's elder daughter, willing to pull rank. She caught Luke appraising her and curtailed her flight of boisterousness. Ella could never play compassion to the workers, thought Luke, even though she was at college planning a career in social work.

When they returned through the lobby, a message came over the loudspeaker: "Paging Sister Carrie Behan. Please come to reception."

Sitting in the lobby, Luke noted a fresh-faced young girl of mixed race and strangely luminous presence. She could not have been more than seventeen going on eighteen. Slightly pregnant, she was drooling over a rag doll.

"I's Candice Quint," said the girl by way of unnecessary introduction as she rose from the small reception couch.

When Luke and Ella returned to the whale's abdomen of a sorting room, Carrie was coming out to greet her guest in reception.

When Carrie returned, she said to Mistress, "Candy forgot her keys."

"Learning difficulties, eh?" said Mistress matter-of-factly.

That weekend, on their early Sunday morning walk in the neighborhood way higher up the hill, Hermione, apprised of the cast at Fast Track Sports, pointed out to Luke a garden on Rigid Road markedly different from the others.

"This is the home of the police chief, Leo Guerra, your co-worker's father."

The outer part of the garden nearest the road had gone wild. Peeping through the gates, Luke and Hermione could see long grass between the flagstones. They could smell dead flowers and dying leaves on the ground. The ferns seemed as high as young trees. The air was pungent with rottenness.

"I know what you're thinking," said Hermione. "That the police chief must have more than enough money to have as manicured a garden as everyone else on Rigid Road. My guess is that what we see here is camouflage for the periphery—the police chief's individual alternative to a gated community. The garden nearer the house is probably as manicured as the other gardens nearby. It's also the police chief's way of saying 'Sucks' to the other big shots here who either come from old money or newcomers who want to ape the old money with stilted perfection."

At the beginning of the next week at Fast Track Sports, Mistress introduced Luke to a new recruit who would only work afternoons. As he went into her inner room, Luke overheard a minder say softly to Mistress, who was fanning herself with a newspaper, "After a serious auto accident left him with multiple injuries, Louis speaks with a slur and is a bit slow to understand. Social Services put him in a hostel and referred him to Remedial Recuperation Services but there's this very determined dame at RRS. She thinks he can cut it—half time—and it will be better for him."

Turning to Luke, Mistress said, "This is Louis, our new co-worker. You know the ropes, help him out."

"Sure."

Louis limped and walked unsteadily with a crutch. But he was physically powerful despite his ravaged face. He always arrived with the minder, a silent older figure perpetually immersed in his newspaper. Louis said little but what he did say came out most deliberate. At the beginning of his second week he asked, "Luke—these tops—Denver Br-Br-Broncos or Cincinnati Be-Be-Bengals?"

"Dunno. Let's check the catalog."

While they were trying to locate football tops and match up logos in the book to logos on the badly wrinkled garments, Sylvie spoke. It seemed the profusion of garments before her with torn edges, broken clasps, and missing buttons had exasperated her nerves beyond her usual control. She burst out with, "It's simply shoddy workmanship. No quality control by the manufacturers in China. None of this—the wrong colors, the mistaken designs, the faulty hooks—need happen at all."

As she tugged upon a bundle of rejected sports apparel, Sylvie exclaimed, "One day, these clothes will break my back—they'll be the death of me."

Luke was surprised at Sylvie's outburst. Before he could prise open whatever lurked beneath her controlled manner, they were taken by another surprise.

Standing across the room, April was casually flirting with the clothes. A roguish idea struck her. She began to adorn herself with scarves and bloomers, more and more, draping them diagonally from her shoulders and crowning the ensemble with two baseball caps, each put on sideways, giving her two chimpanzee ears. This touch ridiculed the overall effect of a sumptuously attired odalisque from the Arabian Nights. So did the radio station playing a recording of the *Sorcerer's Apprentice*. In time to the music, April then tucked other bottoms into her waistband to form a peacock's train of spruce blue amid fir greens.

She sang out, "Don we now our gay apparel," to the tune of a Christmas carol and collapsed with laughter at her joke.

"April has the cruelest mouth," said Sister Carrie.

"For shoppers, Fast Track Sports is a consumer paradise of cuts and colors; for us, it's a penal colony of toil and degradation," added Sylvie without looking up.

48

They were brought up sharp to the truth of this when a security guard rapped the underside of the bench with his baton just underneath Louis. It made Louis judder, reminding him of past incidents when guards had woken him up when he was sleeping rough in railroad stations.

"That's enough, all of you. You stick to your work or it will be the worse for you."

With that, the guard rapped his baton again underneath Luke's butt. Luke rose, startled.

"Sit down, you. Get on with it."

"Or?" piped up Ella.

"Or it will be the worse for you—not you, Ellie, of course."

The little group fell silent.

Luke considered how old factory contraptions of smoking chimneys, glaring lights, and belching pipes of heavy industry in which artisans had toiled in former days had become in this detritus of the Industrial Revolution a scrap yard of flannel heaps in which human cogs scampered in perpetual motion.

April reasserted herself.

"We have plenty of nothing, that's for sure. Our every little pleasure turns to misery. Forget that there was ever such a thing as happiness. Stripes on your backs. Bow your heads before the bosses. If you dare look up, beware the security guards, as you've just seen. Everyone here earns their bread by the sweat of their brow."

There was no response.

Luke tried to concentrate. He could tell these tops were olive green but he could not locate the right set of logos in the guidebook so he did not know if they were the green of the Green Bay Packers or of the Oakland Athletics. There was nothing for it but to ask Mistress for her help yet again. The other senior members of the team were nowhere to be seen. Neither, at first, was Mistress. When Luke entered her work area, she was not in her chair or at the trestle table. He looked carefully in case this unexpectedly empty warehouse was some mirage of his declining eyesight. It was a good thing he did look carefully. For there she was. Mistress had collapsed under the table, a voluminous mass of two loose sweaters, apron, and skirt.

Luke bent down but could not rouse her. He called Louis for help. He and Louis propped her up, then sat on the floor with her. Their co-workers called for the company in-house medical team. Without much examination, they said Mistress had had a TIA, a transient stroke.

"You may have saved her," said the nurse practitioner who arranged hospital transfer and check-up.

Spring

8 Beachcombers

Yuppie social worker Marie Louise Garden loved the beach. Closer to the sand than any but the smallest toddler, to her the seashore was a magical world of sand and shells. She knew, on any regular working weekday when the beach was a semi-desert, that, separated by distance from other beachcombers dotted around the shore from afar she looked to sunbathers, swimmers, and passers-by like any regular beach-goer. Sheer isolation on a blank canvass of undulating dunes blunted others' sense of proportion. Because Marie Louise was reclining and not next to anyone, people could not look down on her socially because they could not compare her.

The mix of beating sun and sea breezes blessed Marie Louise's skin till it glowed. She let her mind drift off into what might have been. Here she felt adored by benign nature. This was her cherished fantasy: an escape into the nirvana of commercially promoted, sun-kissed, twiglet bodies decorated with micro bikinis. Even when passers-by called out "Hi!" as they trundled to the sea, she felt protected from their gaze by the sandy expanse, sheltered by the very openness of the desert.

Some days Marie Louise felt so heartily sick of Remedial Recuperation Services, she felt that it was as if she practically had to flog herself to get to the hated office. But she did.

She thought of Louis Cans's devil-may-care truculence since he had come out of hospital and his sulks.

"It doesn't work with me, Louis. You're simply exploiting disability to escape responsibility for your life. You'll continue the physiotherapy to get you moving better and you will work half time. You'll stick with Fast Track Sports."

Louis was not the first of Marie Louise's disabled clients at work who quickly learnt that her brittle exterior did not yield some easy marshmallow inner core of soft-center sympathy.

As their bi-weekly meeting drew to an end, Marie Louise was surprised to receive a token present from Louis. It was a standard issue of mottled blue soap into which Louis had carved her two first names as a bas relief front and back of the rectangle: MARIE and LOUISE. Her excitement at this little treasure was immense. She promised never to use it to wash and to keep it always with her other treasures on her bedside cabinet.

Much as she was attracted to Louis Cans, he would never prove marriageable material. And, despite her severe manner and implied warning, she wondered if, having placed Louis Cans at Fast Track Sports, he would stay the course.

But today she was off or, rather, her clothes may have been off but her thinking cap was on. Marie Louise knew from her disability-awareness classes that impairments were not only physical and sensory but also psychological. She was disturbed about Louis and this roused her own emotions about the way she saw society regard disabled people. She said, aloud, "It's so unfair. We have so much to contribute. Why won't they let us?"

Alert on the New England shore, Marie Louise sat up and started to play with the sand, letting it run through her fingers. Noting the dimpled imprints where people had passed hither and thither on the beach before her, her mind turned to her beloved brother, Todd's, enthusiastic history lessons. She thought of the sands of Egypt and how desert was the frontier of empire, the scene of battles, making grown men lumber about, moving no better than children playing with sandcastles. She thought how in ancient Rome sand turned an arena into the playpen for cruel blood sports. This last thought was prompted by a postcard she had just received from her girl friend, Cheryl, in Rome, showing the Colosseum. Marie Louise remembered how one of her schoolteachers had told her the winds of time wasted the great empires, one after the other, turning the rocks of achievement into sand dunes.

As she let the sand run through her hands, she thought how these childish history lessons of forever crumbling societies also applied to her. Separated from her family at a tender age, shunted from residential home to residential home, she, like Louis, was thus destined to find it difficult to forge any lasting, personal relationships. Her lifetime's experience taught her that you started with someone, then someone else or something broke up the relationship, and you started all over again. She was eliminative with people as she was, also, with her pet cats.

Coming out of her reverie, Marie Louise caressed her figure with sun lotion. Then, starker consciousness intruded with a loud woof as a somewhat shaggy fox terrier looked askance at her. When he started to lick her shoulder, she panicked.

"Here, Lapak; here, boy!" a little girl's voice called from somewhere in the distance. The dog looked round. As he bounded away, Marie Louise heard a woman cry out, "Lizzie! Leave him be; he's coming back."

As the dog ran off, Marie Louise thought she was safe from more intrusion. That was because someone else was not. The air carried cries from the Sound, playful yells and giggles as frolicking bathers splashed one another. The fox terrier started to bark as it raced forward to the sea. Marie Louise realized that the yells had turned querulous. Some swimmers were converging on two dots in the Sound. Children's cries pierced the air. Marie Louise sat bolt upright and peered straight ahead as best she could.

A small crowd edged to the sea and then broke back in a mini wave of human astonishment. Two burly men stepped out from the sea. One carried a little form and laid it, lifeless, on the wet welcome of a swimmer's sandy towel. Marie Louise now moved forward, her loping gait even slower in the slippery sands. No mother's tears flowed more freely at the sight than did Marie Louise's. Her emotions were at their most raw when poignant drama curdled dull routine. The little body on the crumpled towel gulped. From his mouth streamed a yellow-white mixture.

"We can't get through to the police," said one concerned man, becoming irritated with his unresponsive cell phone.

"Let me help," said a prepossessing woman in a green one-piece bathing suit and matching turban, whom Marie Louise recognized as the mother of the little girl with the dog.

"My name is Bella Guerra. My husband is the police chief. Don't look, Lizzie," she said, holding her little girl back.

"They'll surely respond to me. Besides, I have his private number."

It took all the strength she could summon for Marie Louise to return to her own towel. Then she broke down uncontrollably.

She did not know how long she had been sobbing when she heard a man's voice.

"What's up with you, little lady? Dry your eyes."

The voice came from a black man. He was standing in front of the sun, but, even when he was in shadow, Marie Louise could tell his skin had got a trifle purple from being in the sun. At the same time, he started to look at her a little more closely. First protected from scrutiny by distance, now he was almost on top of her she could tell he had started to measure her in his mind's eye. He knew she was staring back.

"Beg pardon. S'cuse me."

"Forget it. Don't worry. I get it all the time."

Her tears started again.

"Let's get you home."

"I came in my car."

"You're still a bit shaken. Mind if I come with you—see you're all right? The name's Dickon. I'm honest. I work."

Marie Louise weighed up the potentially adverse consequences of letting a burly man she did not know guide her home in her own car but she was too unsettled to respond in any way but a silent assent. She introduced herself: "I'm Marie Louise."

Marie Louise headed off with Dickon into the twilight zone of homeward-bound highway traffic just before the rush hour with its violet hues across the sky punctuated by the torch-like blares of streetlights. She was filled with ecstasy and dread. She had pulled a man but at what cost?

When they arrived, Dickon noted two rows of sunflowers before her street-level apartment, all just coming into bloom. Compared to Marie Louise as she stumped up the steps, they seemed to be reaching for the stars.

When they entered her little apartment, Dickon, who was carrying the bags with beach things, said, "Nice place you got here: real love-nest material."

He looked around at the half-furnished living room and some shelves, empty but for box files from work. There was one half full bottle of red wine on the kitchen counter.

Marie Louise had learnt to drink alcohol at college. At first, this was to be one of the girls and later for a hazy illusion of happiness that sent her to sleep alone. One large glass of red wine sufficed for a night. On nights out, she soon learned that her pocketbook was to be opened only twice and the second time it was only to extract her lipstick.

This time she realized she could, if she wanted to, hit the jackpot. She also knew the swimming accident had made her extra nervous, afraid, vulnerable.

Dickon interrupted her sad mood.

"You don't have books, no? I'm surprised."

"You like reading?"

Marie Louise did not say she would be surprised if he did.

"Exercises my mind. Don't care for girls who aren't educated. I may not look it, but I'm a guy with a sensitive soul. That's why I get bored easily."

"Me too."

Marie Louise started to look on him differently. "I'm too tired to read when I come home from work."

"Me too, most days. I drive a city bus—knocks me out by the end of the day."

"I work for the state in Remedial Recuperation Services."

"You're highly educated, then," Dickon said as if pronouncing judgment.

Marie Louise started to be coquettish. "Haven't we met before?"

Dickon thought to himself, "She likes my ass—torso, too, probably."

"I'm a Romantic," said Dickon, encouragingly.

Marie Louise thought, "That means he's poor and wants to be kept."

Dickon could see Marie Louise's street-level apartment had none of the decorative touches, none of the knick-knacks that even the poorest people could salvage to soften meager homes and make the drab interiors more personal. Instead, there were scaffolds and ramps up which tiny legs could clamber to be eye-level with electric cooker and kitchen sink. Her kitchen was like the bizarre construction of a stage set.

Such humanizing touches as might have softened the environment were provided not by visitors or ornaments but by cats—six of them—feral strays whom Marie Louise had first enticed with bowls of scraps left outside. Once inside, she disciplined them.

Dickon started to look around the room and noticed a photo in a frame.

"Your mom?"

Marie Louise nodded. She went through the familiar story of how her mother, Gina, had been a great beauty in her youth. Even in middle age, her fine features, shapely tight figure, and alluring presence still attracted men. Dickon could see that and Marie Louise read his mind.

"Men go to her like bees around a honey pot," she said as if by rote.

Earlier that week, on impulse, Marie Louise had bought a jar of green olives as a concession to her rising status as a yuppie professional who should also be a consumer. Now, as a gesture of hospitality to her guest, she tried to open it with her little hands. No luck. Then she tried with a knife. But after a lengthy tussle, she realized she was soaked with her own sweat. The cats were in a semi-circle around the table. She started to laugh at her own absurd situation. This brought Dickon into the kitchen to wrest the top off the jar.

"Capable hands," she said, admiring his brawn.

"Why don't you have anything more to drink?" he asked. "I'm broke but you're an educated girl, you were born under a lucky star. You can go to the beach all day, stay all day, and drink wine with ice."

Getting no response, he started to look at the cats and began to count them.

"Three, four, one hiding behind the sofa, five, one under the easy chair, six."

"That's right: six."

"Company."

"I s'pse it would be different if I had a child."

"Yes, me, too, but children come here because two people have been together."

"Huh?"

Marie Louise really pricked up her ears.

"S'pse you have a man? All educated gals do. Meeting you has made me happy. Do you want to play with me—let's hold one another."

Marie Louise started to feel aroused. The sensation spread through her tiny body.

"Don't try it on."

"I'm stronger than you are."

"Obvious. What are you up to?"

His hands were on her waist, and he slipped his right hand up her right leg under her child's smock.

"We've all got needs, Marie Louise—you as well as me. What's your imaginary boyfriend got that I haven't? Arms? Legs? Chest? Face? All present and correct; everything in working order."

He bent down and kissed her and she realized from the mint toothpaste taste of his welcome tongue that he must have smeared his teeth with toothpaste from her bathroom while she was tussling with the olive jar. His tongue felt good and she responded with hers.

While they were kissing, he slipped his left hand down the front of her smock and found her nipple.

"All present and correct, including this monster. You help me and I'll help you."

With that, he yanked open the front of his jeans, gently took her hands and invited her to arouse him with her hand and her mouth. After he moved her little fingers up and down his penis, he moved her hand to his testicles.

"Caress my balls, honey lamb. Take a chance. You see, I travel light—no baggage. The only must-have bag for a man is his scrotum."

This remark sent Marie Louise into peals of laughter and vanquished her inhibitions. She was his.

After oral sex and he had wiped her face clean with toilet

tissue, they laid down on the bed and fell asleep.

During the night, he murmured in her ear, "Best sleep there is: sleep of the just after."

Nestling in the arms of her handsome fox, she giggled at this stale joke.

But when Dickon awoke fully in the morning, he sensed her unease and was ready to turn it to his advantage.

"I had a great time last night," he said when he was fully awake.

Marie Louise was wondering, "Who the hell is this guy?"

He stayed three days, missing work on two of them, and getting her to call in that he was sick. They had sex twice a day. Dickon wrapped his huge arms around her and murmured in her ear, "You're my little Lady Bug."

She murmured something and so he added, "Let me play with your little garden."

But, after leaving on the third day for his bus round, Dickon did not return to her little apartment that evening. After he was gone two days, Marie Louise controlled her disappointment by concentrating on work, taking solace by playing with her kitties, and by deciding that, if Dickon ever came back, she must set her sights low:

"Dusty," she told the mangy gray cat, "you're the most beautiful cat. You are my best romance. When Dickon is out, all of you keep me company. You are my dream love affair—no jealousy, always cuddly. Do you know why? It's because your philosophy is simple—just purr and purr the day away. Aren't you the cat's meow? Better to eat your slices of heart from a can than eat your heart out for a man."

In fact, these cats had to do much more than purr their way through lazy days. Marie Louise's cats were not overfed cats, plumped out through a sedentary life of bozo ease. Marie Louise ate like a bird and she was equally frugal with her stray charges. Although Marie Louise loved the solace of silence, once inside her apartment after work and when she had taken out her hearing aids, she knew there lurked dangers of burglary, fire, and flood. This was particularly true as she was deaf to door and fire alarms.

"Your momma is not some batty old cat woman. You pussies are here to work. And work you will. You babies, all of whom I have christened with proper names, have a special function: to sound an alarm. I'm gonna train you to wake me if I happen to be asleep without my hearing aids when the door bell rings or an alarm sounds."

Once Marie Louise had acquired a new kitty, she would lie down. Using a bedside cord, she would ring the bell, and wait for his scratches, cries, and clambering upon the bed to "wake" her.

If Marie Louise had to travel away to her mother or to a conference, she simply let the cats outdoors and left them there to fend for themselves. If they were around when she returned, she took them in—or as many as came back. If she were short by a few cats, she always found other proto-children.

9 Swimmin' with Women

On Friday night, after a glass of red wine to help settle her, Marie Louise fell asleep. Then she awoke to a thudding noise. One of the cats was tugging at the blanket by her shoulder. She turned on the lamp. It was three in the morning. Dickon was calling from outside.

"Marie Louise. Marie Louise, you inside? You get your tiny ass out here and help me in."

Marie Louise felt a pounding inside her stomach. She was

consumed with fear. Here was her lover, a drunken brute. She stayed perfectly still. But the voice started again.

"Marie Louise. Marie Louise, I know you're there. Get your hot ass to the door and let me in."

There was another loud banging at the door. Then Dickon's voice started all over.

"Knock, knock, who's there? Dickon's here and ready for you. C'mon Marie Louise, I know you're gagging for it. And I'm willing. Get your clothes off."

Marie Louise did something she had not done for years. Involuntarily, she crossed herself. Timidly, she edged to the front door. The letter box opened. She knew two eyes were staring at her.

"Whadda you mean locking me out? You know you want it, my little Lady Bug."

Marie Louise was now too frozen to answer back. However, she unlocked the door and moved quickly back, sensing what would happen next. Dickon did not fall in on top of her but banged into the furniture and almost fell down into an easy chair.

"C'mon, help me. Get my clothes off."

He tried to take off his jacket but succeeded only in getting his arms twisted into it.

"What the fuck? Marie Louise, c'mon. Get it off."

Marie Louise was still paralyzed with panic. Then, somehow, the jacket was off, flung on the floor, and kicked aside like trash.

"Help me get the boots off."

Dickon hoisted a leg aloft for Marie Louise to untie the laces. She came close and started to pick at the knots.

"That's not it, you little critter. You're a real cunt when it comes to clothes. D'ya know that?"

He bent his leering face right down on her. Marie Louise stiffened. She knew she must not show any more perturbation.

"I'm not afraid of you. Shut your mouth."

Dickon was off in his own world with his other women. The laces undone, he kicked off the offending boot by edging it with his other foot. He raised the other leg but he was again in a different world.

"April, give a hand. Why's it so dark, April? I can't see the bathroom."

Marie Louise picked at the laces of the other boot. This second boot was looser. She started tugging it to get it off.

"Not so hard, April," he rasped. "You'll take the foot off with the boot."

Now Dickon started fumbling at his belt. Then he stood up and let his jeans fall down. He tried to climb out of them but his foot got tangled. He collapsed back into the chair, sobbing into the side.

"April, whadda ya done with the kids? You jes disappeared on me. Where are you now?"

As discreetly as she could, Marie Louise pulled off his jeans. She tackled the stockinged feet. They stank. Then, as if taking control of himself, Dickon stood up.

"Why's the light not on, Marie Louise? I can't see a thing."

Marie Louise put the main light on in the bedroom. Dickon turned, reeling. Then, reaching the bedroom, threw himself sideways onto the bed.

"Get me a drink. I need a drink."

"You've had plenty."

"Not enough to blot you out, you little critter. Give me a sip from your yuppie wine."

Marie Louise padded to a little cupboard and poured out red wine into a small glass.

"That's better. It's good to sing when you drink but, when it's all gone, it's not much fun."

He had downed it in one, pulled the duvet over him, and fallen asleep.

Marie Louise was still perplexed. His size, his brutish

unpredictable rage, his loutish manners were all a threat to her home, perhaps to her sanity. Her panic immobilized her.

She told her cats, "Sorry, Bucky. I don't like to admit it, Lemel, but I was better off when I was by myself. I did have some freedom."

Marie Louise recognized the pattern into which she and Dickon were falling. He was typical of the blue-collar men who came back exhausted from work. She was also typical of blue-collar wives—a woman who also came back exhausted from work and then got even more tired through the chore of home-making.

Marie Louise tolerated Dickon's casual attitude to work by treating all this as a secret game in which only they knew the rules. She minded a hell of a lot but, unless she played by his rules, she knew Dickon could move out of her range. He could easily find someone else at work or on the streets.

Far from their physical closeness making frank exchange about their difficulties easier, it made them more difficult. Marie Louise sometimes needed some personal care that Dickon found repulsive. She did not like his habit of spreading his legs out in bed and resting his cold feet on her scrawny ass. But at least he was hot everywhere else and he was there.

This was not going to be a case where time would ease their physical problems—the juxtaposition of his fine muscular physique and her shriveled one—leading to their physical incompatibility. Then there was his feeling every time they went shopping, or his friends saw him with her, that he was being stigmatized.

Marie Louise also felt stigmatized. She felt ashamed of Dickon but she often came to his rescue and thus ensured that he kept his job. However, this only deepened her sense of shame. Inside, she was all apprehension because every day she compromised herself.

A few days later, when Dickon mounted the Delta bus for

his midday shift after another hard night with Marie Louise, he found passengers already on the bus at the downtown Green vociferous after the small delay in the customary changeover of drivers.

"When do we get this show on the road, man?" whined one voice.

"We ain't got all day. I got my sister sick in hospital," piped up another.

"Give me a break!" said a third.

"Give the new guy a chance," added a fourth more equivocally.

"Let's rock 'n' roll," chimed in Dickon, now strapped into the driver's seat. He was already tired by the crack-of-noon chorus although he had only been on the bus two minutes. He was ready for blast off. He opened the bus door for its additional load of passengers, two with babies, one with a toddler, one laden with grocery bags, and two with canes. One cane seemed to be leading the woman, pulling her along to the front seat, running alongside the right window. These extra, new passengers duly deposited their fares in the fare dispenser machine. Then they were off.

Immediately, someone pulled the yellow cord running the extent of the window on both sides to signal a request stop at the next block at the top of the Green.

"Jesus Christ," thought Dickon, "they could've walked in the time they waited for the changeover," but all he said was, "Have a good day, ma'am," as a traditionally built white woman climbed wearily down the steps.

More people got on at the next corner stop between Milhous College's two art museums on opposite sides of the street. All of them, Dickon could tell, were heading for Sizewell Avenue at the point where town met gown but there was no crossover block or two between them, only a sharp shift from preppy white college to the impoverished neighborhood of Louvre Ville.

Like so many of the parallel worlds Dickon moved through, the college was its own closed world, a gated community, forbidding to the outside world, its only signs of organic life beyond the walls being the periodic blue lights that betokened safety-call telephone points for endangered students who had dared to put a toe outside the hallowed walls.

Dickon tried to concentrate on the road, the lights.

"Ida, I don't mind you sitting aside-a-me—like a spider," exclaimed one woman as someone crossed the aisle, "but you could say 'Excuse me,' on account of my sore back."

As another Delta bus from behind moved ahead of them, an old white man on the bus said to his neighbor, "Don't you just love how they niver stick to the schedule, how the bus company just makes up the rules as it bumps along? Bump, bump, bump."

"Ain't this a lovely day? Don't it make you feel jes cheerful," said another woman as if it was a logical punctuation mark in the omnibus conversation.

Dickon did not know whether to chuckle, wince at the irony, join in the free-for-all conversation, or simply set his face grimly. He muttered, "Hey, no one can touch me, I'm the man in charge."

For he had his own strategy—to lead the peasants' merrymaking with offbeat blue notes from his bass clarinet voice. When a woman said aloud, "I jes hope we get to the supermarket before all the best greens are gone," Dickon chimed in with "Cabbages? Cucumbers? Collards?"

She answered, "Collards."

He continued. "Collards are real good for the kidneys. They help clear and flush all the toxics out of your system—better then cranberry juice."

This brought the hubbub to a halt until the woman rejoined, "Where d'ya hear that, son?"

"I read it in the *New York Times*. Homes and Gardens

section. My girlfriend showed me," he added in order to show he was not available.

"You got a girlfriend?"

"Two. April and June."

"What happened to May?"

"Guess that was a lost weekend."

As they headed along Sizewell Avenue, a stringy woman told everyone, "There's a diversion at Pearl. Police out in force. Another shooting."

This shook up everyone—but not with fear since shootings were expected outside the city center; rather it was with excitement that they were all about to witness history in the raw.

Dickon's way of getting through a morning-after-day was to strut his stuff, to josh with the travelers, to play along with their complaints, and thus turn these scenes into a carnival. "Whaddaya say, ma'am?"

"Another shooting. Some guy from Louvre Ville came into the Hill territory. They shot him in front of the junior high school. They don't like people from one area going in another. But, what I say is, this is a free country and we got rights to go where we like. Lookee, the diversion's ahead. Can you see the police lights flashing?"

"Don't ya mean that shooting yesterday? It's in today's paper. Two shots rang out. Boom. Boom. One guy hit in the leg."

"That *was* yesterday. This is today. No remorse. They are cleaning up the neighborhood. Fixin' houses and this happens. We live in terrible times."

Dickon knew he had better make a driver's announcement. He started speaking into the recorded tannoy system.

"People, there's a police barrier ahead. We need to make a route diversion—into Pearl, along Inglewood Nook, back onto Foster, and then back en route to Sizewell."

But, when he replayed the recording, his voice came out booming like a rock guitar explosion. He stopped the recording, started again, and was about to repeat the voice-over announcement for magnified playback, when the chatter started.

"Are we going off route?" asked the old lady. "Can I get to Stop and Shop at the Plaza?"

"Can I get off here?" asked another woman just as Dickon steered the bus to the right from Sizewell into Pearl. "I need to get off."

"Lady, I can't do that. The bus company has its rules for your protection. Only designated stops except in the case of emergency."

"This is an emergency."

"No, lady—for the guy shot in front of the school, of course. For the people on the street. For us, just a temporary inconvenience."

"I wanna get off right here and now."

"No, lady, that's more than my job's worth. I let you get off except at a regular stop and you have an accident, it's my responsibility. I lose my job. I let you off and someone complains or then everyone wants their own personalized stop, it's my responsibility and I'm made accountable. We're turning back into Sizewell in just two minutes."

When they did turn back, yet another Delta bus passed them from behind and zoomed ahead.

"Lookee," said the assertive woman, "the police are waving everyone through. I guess the cordon's over. Now the press coverage begins."

Dickon's head was thumping from his all-night drinking.

Someone pulled the yellow cord for a regular stop.

As Dickon began to slow down the bus, the bell ringer said, "My mistake. I want the next stop."

"Will I miss my collards?" asked the supermarket shopper.

"This is everyday life on the Delta route," thought Dickon.

As the bus turned a corner, with Dickon having given all

the right signals, a kid on a bike—no more than fourteen or fifteen—swerved diagonally across the bus path. It was like a Spanish matador swirling his cape with a mad bull—the bus—in the ring.

"Crazy kid," said the assertive woman. "If they don't want to get killed one way, it's another. Don't envy your job," she added, with Dickon in mind.

And she laughed, slapping her hands on her knees, sending up dust from her jeans.

10 Keep a Diary and One Day It'll Keep You

When the big guy with the gold cufflinks next came back to the tumbledown, clapboard house in Cherry Street, CJ was ready for him in Candy's room.

"Didn't pay last time," said the big guy, extracting a small wad from the breast pocket of his blue check shirt. "Sixty do?"

"More like eighty," responded CJ. "Wanna smoke?"

This time he had a small tablet prescription phial with silver foil and ash on top that he handed to the big guy.

"Best before sex," added CJ.

When CJ loaded the narcotic on the silver foil he said, "There's little pin pricks in the foil. Breathe in through the pipe," indicating a slender white tube sticking out through the side.

"Nice and gently, now; breathe slow. Better? That's it. Better product. Not so harsh."

CJ's name was Cosmos Jones. He got the idea of "CJ" from the way Candy pronounced his signature, "C-O-J-o-n-e-s."

"They call me CJ. My name spells COJONES—do you know what that means? I got cojones. I got balls. I'm fit for anything. But it's not my cojones I got to peddle, if you catch my meaning."

The big guy was sitting on the bed. Candy wrapped her legs around his. Then, she wriggled out of her micro skirt. As he bent towards her, the pupils of her luminous eyes seemed larger, distended. Her skin did not so much glow as ooze sweat. The very room was rank. The big guy with the small gold cufflinks unfolded four twenty-dollar bills and handed them over.

Amid poverty and grime, solitariness and despair, Candy and CJ sat on the bed, trapped in their individual isolations. By their side, the big guy felt triple-trapped in career, marriage, and palling fantasy. When he was inside Candy, he had noticed a fluffy white rabbit perched on the headboard of the bed. It distracted him. He thought of himself as a white rabbit down the brushwood of the rabbit hole.

Outside, the driver thought he heard a scream piercing the air. He bolted out of the car, bounded up the steps of the insecure house and through the open front door, and raced up the stairs. Candy's pealing laughter drew him to her room. She was sitting aside the front of the bed with her tawdry slip gliding from her shoulders to expose her left nipple. Now standing by the open window, the big guy had an unfurling toilet roll in his hand. He threw it out the window, joking that "It's the last rat you'll find in this room."

"Plenty of rats, here," mused CJ. "Spoilt for choice."

When Leo Guerra let himself in back home, Lapak the dog fairly leapt to him, woofing excitedly. When he kissed his wife goodnight before turning over to sleep, he had murmured, "Miss Dainty Spread," as he usually did. She noticed he had a different smell—a sort of musk—on him; also, that his pupils were dilated. This set Bella's mind racing.

"He's at it again," was all she could think. "Who is it this time?"

She tossed and turned until morning.

As she always did when in doubt, she called her sister, Juno, next day. Former model Juno Foster was the wife of Abe Ripemoff, county supremo for blind people at VIPS (Visually Impaired People's Services). Juno knew the score. She had been there with a philandering husband of her own. She and Bella could talk in code. Without admitting anything, they exchanged confidences of infidelity misery.

Bella had the perfect overture for her phone call because Abe, through Juno, had sought makeup tips for himself—one he knew Leo Guerra used, as administered by his wife. When she made the call, Bella had notes to hand.

"I'll send you the makeup tips in the mail but I thought I should go through them with you in case Abe asks questions when he has to apply his makeup away from home.

"Here it is: Clinique. This is super balanced make-up. You use it all, like painting a fence. Don't forget the ears. Get Abe to close his eyes over the lids, and then smooth over everything with the liquid using a pad."

"My makeup days ended when I gave up modeling but this sounds like putting on makeup with a garden trowel."

"You got it in one. Now, here's another effect. Use a powder and apply dark terracotta Guerlain all over. After that, simply slap on the fake tan bronzer. Heightens the butch effect—so I'm told. It works for Leo."

"Bella, that's helpful. I'll explain everything to Abe."

Upstairs, Bella could hear her two daughters giggling as older Ellie applied some of her makeup to young Lizzie's face.

Bella found she could contain herself no longer.

"Juno, he's off with someone again. I recognize the signs—controlled absent-mindedness, firm grip on formal salutations—and a strange perfume. Is it Carla?"

"Carla's on the West Coast with her new husband—it's their honeymoon—been away for well over two weeks."

"Julia?"

"Julia's real hard pressed: some state report and there's a very tight deadline. I don't think she's got the time or energy."

"So, it's not Julia. But who?

Who indeed? From the comfort of his cage, the African parrot blinked as if he could tell the future.

That day, at work in the precinct, Leo Guerra, errant husband and police chief, the big guy with the small gold cufflinks, was in his office, discussing police strategy against the Louvre Ville drug gang.

Unintentionally interrupting his boss's reverie, McBride, his second-in-command, said, "Cocaine's a very insidious drug. Takes hold of you long after you've stopped taking it, long after you're no longer high. It warps your ability to handle situations and see things in perspective. Don't you think so, chief?"

The good shepherd wondered if he was meant to rise to the bait. Or was he just imagining things, sensing a threat where there was none?

"Listen, Candy."

A social worker was talking at her.

"We were here just two days ago. Your baby has been fed but not changed since then. Her diaper is wet and soiled. The bedclothes are stained with feces."

"Fee—?"

"Shit," said the social worker's aide.

"There are bruises on her arm. The constant wetness has given her sores. The neighbors called because she cries all the time. We came and found her in this terrible state."

"I try my best. The crying sure gets on my nerves."

"You're not the only one," called out CJ from the next room.

"Your best is not good enough. The darkened rooms, the lack of fresh air, the parade of men as you do business. It's bad for the little one. We're going to take your baby into care. The official papers are signed. Here's your copy. Make your mark here."

The social worker pointed at a dotted line. Candy did as she was told.

"But it's not fair. I'm becoming a better mom. I know important people."

"You've had three official warnings. Our primary concern has to be the little girl's health and safety."

The social worker put on plastic gloves. Her bodyguard stood to attention. She unfolded a wad of clean baby sheets. She took off the baby's own soiled clothes and put them into a plastic bag. She raised the little girl tenderly into her arms, wrapped her in new swaddling clothes. Most business-like, she made for the door as Candy slumped listlessly onto the dirty bed.

CJ stood aside.

As they got into the state car, the social worker could not help saying to her guard, "Made it. Just in time. Did you see the way she looked?"

"Looked at us?"

"No. Just looked. She's pregnant again."

The big guy with the power tie knew he was getting too deeply involved. He also knew how to play the young whore's game, or, if it were not her game, her pimp's game. He did not want to give up his nocturnal trysts with such a pretty, accommodating piece of flesh but he had to take charge. The next time he sought out Candice, he had his driver park the car directly in front of the next house on the street and toot the horn. When there was no response from the darkened house, he took a risk and had Phil the driver toot the horn again.

Upstairs, Candy was impatient. What could be keeping the big guy with the power tie? By his fine clothes and his insistent touch, he always made her feel so needed. Still he was not there. Then a horn sounded. She thought nothing of it. Then there was silence. She got up from her bedside chair and peeked out the window. There was his car. Then the horn tooted again. He wanted her. She would go. She practically flew down the stairs, out the front door, and onto the curb. The car window was down.

She said, "I waited. I put everyone off."

From the back seat, the big guy with the power tie, said, "Get in," and opened the door.

That was all she needed.

"Don't you feel pleasure? Don't be afraid. There's no shame. We need each other. Our pleasure is our happiness."

All this was new to Candy. She wondered where the big guy had found these words. Still, her endless anxiety was becoming exhilarating ecstasy. Her top was off and he was tugging at her bottoms, feeling her firm flesh underneath as he pulled off her tight pants, and feeling her lovely growing bulge. Then he fumbled in the pockets of his dangling-down trousers. She did not want to wait.

"Use these. CJ had them ready for us," she said as she pulled out two condoms and handed them to the big guy. Eagerly, he undid the sliver of the first sachet. She was as greedy for love as he. That was good.

But CJ had thought he was ahead of them both when he told Carrie as he held up a condom, "All it takes is one prick."

Carrie said, "She's pregnant, already—two months since."

"Well," he answered, not wanting to lose the initiative, "the next little baby will make our fortune. Keep us safe. Wait and see."

11 Eyesores

Marie Louise's ecstatic trysts with Dickon were interrupted by her having to spend a weekend away with her mother and get to know Gina's new husband at their home in the west of the state.

Just before she got into her car, Marie Louise ran back up the little path aside the emerging sunflowers and leapt into Dickon's arms.

"Dickon, you do love me, don't you? Really love me?"

"Sure. Dry your eyes."

"I'm plucking up my courage to tell my folks. The flowers will be fresh while I'm away. Just promise to love me, like I love you."

"Sure thing, my little Lady Bug."

Gina's latest husband, Harry, was twelve years younger than she was. At sixty-five, she could pass for a swinging forty. At fifty-something, he could pass for sixty. With a full head of white hair and dapper figure and clothes, cultivated manner and homespun words, he might have acted the idealized American president of a daytime television soap— so much more preferable to audiences than many of the real presidents they had to endure. But Harry only had one acting card—an adoring manner. For he adored Gina as if she were a Broadway star, which, in the life of her own soap opera, was what she was.

Harry had a comfortable pension from years of insurance work in the state capital, a town apartment in the night-time downtown desert by the Capitol building, and a converted country farmhouse in the west of the state where he could live to serve and service her.

Over the weekend, it dawned on Marie Louise that Gina's palpable unease had nothing to do with any nervousness about her meeting her new stepfather. She sensed what was coming.

Marie Louise and Dickon had exchanged sweet nothings on the phone several times over the weekend. When Gina overheard Marie Louise blowing a kiss into her cell phone, she decided to ascertain what her cunning little vixen was up to.

"Sit down, Marie Louise. Let me get to the point."

"Please do," interjected Marie Louise, critically rather than politely.

Gina broached the subject with a studied air of more-in-sorrow-than-in anger: "It's about this Dickon Young."

"Don't judge me. Who told you this, anyway?"

"I've heard you'll go with any Tom, Dick, or Harry."

"But I prefer Dick."

Before her mother could round on her for this impudent remark, spat out with brazen assurance, Marie Louise was ahead of her.

"Yes, it's true. I have a regular guy. His name is Dickon; he works for the bus company; regular job; regular guy."

"Is he—" Gina paused.

"Black? Yes, mommy dearest."

"You say he has a regular job?"

"Hard working, salt of the earth, protects me, utterly loyal."

"Another try? I hope this time it will all work out."

"I'm glad you have no objection, mommy dearest. That takes a load off my mind. Had you objected, I would have been miserable."

Marie Louise's unctuous words amounted to more defiance but Gina decided not to rise to the bait. This allowed Marie Louise to extend an olive branch.

"Mommy, I know it's inevitable that you will worry over me but this time I've found a good guy, true to me."

Marie Louise was tired with the two-hour drive from the western side of the state back to her little apartment in Norse Hoven with her lover and her cats. All she wanted was to climb into bed. As she parked the car, her heart bustled with excitement, she was thinking, "Here comes the moment of intense pleasure with my beautiful black lover."

Marie Louise turned the key in the lock to open her front door. Surely she could hear laughing from inside?

Inside, Dickon was on the sofa with a woman sitting on his lap, one leg crossed over his and the other dangling over the sofa seat with her sandal half on and half off. It was clear. Over the weekend, Dickon had installed an old flame in Marie Louise's apartment.

"Della's all right," said Dickon by way of introduction.

When she rose, Marie Louise could see Della was very tall. In her Tina-Turner-like-chicken-leg stance, she seemed all legs reaching into infinity, then all white teeth shining brilliantly against her dark skin, breaking alternately into smiles and snarls. Marie Louise tensed. She did not know which she dreaded the most. Marie Louise thought that, under their dark skin, both of them were blushing. Over in a corner, three cats sensed her trepidation and this added to her unease.

Della nudged Dickon. Thus prompted, Dickon continued, "Della's boyfriend threw her out. She can't go back to her folks. What with the dogs, there's no room. I said she could lay low here for a few days."

"My name's Della Ware—like the state if you say the two words together fast enough."

"Like the song, too," added Dickon.

"But I'm actually from South Carolina. My girl's with her father. I can clean and tidy the house," offered Della, this time with a sullen smile. "In the evenings, I'll be gone."

Marie Louise interpreted this to mean that, come nightfall, her unwelcome guest would be working the downtown streets.

"It's Tuesday now; you have till Saturday noon. My folks come here then."

Marie Louise had put down her two bags. Dickon took the one with the polka dots into the bedroom. One of the cats loped across the room, jumped into Marie Louise's armchair and then onto the rim of the back as if to say to the intruders, "This is Marie Louise's seat and I'm here to keep it warm for her."

As Marie Louise was about to sit down, Della rose and said, "Let me help you with the other bag, dearie."

Marie Louise shrugged and climbed into her chair to survey the scene made by the canoodling lovers. Dickon was now back in the room, caressing Della's rear as she was on her way to the kitchen. It was clear Dickon had been drinking. Despite her dread of his alcoholism, Marie Louise felt her desire stirring, her jealousy rising, and her humiliation forcing her tears. She realized she was now a prisoner in her own home—at least until morning when she might get help from her co-workers.

Della had also been provident: "I'll get us somat to eat," she said. "You must be hungry after your journey. How many hours is the west of the state?"

"Time-wise, two."

But Della was not listening. From the kitchen she produced three trays and on them three plates of scrapple, each with a fried egg on the side.

"Like I said, I'm from South Carolina. My little girl's with her daddy," she added as if it was inconsequential. "Like music, Marie Louise?" she asked, switching on the radio without waiting for an answer. A crooner had just started "Summertime."

"Marie Louise knows all antique music," put in Dickon. "It's from *Porgy and Bess*, right, Marie Louise?"

"What's it about?"

"A drug-dependent vamp moves between three lovers: a brute, a hustler, and a cripple," was Marie Louise's plot summary.

There was an awkward silence until Della asked, "You like *Porgy and Bess*?" as they settled to eat.

"Yeah, I like it; but I don't want to be in it," came the tart response.

"A bit late for that," added Dickon. "What did I tell you, Del, flits like a butterfly but clings like a flea."

This said, the sad trio finished their meal in silence. Then Dickon, as if on cue, said, "I'll clear up."

"That'll make a first," thought Marie Louise.

This left Della alone with Marie Louise, who sensed her hope of eviction, even by Saturday, ebbing away.

"Marie Louise, I have to be out this evening. Dickon says I can come back."

"Do I have a choice? Let me repeat myself. You have to be out by Saturday."

Della looked herself up and down in a tiny pocket mirror, titivated her makeup, and frisked up her orange-streaked hair. From the coat rack she plucked a frowsy blue coat and sidled over to the front door. As she turned the latch, looking over her shoulder suggestively like a stripper letting go of a loose bra strap, she added, "'Bye, dearie," and waltzed out into the cool night air.

When Marie Louise's eyes started to well up, it was involuntary. She waited momentarily, then she shouted to Dickon, now skulking in the kitchen, "Dickon, get your black ass in here."

Dickon did so and hulked his frame before her to increase

his size. He had an open beer can in his hand and glared at her.

"I want a commitment: you're the only man I've ever cared about."

"You mean I'm the only one who hasn't rejected you. Okay, do you 'really' love me?"

"You mean you've done something really stupid and you got found out. I get it all right! Well, the one thing this Delaware doesn't wear is a brand new jersey. Not in my house. How could you? I gave you a home."

"How could I? I'm a regular man with appetites. A mouse can't satisfy me. Takes a healthy young girl."

"Back to *Porgy and Bess*."

Marie Louise wanted to scream. She sensed she was shaking her meager voice at him like a tiny, clenched fist of impotent rage.

"You want a guy to see how your inner soul is beautiful? Someone without his own physical needs? Well, I'm not one of your social services friends. Your soul is as shriveled as your body is deformed."

"You're not a healthy stud. You're a parody of a drunken street punk."

"You're not a fine figure of a woman. You're a parody of a human bean, a squat little lump."

Marie Louise could stop her tears no longer. She collapsed back on the chair, kicking her legs in fury. She was also so scared that she now had no energy. All she wanted was for her mother to hold her.

The cats scuttled under the side table.

Marie Louise went to her bedroom and locked the door. Eventually, the exhaustion of traveling overcame her fear and she slept, albeit sick at heart. Next day, in her inner sanctum, her bedroom, she dressed punctiliously while the room got the morning sun.

"Poor thing," thought Marie Louise as she looked at the

pallid orb. Although it was still early morning, it was as if the sun was already saying farewell to its own light, declining into a haze so that the very street looked as if it was about to dissolve into humid twilight before day had even taken hold.

Then Marie Louise brushed her abundant hair as they had taught her at the school for crippled children.

Outside the bedroom, the newcomers were ready for her, all political polish to play on her generosity.

From the sofa, Dickon said, "I like Della and you will, too, if you give her a chance. She's ruled by one instinct—security. She's a healthy specimen of female flesh."

"Thanks a heap," said Della.

Marie Louise realized that Dickon was not only trying to wheedle her into accepting Della, but also sculpting his remarks with a vindictive edge as she clearly wanted to resist his scheme of setting up a harem in her apartment.

His physical stance, capped by a bitter, sneering expression seemed to be daring her to leave him, allowing him to take his pleasure where he chose. So, that was it. Marie Louise was there to have her own garden tilled at his convenience. Suddenly, she could well understand how brutish husbands provoked abused wives to murder.

Making sure she could stay in her new nest, Della resumed the attack.

"Don't think that to be happy, you have to put all your eggs in one basket. It's not dependent on being occupied with just one other fella. Start living for yourself. You give men—all men—the moon—everything you have—and they get bored. You join the company of the walking wounded if you must. But it's not my destiny."

"It's true. I don't want a life spent between the bed and the stove. But, but—it's not very romantic."

"Don't confuse romantic love with the practicalities of life."

Then there was work. Dickon's fickle attitude to work was another matter. Here, Marie Louise unexpectedly discovered Della Ware was her ally. When Dickon asked, first, Della, then, Marie Louise, to call in for him to the bus company and declare that he was sick, each, independently without the other knowing, said "No"—and none too politely.

"Get your ass outta there!"

While he was gone, Della persuaded Marie Louise to play a practical joke on Dickon to bring him to heel—to show him that having two wives meant two sets of responsibilities, two wardrobes, and two extra mouths to feed.

They knew he would come home that night drunk from the neighborhood bar. When he did, he was mumbling about his former girlfriend, April, before either of them knew him. As Della told Marie Louise, he imagined he saw April in the sunflowers outside the front door.

So, to tease him, Della had tiny Marie Louise crouch behind the waning sunflower, rustling it slightly and make it move. Dickon did what Della had told Marie Louise he would do. Because he thought a flower was his girlfriend, he reached out to touch her but she was not there.

"April," he said, half asking.

The sunflower was brittle from a snap of cold weather. As Marie Louise moved them, the leaves cracked and blew off into a hundred shivers. It was as if April was evaporating before his eyes. Dickon fell over and banged his nose. Then, Della was there, standing above him with her blatant chicken-leg stance and laughing.

"Get your fat ass inside; this is Marie Louise's home and you start to service her."

Marie Louise was now much taken with Della's streetwise patter and thought, "I better save that, set it aside for future use—especially in hospitals and airports."

"Where did you get the idea about the sunflowers?" she asked Della.

"From your kids' book on the shelf, dearie—about your little foxes."

12 Party Animals

Luke's unexpected reward for coming to help Mistress at Fast Track Sports was an invitation to Mistress's home for a cookout one evening, along with Louis—arranged by Carrie.

It was a dull, gray-clapboard, two-family house with many clapboards missing, some broken concrete steps to the front door, and a dingy entrance hall and front room. Carrie Behan was at her most expansive when she introduced Luke to her young half sister.

"We live two streets down. She's the real pretty one. Look at the face and those bedroom eyes!"

Once again, that tantalizingly well shaped teenager, Candy, stepped forward. She had dressed in a hurry. There was nothing remarkable in her black halter-top and denim bomber jacket but her sculpted jeans proclaimed designer label. They seemed strangely out of character with the rest of the ensemble. She was halfway through her pregnancy.

Carrie caught Luke trying to eye the shapely cut of the jeans and legs and butt inside them. She answered his unspoken question by saying, "She got the designer-label jeans from an admirer. Won't say whom. She's a quiet one but she always gets what she needs. Ain't that right, sis?"

"I's Candice Quint," said the girl, as if they had not met before.

"Pleased to meet you," said Luke.

If he expected Candy to say something such as "Likewise," he was more surprised by the way she repeated her first remark, "I's Candice Quint."

It was not exactly like a clockwork doll but not dissimilar. Yet there was something about that repetition as if there was also a hinted subtext: "You must have read about me."

"Hush, child," interrupted Mistress. "Luke don't know you yet."

"I's Candy. I ain't a child. I got experience. I got a child of my own."

Luke stared at Candy. Carrie Behan whispered in his ear, "Got it taken off of her by social services. Couldn't cope."

From the comfort of a shabby armchair, Mistress added, also ominously, "Said she wasn't a fit mother, if you follow my meaning."

While Luke pondered this, Candice interrupted.

"That was my first born. My little girl. My second one will be an important baby boy."

"You think she's young," chirped in Carrie.

"I'm eighteen," said Candice for the world as if everyone there regarded her as too young or too old.

"She may not be the sharpest kid on the block," added Carrie somewhat waspishly. "But she's a high flier when it comes to sugar daddies."

Then she drew Luke aside into the kitchen. "It was a difficult labor," said Carrie.

Luke thought she was talking about Candy and her lost baby. He soon realized that Carrie meant Candice's own mother giving birth to Candice herself.

"Candy came early. There were complications. They had to use oxygen and forceps and somehow Candy's brain got—just wasn't right. Given her problems, she's done well—special schooling and all."

Luke took it in.

The cooking was done al fresco over an old barbecue

borrowed from next door amid the tumbleweed garden of dilapidated ferns.

In the main room, Mistress was discussing the police chief's current war of attrition on the Louvre Ville drug gangs, a war supposedly coming to its climax with a forthcoming raid.

"Jail's the ideal home for these criminals—solitary confinement in a steel-barred cage."

Turning to her hamburger, she added, "Forty years in jail should teach them how to use a knife and fork for eating—not stabbing. Maybe they can start reading the good book."

"Police chief?" said Carrie. "Have I got news for you! You think the temperature's hot—well, the temperature's certainly rising and no mistake."

There was an awkward pause that Luke did not understand—like being excluded from a private joke. Somewhat lamely, he added, to start the conversation again, "Well, if it's not the heat, it's the humidity."

"Talking of heat wave, here's Louis," announced April, who was also there.

Indeed, after Louis entered the smoky downstairs room, the little party took to joshing about beer swilling, and more yet again on the rival physical claims of Hollywood's photogenic stars. When Louis was introduced to Candy, he recognized her immediately.

He said to Luke, "When I first went to Re-Re-Remedial Re-Re-Recuperation Services, there was a scuffle with a weirdo in a leather jacket—all made up for Halloween. He had come to make a scene in the lobby. The p-p-police carted him off to the pr-pr-precinct but he dropped a photo that I gave to my rehab officer—that's her, Candy. Something about how the co-co-cops had knocked up his sister."

Before he could say anything in reply, Luke and Louis were introduced to the card game of Pitty Pat, a diversion that ended with uproarious laughter over trifles. After they finished a hand, they dined on hot dogs with mustard and fried onions.

Mistress changed the subject. "How's your eyesight doin', son?" she asked Luke.

Her straightforward, open question troubled Luke. He was in no doubt that he was losing his eyesight progressively. But if his co-workers had guessed that it was getting yet more serious, surely his employers—past and present—must have guessed it, also.

Luke was on the horns of a dilemma and no mistake. While he was crossing the boundary into disabled status, step by step, with every new downward stage in his condition, his worst fears were psychological. It was as if the world of work seemed to disbelieve everything worthwhile in his previous career in publishing. He was a temp without qualifications who could not drive a car, had no money, no prospects, and lived off the charity of his mother's best friend.

Hitherto, Luke had kept his self respect by trying to minimize the impact of his sensory loss by revising his biography to himself and others—marking the important boundaries of his young life, not by successive educational stages but according to the successive crises of his deteriorating eyesight.

Luke's bitter experiences of stop-start, staccato work seemed to be telling him that he should now openly acknowledge his impairment. This would make legitimate and more palatable the abrupt decline in his income and his bleak future prospects. Could he try and come to terms with his reduced circumstances?

"You could go to Re-Re-Rehabilitation Re-Re-Recuperation Services, like me," suggested Louis, who, to Luke's surprise, was also a party to Luke's problem.

"They got me the job at Fast Tr-Tr-Track Sports—I know you don't like it but it saved my ass. They'll help you."

But before Luke could follow up this suggestion with

questions, Candice, appearing from nowhere, pressed a rose and stem in a plastic sheaf on him and kissed his cheek, almost like an anointing. This seemed to be some sort of signal to say goodnight. Mistress was getting tired.

She said, "If we call for a cab, they'll give a ballpark figure of twenty minutes for coming but won't come—not to this neighborhood. But if you walk three short blocks up to Olive, hone, there's an auto repair shop. This rose will tell them that we've sent you and they will get you a cab."

April added for good measure, "Rose's are red, Violet's are blue—what color are yours?" and the women fell about giggling until someone explained the joke to Louis.

It was time to go into the purple night of Louvre Ville. Luke carried out Candice's rose as if it were a little child.

"Watch where you're going, you two," called out Mistress as the two young men left to go their separate ways up and down Sizewell Avenue. Luke went up and Louis went down, disappearing into the mauve spring night.

Luke's eyesight was a hazard for walking straightfor-wardly down a street, especially at night and in rain when reflections multiplied the number of streetlights and car lights and the number of autos he saw on the road. But it also gave him the sense he was seeing things from several angles at once. These impressions were heightened by the frustrated energy amid the stifling sloth of spring life on house porches.

After five minutes or so, as Luke was crossing the road, he realized he had missed his way. Then, a kid riding a bike fast glanced him at his side and struck him square in the face crying, "Whitey, off the street!"

When he got to the far sidewalk, Luke knew even in the bluish-purple twilight that he was unfamiliar with this dark brushwood. Two shadows, little and large, passed him by. As if by instinct, he crossed the road again, this time to the kitty-cat corner opposite. It would be best to keep walking until he reached a street with brighter lights. He thought it would be a mistake to ask any passer-by for help. That would invite attack. Then the road turned but it seemed that he was reversing his path.

The two figures—he thought they were the same—were now in front of him. This time they were wearing hoods.

The taller one said, "Hey, punk, give over what you got."

Luke froze. Then he felt something hard in his gut, a rod. The taller hood then withdrew his arm and said, "Give us what you got. Or I'll use this."

It was clear—as if Luke could still see properly—that the hood was stroking his cheek with the metal cylinder. Luke stood as still as he could. Was there a gun? Was it a toy gun? The hood edged even closer. This time he slapped Luke across the face. Then again.

"Don't do that," was Luke's broken response.

"Do I have to repeat myself? Give us what you got, punk."

"All I've got is seven dollars."

"Sure thing, punk," said with sarcastic disbelief.

The second hood grasped the plastic sheaf with its pink rose and caressed Luke's face with it. He felt a sharp prick and realized that a thorn had torn his cheek. That would be the least of his problems. Luke fumbled in his right jacket pocket and handed over the money. With that, the hood slapped him again.

"Don't do that."

Then the hood raised his hand and cracked Luke across the top of his head.

"Don't do that."

When the hood did it again, there was a snap. Something fell to the ground. The smaller hood flicked a cigarette lighter, bent down, and shone it on the grassy ground: "Here."

The taller hood picked up the two pieces of the gun.

"It's broke."

"So," thought Luke, "it can't be a real gun—it must be a toy pistol."

Turning to Luke and shining the lighter in his face, the taller hood said, "Now you're for it." But, as he was retrieving the broken firearm, from somewhere in the distance came the unmistakable scream of a police siren.

"Quick!" was all Luke heard as the hoods hurried away into the shroud of darkness.

"Chance has saved me," he thought.

Luke tried to get a grip on himself. Once he felt safer, if only a little, he bent slightly, as unobtrusively as possible, to pat his left leg at the sock where he had hidden his last twenty dollars. Then, as he started to walk back somewhere—anywhere—it started. He felt wet running down the side of his head. He knew it was blood.

"If I can get back to the tavern on the avenue, someone will have to help me."

He held onto his thought. He took out his handkerchief and wiped the side of his face. The handkerchief was soaked. Lights in the distance got closer as the main street beckoned. Now Luke sensed there was light at the side.

"Hey, guy! What's happened? You been hit?"

Suddenly, an elderly black man was beside him, taking him by the arm. He led Luke to a car-repair shop at the side of the road. Then an elderly woman was moving toward them.

"Sit here, son," she said, motioning him to an empty wicker seat.

"Rose, call for an ambulance," said the man.

Luke sensed there were several vehicles inside and out of the shed.

"We repair autos here but, if a car's in the shop, it's stranded, come to the end of the road," added the man.

"I haven't any money or insurance."

"That doesn't matter, son," said the man. "Your head's cut

open at the back. You'll need stitches. The lapels of your jacket suit are getting soaked."

As Rose hobbled back from a wall phone, a police van drew up with screeching sound and blaring lights. A policeman was in conversation with the old man. Then he came over and asked Luke for details.

"Where did this happen?"

Luke was not at all sure. He fumbled over details—the hedges, the brushwood, and the wire netting. By his auto, the cop ordered, "Get in the front."

Luke got in and they were off, blaring away. Luke thought his ears would melt.

"At least the flow of blood seems to be over," he mumbled.

"That's a nasty cut," said a policeman. "You'll need stitches. The ambulance is coming. First, we need you to show us where. This the spot?"

They all got out.

"Looks familiar. Can't be sure. I don't see well."

"That a 'yes'?"

"Yes."

"Bad news, I'm afraid. Sorry kiddo. This crossroads is over the town line. We're Babel City Police. Not Norse Hoven. It's their responsibility. We'll have to hand over the investigation. You can either wait here or go back to the car-shop where we picked you up."

With that, and without waiting for Luke's answer, they were off. As the car sped away, Luke sensed his heart thumping. He was stranded in this infernal blackness just like before. There was no one around.

First, he sensed little specks of light, then bigger ones. He seemed to be heading back to the car-repair shop. Was he mistaken? Was it an ambulance? Was it a small group of people in the midst of blazing lights?

Then Luke heard something fizzing nearby and noticed a small flickering light. He paused. Then silence. Then he heard a noise, like someone blowing out. He stopped dead. Had they come back? Someone tall rose from the bushes and came up to him—big head, huge hands, and when he opened his mouth, chipped and broken teeth.

"What's up?" asked the man.

"I need to get back to the auto shop on the corner of Sizewell."

"Injured?"

"Knocked down."

Luke thought it would be better not to say more.

"I'll get you back. Let me settle my business first."

"Business here?"

"Ask no questions and I'll tell you no lies."

They walked back along the road Luke had come earlier in the police car. Soon, they were beside a row of shanty houses with more badly peeling paint and more broken clapboards. The big guy went up a side drive and tapped at a window.

"It's Rob. Let me in."

"I can't," answered a muffled woman's voice through the summer screen. CJ's here." Then, more softly, "On the ledge."

There was a bang from inside. The front door was flung open. A tall man stood silhouetted against the paltry inside light. "You want something? Something for the weekend? My lady? Or something to smoke?"

Luke realized that here was yet someone else brandishing a firearm.

"Stay still," muttered Luke's new friend back from the side window ledge and from behind clenched teeth. "Don't move. I'll do the talking."

He turned back to the man on the porch.

"It's Rob. Rob Burr. Markus sent me. We don't mean no harm."

"You better not," responded CJ.

"What you doing bringing a white dude here? You homo? Let's see what Carrie has to say 'bout that. Now, you back off or I'll blast you."

Rob edged back three paces, still facing the drawn gun. Luke did the same.

"You cause me trouble, I'll give you hell," continued the man on the porch.

"We're moving off, taking it steady. We'll be gone, out your way." Turning to Luke, Rob added, "Start walking slowly, and then take the right."

Luke did as he was bidden. Rob, if that was his name, also turned. They both moved cautiously with Rob glancing back occasionally. When they turned the next corner, he said, "Move faster—quicker pace."

Luke could not be sure where he was and what was around him. Were those twinkles of light ahead street lamps? Was that angular, dark shape to the side a truck? Was the swell of the ground the beginning of a hillock or just a bump in the scrub grass?

Surreptitiously, Rob raised his arm and slipped something into his mouth.

"You copped?" said Luke, more in surprise than as a question.

"Ah-ha," answered Rob Burr.

"But the window was closed. The girl hadn't enough time before the big guy emerged."

"What the eye don't see, the heart doesn't grieve over. So my mom told me. Now, what you got for me saving you?"

Rob bared his rotting teeth and it was not a smile. Involuntarily, Luke inhaled Rob's bad breath.

"I got nothing."

"I bet you still got your wallet. Give me that. I saved you."

Luke was dumb with fright but he pulled out the old wallet. Rob took it and scanned the contents.

"These the pin numbers? Convenient."

Rob had moved away from what might have been a truck and was advancing on Luke. Suddenly he fell, knocked down by someone banging open the truck door. He dropped the wallet.

"It's okay, Luke."

Luke would have known that vodka-martini-soaked voice anywhere. It was Louis. He could have leapt for joy.

Rob started to rouse himself.

"What the fuck!"

"You lay off Luke. He may be white and pr-pr-preppy but he's co-co-cool."

Turning to Luke, Louis said, "I thought I should come back, meet you at Ro-Ro-Rose's place—see you got that taxi home."

There was a slight moaning. It seemed to be coming from the open back of the truck where there was a solitary black trash bag.

"There's someone inside," said Luke.

The pain in his head was beginning to sting real badly but Luke pressed ahead, ignoring Rob Burr. When he moved closer, he tumbled slightly over the sodden earth with its treacherous little hillocks and their tufts of grass. Gingerly, Louis tore at the bag. Whatever it was inside groaned, "Help me, help me."

As Louis tore again, the plastic of the bag seemed to moan with every tweak.

A man inside looked petrified and spluttered.

"They got me, first on the head, then on the leg."

He gestured to his jeans, torn where a bullet had gone through.

Louis said, "It's Sp-Sp-Speedy the Vampire—Candy's brother. He's the dude who caused a scene at R-R-RRS when I first went there to see my rehab officer—tr-tr-tried to sc-sc-scare them by threatening to sp-sp-spray the walls with infected blood."

Rob Burr, out of his daze, realized there were lights to the side.

"Your ambulance is there. I'm off," said Rob.

"What about this poor guy?"

"What you goin' to tell the cops? That, after being robbed at gun point, you stopped over at some drug dealer's on the hill for some R and R?"

Rob Burr laughed. With that, he disappeared into the night. Now Luke had to concentrate. He leaned down to search around for the wallet in the brushwood. The man in the truck was sitting up, helped by Louis.

"It's no use, I can't move."

He was whimpering.

Luke's head wound started to ooze again as he bent forward. He was swinging his arms and hands forward and sideways to try and detect the lost wallet by touch. Then in the distance he heard someone say, "That's him—over there, moving about on the ground."

Luke stood up and the ambulance trundled nearer.

"Say, bud, what you doin'?" asked a paramedic. "They say you're injured. You need to keep your head still."

"My wallet."

"It's not important."

Someone was shining a torch. There was a ripple of a glint on the ground and Luke realized this must be the broken rose stem, still in its plastic sheaf.

"Who're your pals?"

"This is a friend, Louis. The other guy we found in a trash bag. He's been hurt real bad."

"First, they knocked me out with a stone," stuttered the man. "I'm Randy Quint. I got evidence."

"The wallet's here," said another paramedic.

"This it?" asked the first voice.

They passed the wallet across Luke's face.

"Let's get you both to the hospital. The Norse Hoven police will be there."

A paramedic pulled Luke into the ambulance. Another produced a stretcher for Randy Quint and the first paramedic helped him hoist the injured man inside.

Luke said, "I haven't got insurance."

"You've got a nasty cut. You need to prevent infection. There's no choice. Look at this poor guy beside you."

There was not room in the ambulance for Louis.

"That's okay, Luke. No pr-problem. Call me tomorrow."

As the ambulance paused at the main street before turning, the old man from the car shop came up again and said, "The Norse Hoven police will meet you at the hospital."

"Nobody could've been kinder than you and your wife."

With that, they were off.

In the emergency room a young medic scrutinized Luke's head.

"This will nip a little. We'll give you a local anesthetic. I have to clean the wound then stitch it."

Luke heard just outside the cubicle curtain, "Dave—a word. The other guy."

"I'll be with you momentarily," said the young medic. When he had finished cleaning Luke's wound, he went outside. Luke half-heard some discussion about stitches, clamps, and butterflies. When the doctor reappeared, he said, "We were talking about how best to secure the gash: I prefer stitches. I'll need to cut away some hair first."

He took a razor blade from a drawer in a side cabinet and started shaving away. By now, as the analgesic began to work, Luke felt relaxed. As the doctor started stitching away methodically, he suddenly found everything silly. The doctor kept him chatting about differences between American colleges.

When his scalp was stitched and bandaged, Luke needed to go to the men's room. In the corridor just outside, he heard a police officer talking to a man dressed as a hospital orderly. The cop had brown hair and a handlebar mustache. He was saying, "Randy's too badly injured for us to move him out of hospital. It means a guard twenty-four-seven. You have to get to him somehow before the taped interview with his lawyer beside him. Assure him he'll get full protection in exchange for his evidence against the Louvre Ville boys. But he has to button it up about the kid on the way."

"Otherwise?"

"Otherwise, we feed him to the dogs."

Luke returned to the cubicle and the doctor let two policemen in to see him. Luke adopted a mask of composure while he told his tale. The only thing Luke was clear about was the cops' final instruction, "We'll need you to try and identify the guys from ID photos and give a more detailed statement."

"What about the other guy? He's all right?"

"Don't concern yourself. It's already early Saturday morning. Go home. Get some sleep. After the weekend—Monday or Tuesday—come into the main police precinct on State Street. Ask for Sergeant McSweeny."

When the police had left, the young doctor reappeared and gave Luke antibiotics and a prescription for more. He also made arrangements for Luke to return to the hospital to have the stitches removed.

"Randy, can you hear me?

The supine figure on the bed swathed in bandages and tubes as his body was being fed by drips looked like the outsize chrysalis of an insect. But it did not stir.

"We'll do everything to help you, keep you safe," said the cop in hospital uniform. "If you can hear me, just tap my finger while my hand holds yours."

There was no movement.

"Randy, all we ask of you is that you say nothing about the

95

kid. Don't get your emotions confused with your safety."

McSweeny felt the slightest hint of a tap.

When Luke awoke with the watery sun, he wondered how he would explain himself to Hermione, first the blow to the jaw in New York, now the gun crack to the head in Norse Hoven. Would he have another eye hemorrhage? He could not hide the plaster and bandage. Hermione, who was leery of illness, might think all he did was cause trouble.

Luke found her up before him sipping coffee with the *Norse Hoven Courier*, its news section spread out across the kitchen table. But Hermione had other things on her mind.

"Luke, you remember that story we read the night you came here—about the delivery guy killed in a case of mistaken identity?"

Luke nodded.

"Well, here's the tragic sequel. There was a long delay to the funeral while the police held the body in storage for forensics and they wouldn't release it to the family. Now, at that poor guy's funeral, there was a drive-by shooting. The press report says, 'Shots from a car claimed the life of Markus Ramirez, 22, and injured two churchgoers. Terrified mourners ducked for cover among parked cars as gangsters sprayed the walls around the church cemetery. Markus died in hospital from a wound caused by a revolver bullet that struck him in the torso. Police think this may be another tragic episode in a gang feud and also that it may be yet another case of mistaken identity.'"

"Jeez!"

The next paragraph was marred by a misprint:

"Police Chief Leo Guerra says, 'We will leave no turd unstoned to apprehend the criminals behind this killing of an innocent man.'"

"Whaddya think?"

"I think, in addition to the personal tragedies, the press

report is a signal to us that there is also some underground police operation ongoing—not that it's going to be wrapped up tomorrow but there's a decided strategy to break up the drug gangs. The police chief won't rest until the gang culture is destroyed."

So, Hermione realized there was more to this story than the circumspect account in the *Courier*. Steve Sharp opposite was in her debt for her looking after young Dennis. She knew that, as editor for Network News Norse Hoven, he would know the underside of the story. So, she pumped him.

"Right across the state, the governor's chief secretary has told press, TV, and radio stations to report the investigation of the Louvre Ville gang as minimally as possible so as not to prejudice a forthcoming raid and subsequent trial. We've complied.

"Now, as long as this doesn't go any further: These two apparently random, unconnected street murders are part of the inner story of the Louvre Ville Gang.

"The family of the first victim, Zack Flower, denied that he was a gang member. In fact, he was studying at college to become an engineer. He was delivering pizzas part time. He was the victim of indiscriminate shooting. His sister, Violet, was the girlfriend of Markus Ramirez, the second victim. Markus Ramirez *was* a minor gang member. He, too, had enrolled on a junior college course aimed at helping young adults with criminal pasts. To stay on the straight and narrow, he avoided all his old haunts. He had only returned to Louvre Ville for the funeral of Zack Flower— remember, his girl was Zack's sister. He was shot coming out of the church. Violet was pregnant with their second child.

"It all ties into the general picture the police have of the Louvre Ville gang. A complex web of cell evidence has led police to the killers of Markus Ramirez and Zack Flower.

The suspects are all big shots in the Louvre Ville Gang. Two brothers lead it: Anton and Rafael Purgatori. The police have been shadowing them for months through cell phone messages, sightings, and so on."

When Luke took this in, he was thinking, "How does the brutalizing of Randy Quint fit into all this?"

13 De-Selections

The next Tuesday Luke did as the police had asked him. He arrived at the police complex on State Street, a large, anonymous-looking building. Its vast surfaces of poured concrete with ridges had no street windows. Luke ascended the formidable cascade of front steps.

"What you want, boy?" asked a cop on the front door.

Luke explained his business.

"Straight ahead, take the right, first office on the left."

When Luke arrived at the enquiry point, he handed in his police notice with the incident number. He was startled by a voice from behind.

"Have no doubt about it; the thugs who led this gang—especially Rafael and Anton Purgatori—are among the most dangerous men in the county."

Luke knew who it was from the flash clothes and the commanding manner. It was Leo Guerra, the police chief, Ella's father, across the way, just inside an open doorway, holding forth to two reporters.

"These hoods have created an entire network of criminals. They have easy access to firearms. They are ready and willing to use violent death every day to enforce their overall strategy of settling scores with rival gangs. They simply don't care whom they injure or kill. They've subjected entire neighborhoods to a reign of terror."

Luke was brought up sharp by another voice to his side: "I'm Sergeant McSweeny. Come to my station."

Luke recognized McSweeny as the cop with the handlebar mustache from the hospital corridor. McSweeny recognized Luke. He did not want this witness to the conversation about Randy Quint anywhere near the precinct. He steered Luke to an inner chamber with a sequence of interlocking, gray, shoulder-high cubicles like the publisher's office in New York but less swish. The garish blare from overhead neon lights was overpowering. Some men were chatting in pairs, others tapping keyboards, their faces obsessed on computer screens. Others were rapping out orders on phones.

"Sit here, son," ordered the sergeant.

"Paging Sergeant McSweeny: come to the chief's office," rang out a voice over the harsh intercom.

"'Scuse," said McSweeny as he rose and left.

While McSweeny was away, Luke caught sight of a sheet torn from a lined yellow pad on his desk. He edged his chair forward and peering his eyes, he read:

NOWHEAR THIS ALL U HATERS: YOU WANT THEM BANGED UP BUT THEY WON'T BEGONE FOREVER SO SHAME ONYOU: 39 YEARS! MIGHT AS WELL BE GONE FOREVER!

Luke was pondering this note with the threat, probably related to the weekend gang story, when he overheard McSweeny say to someone as he was returning, "It's a curious thing. Both our new informants tell the same story. The Louvre Ville Gang leaders like to act out they're real dangerous fellows but, what do they do with their time?"

"Smoke the product?" asked someone.

"Naw, they stick to marijuana—make it a point of honor. Besides chasing girls, they while away their time playing computer games, and, against their bad boy image, in watching kids' DVDs like *Toy Story*."

When McSweeny was back in the little cubicle with Luke, he carried on with their conversation as if he had never left.

"See, here, boy, we don't ask members of the public to come in at will. Victims or not. This here is a well-run orderly precinct. We don't need a statement from you or for you to try photo identifying at this here investigation.

"When we nail our suspects, then we'll consider—I said 'consider'—notifying you for more details. Let me escort you out of this, here, emporium."

Sergeant McSweeny rose, signaling to Luke that he, too, should also rise. With that, he sent Luke away with a flea in his ear. As Luke descended the cascade of steps, he heard McSweeny call out, "It was nice you could drop by."

The loitering druggies, leaning on the waist-high balustrade by the steps, laughed.

Then one of them stepped right in front of Luke's face. Even without the rotting teeth, Luke would have known him from his bad breath.

"You didn't think I would forget what you owe me, did you, my friend?" said Rob Burr. "Going my way to a cash machine, perhaps?"

Luke felt his stomach churn. It was broad daylight and yet he was being intimidated all the same and there was no one to help.

"I'm going to the hospital," he stammered and started off, walking as fast as he could since to run was impossible and he knew that Rob Burr could take him down. Rob shadowed him, stopping from time to time to spit into the road. When Luke quickened his pace, Rob quickened his.

"There's a cash machine in the hospital lobby. We can stop there," Rob called out.

Inside the police precinct, Police Chief Leo Guerra was

about to do what he did best: managing meetings as surely as he managed his troops of police.

"Yes, dear," his wife, Bella, had asked when he had told her about the meeting, after giving her a reluctant peck on the cheek the night before. "But what will you wear?"

"Leave that to me, Miss Dainty Spread. I'll make sure I look damned good—dressed to kill."

Leo Guerra surveyed his array of belts and ties before choosing ones for work that day. His wife was pondering who might be his current girlfriend, chosen at random from among her girl friends.

And now there he was, snakeskin belt with studs, power-red tie, contrasting nicely with button-down collar, striped blue shirt to minimize his paunch, and fully in command.

As he entered the strategy room, Leo Guerra glanced round, taking them all in, the loyal supporters, the indifferent cops just there for regular paychecks, the deputy who coveted his job. At least there was no hack journalist there.

His colleague, Barker, was holding forth when he arrived.

"My guess is that Markus Ramirez was killed because Rafael and Anton Purgatori believed he was still a member of the rival gang, the Hill Crew. It was the Hill Crew who shot Markus Ramirez's brother years ago while Markus was in jail."

Calling his war council to order, Leo Guerra announced with satisfaction, "We've had two breakthroughs in our campaign against the Louvre Ville, thanks, unfortunately, to the murder over the weekend.

"First, there's Lennie DeBoeuf. He's the one who runs the drug dealers. But he's not the sharpest tool in the box. While running from the Chevrolet car used for the killing, he snagged his woolen hat on a hedge. The lab has recovered his DNA from the hat and matched it with our records from when he was involved in an assault a couple of years back. Also, a fiber of his hair was found inside the Chevrolet used in the ambush where there's also telltale firearm residue.

Running for cover from the car he threw off his gloves and they've also been found with his DNA on them. So we've placed him at the murder scene."

"He's in custody?" asked the note taker.

"Yip. And here's the onion. When he was arrested and inspected in a very private place, we found he had $2,000 worth of cocaine stuffed up his ass.

"Second, we've now got a potential star witness against the Louvre Ville Gang."

"A super grass?" asked the note taker again.

"Exactly so. This is Rayard Quint, age twenty."

The police chief seemed to hesitate slightly at that name. He collected himself.

"During the affray last week he got himself shot in the leg. He was later spotted limping at the back of Sizewell. He was traced to an address in Pearl Street. Later, he was found collapsed, banged up in a trash bag by the preppy guy the paramedics took in after being hit on the head."

"Randy Quint's ready to turn state's witness," added uppity Barker for good measure. He continued.

"It seems he's been tortured in some hell-of-a-row over drugs money. Randy says—and he's ready to testify—that the Sizewell Gang's enforcer, Chucky Shah, was responsible. Randy claims he was knocked unconscious with a large stone. Then, they tied him to a tree in a side road off Sizewell. After the medics took him in, they found cuts ripping up his precious six-pack. It was as if Chucky had been playing with him while he was out stone cold."

The deputy smirked at his bitter joke.

"All this was just after Markus Ramirez was shot dead. Randy thinks that he's gonna be next. That's why he had a woman friend come in—she's a friend, not a girlfriend: Simone DeBoxer. They've started to open up about the gang's murders and drug dealings."

McSweeny, who had been there with them all and then

disappeared, reappeared without explanation. Leo Guerra glared but continued more forcefully.

"This dame, Simone DeBoxer, has two kids and she's addicted to crack. God knows how they manage—get the kids to school and stuff. We've had her house under surveillance for some time. It's behind Sizewell. The gang has turned it into a safe house where they use the kitchen to chop up the cocaine for distribution. They let her use the stuff—to test it, see if they can get away with excessive cutting to dilute it."

Barker wanted to show he was up there with the chief.

"You can bet your bottom dollar, it's the usual story: gang members use pay-as-you-go cell phones to conduct their business deals. They drive by in hired cars with dark-tinted windows to patrol their patch. All this leaves its trail of evidence."

The chief took over.

"Right, here's Plan A. From the information we've got so far, find out if anyone else wants to escape the gang's clutches. Assure them of immunity from prosecution and protective measures, if they will give evidence."

Barker prompted his boss again.

"We'll need to get the state to assign one of their attorneys to baby-sit the witnesses, make sure they don't get the jitters. There'll be those witnesses we won't be able to protect once we reach trial in court because of the intimate nature of their evidence. So—"

"—Well, the usual. Beforehand, they'll live in safe houses in different towns across the state. If they have to be named in court, they'll give evidence from behind screens or via TV links, so the defense can't intimidate them. The hi-tech guys have all sorts of devices—voice distortion and video links.

"There's another trail. The gang spend lavishly. Some things we can't quantify so easily—house parties, night-clubs, liquor. But others we can. They buy jewelry—gold chains, mostly—and fancy cars. Even if they pay by cash, the car dealers will remember them."

McSweeny spoke up, anxious to show he was still a player.

"Chief, if we get hold of their cell phones, by using cell sites—they're the antennae locations that route calls and text messages—we can place gang members at specific locations for drug deals, shootings."

"Right. Not least, we need to assemble our crack teams for taking the Sizewell Gang down when we arrest them.

"There's another thing. When we nail the gang leaders we want to make sure the charges stick. It won't help our reputation and our mission if we seize six or seven hoods, press charges, go to court and some of the hoods get off on a technicality or because the jury isn't convinced. We need a full sweep. So, to avoid confusion, we're going to leave the lesser players, like Mr. C. O. Jones and Mr. Rob Burr, alone for the time being. They won't know that, of course, and will be nervous and may do something stupid. If and when they do, we'll take them down but later in separate arrests and for separate cases."

Stung and already feeling that he was being rebuked for his sight loss as much as his temerity in thinking the police would listen to him, Luke arrived at the university hospital out of breath. As it bore down on the paved forecourt of the hospital, the sun did not seem so welcoming, more like another accuser.

Although the security guards waved Luke with his bandaged head inside, they stopped Mr. Burr to question him and, with that, Luke made his getaway inside to have his stitches taken out. However, his hopes that he would be treated by the kindly medic who had sewn up his scalp after the attack were soon dashed. A young Chinese-American doctor stared at him with blinking hostility.

"My name is Doctor Noh," she said blowing out her exclamation in a way that set her hair bangs fluttering. "And you are who?"

Luke explained. Dr. Noh led him to a curtained cubicle. She removed the bandages and sighed involuntarily.

"This is serious. I'm no expert in taking out stitches."

Luke took this to mean she had never taken out stitches before and was balking at a first, unsupervised attempt. She started to snip the first stitch but it would not budge. She tugged to no avail. Luke winced. The very stitches seemed to moan in protest. Dr. Noh was startled. Alert as ever, she seized an opportunity to find help elsewhere.

"I look-see for my colleague in the next station," she added, her evident apprehension breaking up her English. "I new here."

Luke clenched and unclenched his fists in the few minutes she was away. He tried to focus on what seemed metal plates in the hospital ceiling. His unease deepened as he overheard a spat in another cubicle between a patient and a nurse.

"I came here to get help. I know what I want and what's my entitlement," said a man with a southern drawl.

"You entitled to nothin'," answered a male nurse. This was also with a southern drawl, but Luke wasn't sure if it was the genuine article or an attempt at sarcastic mimicry.

"I know my rights," continued the patient.

"You always trouble. Sit down or I'll make you," came a retort from a woman's voice.

"I won't."

"Do as I say," rasped the woman's voice followed by the unmistakable sound of a slap across the face.

When Dr. Noh returned to Luke, her face was grim set.

"My colleague unavailable."

She clutched pincers in her right hand.

Luke faltered, anxious both to postpone any ordeal and, simultaneously, to have it over with as quickly as possible.

105

"If you want me to wait, or come back—"

He had a sinking feeling in the pit of his stomach.

"You racist, then, boy?" said a male nurse who had appeared and whose voice Luke recognized. "You think because the doctor's Chinese, she's the chink in the armor of the hospital?"

Dr. Noh advanced with tenacity beyond her skill.

"No anesthetic. I proceed like an Asian panther."

And so she started to snip.

She stood at Luke's side, the pincer hold of her legs on his chair echoing the pincer cuts of her snippers. There was no hesitation. This time, when she tugged, she pulled this way and that. In a minute, the first stitch was out.

"Here, I mop your blood."

Luke was not sure if this was a misfired, flickering attempt at kindness or another assertion of control. The second stitch came out easily But not the third and fourth. Luke wondered if he was sinking. The doctor wet some tissues and wiped his face, before using them to wipe the little shaved spot on his scalp to clean away its sprinkles of blood. So they proceeded until the process was over. Luke slumped forward.

"Wake up, blind boy," rasped the nurse from somewhere behind him.

Dr. Noh added, "You are free to go and not return here again."

Luke rose and groped his way to the reception point and sat down again. He was sure the threatening Rob Burr would still be outside. Just as he plucked up his resolve to face him down in the forecourt, Steve Sharp was suddenly by his side.

"Hi, Luke! Hermione called and asked me to give you a ride home—said you might feel dizzy. I'm on my lunch break, so I'm happy to oblige."

They left by a side door to reach the hospital car park.

Luke breathed a sigh of relief. But his second encounter and escape from the petty hood set his mind to work. Throughout his progress from one meaningless temp job to another, Luke had been trying to regain control over his professional life. When he faced up to them, he realized that the consequences of his sight loss and his recent brush with death opened up opportunities because his priorities had changed. He decided he would not go back to Fast Track Sports. But before they were to get better, things got worse.

Summer

14 Learning to be Blind

It was hardly love at first sight. But, in their first conversation as officer and client, Marie Louise Garden and Luke Reader recognized an opportunity in the other. That was enough.

For, stimulated by Louis's suggestion, and encouraged by Hermione who remembered how one of her old school friends had had her life first turned upside down by an auto accident and had then been rescued by retraining and job protection provided by Remedial Recuperation Services, Luke made his way to the RRS office for the midweek introductory meeting.

And this was how Luke met Marie Louise Garden.

Luke stared and stared, as much as someone with his eyesight could do. Who was this? There was none of the squat pug-faced or regularly proportioned but compact figure of the two usual types of dwarfism. Louis had said nothing about this. Whoever she was, she had grown up— what a term!—lop-sided, barrel-chested, loping-gaited. She was so wizened, it was like someone old at seventy.

In her office, Marie Louise listened to Luke's career biography with its two crucial points—that he was progressively losing his eyesight and that this had led to "discrimination in the workplace": publishers did not want him and temp agency work was also too difficult.

"To begin with, after the diagnosis there was basically nothing—nothing at all. At the eye hospital the doctor's attitude was, 'So, you've got eye problems. Sort them out.

Goodbye; Au revoir; Ciao; Dasvidanya.' I was offered nothing. I panicked because I couldn't run my apartment in the city; couldn't even prepare dinner. Those were the really scary times.

"It's not just a matter of trying to cope financially," added Luke, "but also of trying to retain some purpose, and get some protection against adverse office politics. In the temp jobs I always feel that, when they discover I've got problems with my sight, they start to regard it as another inconvenience. I was starting to get frightened to go out but Hermione—she's a good friend of my mom's—helped me."

Marie Louise nodded then ran through her range of routine official questions.

"Does your sensory impairment affect your ability to do your work? Do you have problems at work on account of difficulties in the physical environment?"

After hearing Luke summarize his sad experiences and answer "Yes" to each question and noting his anecdotal evidence, Marie Louise summed up the situation with a formulaic conclusion that, to Luke, now came as manna from heaven:

"You have sensory problems—okay?—but it's the way your employers—like the publishers—condemn you for them that makes you disabled."

Marie Louise shuffled forms on her desk. This pause allowed Luke Reader to stare around the gray-blue office with its many adaptations.

"First, for us to proceed we have to find out exactly what's wrong with your eyes medically. The hospital in New York is currently closed on account of financial problems, so, no luck with your records there. We'll have to get you appraised at the university hospital here. But, if they confirm that you should be on the blind register, then RRS has to pass your case to VIPS—Visually Impaired People's Services."

As they neared the end of the interview, Marie Louise held out her arms for Luke to assist her getting down from her perch to walk to the door. As she did so, she leaned very slightly towards him and pushed herself onto his thigh. Luke was startled as if he was receiving the flighty intentions of a family pet. He felt uncomfortable.

But his discomfort was complicated because, as Luke realized from their conversation, it was clear that he and Marie Louise were drawn to one another through shared ideas. Luke had already begun to draw parallels between his unfortunate series of temp jobs categorizing things and his own present position of being categorized himself. Later, he would leaf through articles on disability Hermione had found for him on the Internet.

"Erving Goffman says that those who become stigmatized in later life are in a quandary of re-identification. It's like when people become immigrants in America. They have to learn and abide by American values if they are ever to be accepted here."

But there was practical work to do. Luke now had papers to complete to apply for a federal disability pension and more papers for supplementary state aid. There were offices scattered across the county for Luke to call at to register for this, that, and the other. He felt he was being sucked into a wind tunnel, that his life was being rolled out, stretched out to ever greater lengths like a pastry sheaf for baklava, and extended so far it was as paper thin as his overstretched retinas.

As to the pension, Luke knew that might not be straightforward.

"In thirteen years in RRS," Marie Louise had told him, "I've only once had a client approved for a federal pension the first time round. What happens is: you apply and they reject you. Then, you ask for a review. After two or three attempts, they agree."

If Luke were to achieve any of this, he needed Marie Louise's help not only in guiding him through the forest of applications but also to secure the crucial certificate of legal blindness.

This depended on two independent eye doctors determining whether his eyesight—with each eye assessed separately—met one or both of two criteria: the distance he could see objects on an eye chart with letters and the visual field—assessing what sight there was right across each eye. Having one very bad eye or one entirely blind eye was not enough. The state government determined the state of your vision according to the better eye. The federal government then decided whether or not to award you a disability pension. The state decided whether to offer financial succor while your federal pension was being processed. After it was granted, the state decided if you required additional funds.

Because of her own menu of health problems, Marie Louise was well known in the downtown hospital fraternity. For his VIP classification, she arranged for Luke to be examined by her preferred eye surgeons, each with different specialties. Here she did not strike gold. The first doctor and his team, whose notes, as was the practice at the hospital, were kept separate from the other teams there, were simply jaded about myopia no matter how extreme.

One dismissive doctor said, "Because of your series of eye injuries and all the laser surgery, your peripheral vision is reduced. Then, you have this distortion in the macular of both eyes. Overall, you probably have about a third of the visual field in each eye. We'll run Goldman tests to determine the pattern of both visual fields."

Yet Luke's double vision fascinated them. The shift upwards in the left eye and downwards in the right registered immediately when the doctors used blinkers to close or open sight in either eye alternately. Luke's response to the central pillar of red light in the test was automatic and involuntary.

The numerous allergic imperfections, abrasions, and diminutive pustules over the whites of his eyes also excited the doctors. They knew the cause:

"You live with cats—several cats—and you are allergic to them. You and your friend need to think about that and maybe reduce the numbers, cut down the cat size."

Luke caught the unintended wordplay on "cat size" and "cats' eyes"—the small studs on highways that beamed reflective light from car headlights to help guide night-time drivers—and he found it funny. He tried to explain it to the surgeon who neither understood nor appreciated the joke.

As to his overlapping double vision, higher in the left eye than the right, Marie Louise made arrangements for him to have hospital inspections for a correction by prisms. One day, Luke found himself at a clinic seemingly knee-deep in pre-school children running around their concerned parents. The doctor preferred to use a Fresnel prism, a plastic lens with optically determined corrugated strips affixed by natural suction to the glass in the specs lens for his weaker eye. After experimenting with different strengths and getting Luke Reader to make his own judgment in the adjacent corridor, the better to test length of vision, they found a prism with a strength that eliminated the double vision. However, after trying it at home and on the street, Luke discovered that the Fresnel prism had different, newer problems. It made his sight darker, more occluded. The effect on him was to turn the eye inside out so that he seemed to be projecting the various interior pathologies of the eye—floaters, repairs, sealed tears—onto his outer vision. It really was like looking through a glass darkly. In addition, the Fresnel prism got dirty and discolored after ten days. Looking at the world in Luke's eyes with the prisms was like staring outwards from inside a murky pool. He preferred the sharper if more distorted vision of his regular eyeglasses.

From Marie Louise's perspective, the one important conclusion after the various eye examinations was going to be the doctors' final verdict. Marie Louise's professional experience and her insight were such that she could detect medical differences of opinion and any qualification through the subtlest shifts in prose. She found the first report negligent in particulars that the state needed to make a determination on legal blindness. Therefore, the second report would be doubly important.

After Luke had his second inspection with one Dr. Chicago, Marie Louise knew Dr. Chicago concurred with the medical consensus on Luke: blindness caused by pathological myopia. But Luke's social case could not advance to blind certification, state recognition, social rehabilitation, and pension award without this second medical determination that she had arranged to be paid for by Remedial Recuperation Services. And it had to be written and signed by Dr. Chicago.

A constitutional procrastinator, Dr. Chicago did not write the report immediately. He put his notes on top of a bulging in-tray. As days passed into a third week, Marie Louise wondered if Luke would ever receive his due after years of work and taxes.

Marie Louise went to Dr. Chicago's clinic and took command.

"Dr Chicago, this is what we have to do about Luke Reader. If the delay in your assessment goes on much longer, Luke's federal application for registration and benefits might have no validity because the documents will be out of time. Let me help you. This is what you need to say."

She took a sheet of paper out of her pocketbook and began to dictate what Dr. Chicago should write down, starting with her emotional response to Luke's personal qualities and refined education—everything, in fact, that would make him marriageable material in her mother's eyes. Dr. Chicago was putty in her hands when Marie Louise was at her most winning.

Although Luke had groaned inwardly when he started the process of benefits applications, he heard within two months that the US federal government would award him a pension; his first attempt had been successful. The money he would get was based on some actuarial system that, when translated, relayed his past earnings as a student and as a professional editor into a federal pension of $595 per month.

The pension was to start in five months' time after the date it was approved. Luke would be paid on the third of each month either by check in the mail or electronically into a bank account. Each January the payment would rise according to the rate of inflation as determined by the federal government. There were restrictions as to how much extra money recipients of a disability pension could earn.

"Don't even try; don't even think about it," Marie Louise warned him, "at least, not to begin with. You get the pension on the grounds that you aren't capable of work. If you try and work—although regulations allow it—they might suspect your grounds for applying."

Luke saw the system was moving him along, up and down the snakes-and-ladders' checker boards. But it was not getting him anywhere in terms of a job, which was why he had applied to RRS. In learning to be blind, he felt he was entering the world of the invisible man. He wanted to scream to become visible again, to be electrifyingly audible.

Marie Louise also told Luke that, in the five or six months before receiving the federal pension, and the two or three months before that, when his state application was being assessed, since she insisted he did not work, his only source of income must be provided by the state. To get state aid entailed another set of applications and state assessment of what resources he might have—savings in the bank; any unearned income; any assets such as property or stocks and shares. If he had nothing, the state would determine his needs based on cost of board and lodging and any legitimate medical expenses.

Hence, Marie Louise set Luke Reader on a revisionist program of behavior: learning to be blind.

"We have to present your medical difficulties to the state in such a way as to ensure that they will not use your social interaction with other people against you—imply there can't be much wrong with you if you have a social life. At the same time, you have to set limits on your socializing with regular people. Don't do anything that will embarrass them. Above all, try and avoid expressions of anger or self-pity."

"You want me to adopt an ingratiating manner?"

"That would be best. What it amounts to is this. Disabled people who are nice and respond to everything dutifully— those who are compliant—are rewarded. But those who try and keep a strong individual identity, or who have presence or a distinctive character, or who protest about things that are wrong or unfair get themselves disliked in the workplace, in social services, and by local and state government. One way or another they soon get cautioned. In effect, they are punished."

Luke realized when he attended one of their group meetings that, inside Remedial Recuperation Services, people were just as incapable of settling down and completing anything as the discontented underclass of temp workers at Fast Track Sports. Like the flotsam and jetsam temps, the longer people stayed in the unfulfilling environment of RRS, the more likely they were to deteriorate in body and soul.

One day Luke stood waiting for Marie Louise at the back of the room during an induction meeting led by Rod Fortune. As the applicants started to fill in their forms to join RRS, Marie Louise at the side and Luke at the back listened to two men who had finished their forms ahead of the others. They were talking about retirement pensions. Evidently burnt out by work, they were both trying to parlay long-term ill health into "disability" so that they might receive a pension before they reached retirement age.

The younger one with regular features and jet-black hair without any gray, Marie Louise found attractive, if podgy.

He was saying, "I'm fifty-two next year. I want to retire but I can't afford to. My back still hurts badly from the industrial accident but I can't touch my pension plan till I'm sixty-two. Plus, they've started to delay the start of federal pensions. It no longer begins at sixty-five. I have to wait until I'm older. Besides, the gap between Medicare and the cost of health treatment is too high for me even to think of retiring."

His companion was older, a man with a weather-beaten face and straggling wisps of gray hair peeping out from a dirty baseball cap. He chimed in with, "That's right, son. My eyes ain't that good. They let another guy go from the clothing store after eighteen years' hard work just because he was due for their benefits scheme. Let him go. No compensation but Social Security unemployment."

"You see," resumed the younger man as if his friend had never spoken, "at one time, they said the trouble with American business was that you were just a number. Now, you're just an overhead."

"That's right," said Marie Louise to herself. Then she thought, "And Remedial Recuperation Services has to pick up what's left over."

"Marie Louise certainly set the ball rolling," observed Hermione.

For, after the state issued Luke with the due certificate of blindness, Luke had three visitors.

The first was a Puerto Rican showman. Eddie Carreras arrived in a glossy car with a chauffeur guide guard who said nothing. Unobtrusively, he led Eddie up the dusty, dusty stairs without drawing attention to Eddie's needing him or the house needing cleaning and repair. Yet his blunted features and retiring manner did not hide the fact that he provided Eddie's sense of sight. When he bared his teeth, he looked intimidating.

Both men wore sunshades. It was only by staring that Luke realized that the VIPS man's eyeglasses were completely blacked out and that one side of his face was badly scarred.

"Auto accident," remarked Hermione later. "All down his left side—pitted, nasty lacerations."

Eddie Carreras was all glinting smiles with razor-sharp, white incisors and canine teeth, ready to demolish any fabric of dissociation.

"You're blind, my friend; you're blind—get used to it," announced Eddie, more to draw Luke into his web than as constructive advice about the rest of his life. Luke responded to his questions with as pithy an account of his family, his schooling, and so on as he could manage. He turned his progress through college degrees into something as easy as rising each day, washing, and making breakfast—something he did not always do.

"See, guy," said his interlocutor. "VIPS and me, we're in the position of educating you."

Luke started.

"Then, of getting you to front our organization and indoctrinate—teach—people to be good, blind citizens for the benefit of all."

Eddie flicked not-so-imaginary dust from his trousers as he sat in the tottery wicker chair among the crumpled wreckage of Luke's books and papers—journals, letters, bills, and detritus—that might, henceforth, be immediately to hand but out of sight. To Luke, they represented an ever-darkening woodland glade of business and private responsibilities—unseen, potent reminders of financial and legal demands with ever-shifting goalposts.

"What you need, guy," said Eddie, unintentionally interrupting Luke's silent reverie, "is more education. You're an educated man, I know. But how's your IT skills?"

"OK, I suppose."

"OK isn't good enough; we need you to be super-duper on PCs to front for VIPS. I'll arrange it. Take a note, Matt," he said to the sidekick.

"Someone will be in touch. You'll go to private class two days a week. This is Plan A. You complete the course, we see how you do, and then we try and move you into position as a front man for VIPS."

Eddie was as sure as his word.

Two days a week Luke found himself on the bus to a coastal town, a journey of no great distance in miles but two hours along winding country lanes, some gas-infested stretches of highways, aside coastal vistas, quaint blue-collar neighborhoods, and bourgeois suburban sprawl until the bus deposited him. Then he was on a strip of interconnected shopping malls, all 1990's bland, post-modern vernacular interspersed with remnants of 1970's brutalist modernism. In Luke's particular eyesight, the mix was like small-town America's reassertion of practical coziness to soften the flattening impact of corporate capitalist anonymity.

"Forty-Second Street, here we come," thought Luke with never a thought that this was like the Disneyfication of the Deuce, 42nd Street's most notorious block.

Sometimes he had to wait for a few minutes after he arrived while the previous class finished. So he had time to appraise other disabled students.

Whether, before they came to the IT classes, they worked in dreary office or factory sweatshop, they would disparage their work to others while pretending to their supervisors that they enjoyed it all. Wedged in the net of Rehabilitation or Disability, they quickly caught onto set words and phrases, politically correct for the moment, as appropriate for disabled people as the equivalent jargon on Publishers' Row.

Luke concluded that this society was very much like the worlds of pictures-for-publishers and clothes-in-categories. People passed through the stewardship of rehabilitation and disability as others did in publishing or sports apparel but with no more self-determination than laboratory animals in experiments.

It was evident that disabled people were big business—not like spectator sports or rock concerts—but big enough and providing employment and economic opportunities for those who serviced and managed them in the public and private spheres. It seemed that disabled people needed special education and special equipment so that they could access the expanding world of Internet communication. Also, they were supposed to acquire the personal skills to master the modern tools of the sophisticated office workplace of electronic gadgetry. And there to help them, purely out of the goodness of its heart, was Corporate America, providing computers, enabling software, and personal training in the capitalist gym of all-American business success.

And what about the rehabilitation officers, social workers, and VIP counselors? What they needed to do to fulfill their contractual obligations under state scrutiny was to move the pawns across the chess board as if they were so many sheets of paper being moved from Inbox to Outbox.

Luke thought of Louis and his co-workers, protected by condemnation to a life of always-minimum wage while their minders received double the sum. Thus, disabled people were fodder for government employees, whether federal or state. RRS worked when it came to locating low-grade jobs for people broken in mind or body. It also protected them from adverse politics of disability discrimination. But there was no far horizon with a promise of better things to come.

Luke's second home visitor from VIPS was a mild-mannered middle-aged man with a mane of silver hair restrained by a red bandana across his forehead and a red ribbon at the back to knot his effulgent strands into a streaky pony tail.

"Left-over hippie," Hermione told Luke later.

"My name's Pierre—Pierre Lafarge," he said by way of introduction. "I work for VIPS as a mobility instructor. You're lucky to have me," he added with self-satisfied insouciance.

"Normally, in the summer vacation we concentrate on training school kids. But there was a cancellation—some summer-bug illness. We've only got forty-five minutes. Let's rock and roll."

As they left the house, he paused to ask Luke what two routes they might attempt.

"I need some basic long-cane training and find out how to cross White Water Avenue down the block—I need that in the rush hour, and then to get up the hill on Spliff Street as far as the supermarket."

Pierre undid a large holding bag he took from his car and measured Luke impromptu for an appropriate size of red-and-white cane. He made his selection and folded Luke's fingers round the top of the cane:

"The colors of the cane announce you to everyone else on the street but its real function is to help you navigate left, right, and center as you move along the sidewalk."

As Pierre and Luke set off down the steep breast of the hill to the main avenue at the end of the block, Pierre began by moving Luke's arm so that the cane almost skimmed the surface but tapped the ground on either side of his body.

"This way you perceive objects en route—such as garbage cans, bottles—any impediments—but also variations in the surface ahead—not just road works with barriers but also dips, holes, ridges, indentations.

"Now we've gotten started, I want you always to be aware of two things: first, the way you handle the cane ahead of you; and, second, rhythm. There's a rhythm to the movement. Your swing should be offbeat with your step. People who've worked as professional dancers find this easy. That's because they know how to swing it."

"Like being in the groove."

"Exactly so."

But Luke felt far from relaxed. He tensed up so that his tapping left, center, and right was stilted and erratic. He simply had no swing.

"Let's rest momentarily," ordered the ever-helpful Pierre.

Luke tried to broaden the chitchat.

"Can I ask you? Why did you go into this line of work—helping blind people?"

"Sure. I was training to be a civil engineer but suddenly we were in a war. So—to get out of going to Vietnam: to evade the draft."

They walked to the foot of the hill in silence, Luke still tapping away until he felt they were on level ground. By the mailbox on the corner of White Water Avenue, he found he did not need to explain anything.

Pierre stood, legs akimbo, patting the back pockets of his slacks, surveying the torrent of traffic, and remarked, "Seems you've got an endless supply of difficulties on this road and it's not even rush hour. The traffic pounds along in both directions. The bus stop you need for downtown is directly opposite so it would just make it too much extra work to walk three long blocks to the next crossroads where there is a pedestrian crossing, especially in bad winter weather. Doesn't the traffic ever cease?"

"Not during the day."

"Then, you'll need to navigate by gauging the pulse of the traffic controlled to the left by the lights at Spliff Street and to the right by the rhythm of access from the highway slip road. There will be a pulse. If only we had time."

Then, seizing an opportunity that he sensed but Luke could not, he almost yelled, "Quick!" and pulled Luke along with him to dash across the road in a flickering break in between both streams of cars.

"That was a close one," Pierre gasped when they reached the far sidewalk.

Luke was not sure if this was meant to bolster his sense of self-confidence or heighten his sense of social need.

They proceeded to Spliff Street. They discussed Luke's need to get to the supermarket almost every day, this time up a hill. Negotiating the sidewalk with the cane was nigh impossible as the sidewalk on one side varied between short bands of paving and extensive, unmown grass verges with bushes and brushwood just in front of clumps of trees to the side. Luke's cane snarled and tangled in the undergrowth. He got exasperated and, well before they reached Spliff Street, he had given up using the cane as navigator. Pierre had already filled him in about coping with the mysteries of an uneven disappearing sidewalk.

"The principle is always to walk on the sidewalk opposite the flow of traffic. You can use what sight you've got to respond appropriately when you're facing the traffic."

Pierre gasped. For, on Spliff Street, because of the overhanging trees, drivers on the road could not see who or what was on the side.

"The problem is you need to climb the hill but there's no sidewalk going up opposite the traffic flow. Whether you're going up or down the hill, you will always need to use the one side that has a semblance of a sidewalk."

Luke and Pierre advanced gingerly. When the allotted

time had elapsed. Pierre returned Luke to his home street.

The back of Pierre's estate wagon had dozens of white canes, bundled together like witches' broomsticks. He shuffled among them.

"Also, there's this—it's a shorter walking cane. Very popular with seniors. I have an elderly lady on the shoreline. She told me she kept losing her cane. But that couldn't be right. I found out that she'd being giving away VIP canes like lollipops to her girl friends. Imagine.

"Remember to practice using the cane in your own neighborhood—about fifteen minutes at a time. Also, I want you to use these."

He handed Luke a pair of blacked-out eyeglasses.

"Try the safest part of your walk wearing these and using the cane. First, just up and down your street; when you're more confident, your street and the three blocks along White Water Avenue. Bonne chance."

Pierre got into his estate wagon and sped away.

"It's as if they're teaching me to be blind," Luke said to Hermione.

When they talked it over, he said, "It's one thing to conform to the medical standard of being legally blind. It's another to become socially blind with the way rehabilitation officers train people like me who have some useful residual vision to become dependent."

Luke felt he was falling into a bottomless abyss. Pierre Lafarge's diligent instruction, the IT classes, Marie Louise's edict against him working—it all opened a yawning chasm of nothingness.

Nevertheless, Luke thought there was no time like the present to follow through Pierre's instructions. He unfolded the cane and retraced his steps down the hill and along White Water Avenue to Spliff Street. Then he let the cane drop to its full length. He tried to use it as Pierre Lafarge had shown him. To the left, tap, back to the center, to the right, tap, and reverse. Luke's sense of purpose and control wavered. At first, he thought he must be imagining things but he had the sense that he was being followed.

He stopped to glance up and down the main road. Was that Marie Louise's specially designed little buggy ahead of him? Surely not. He thought he must have been imagining things. But the feeling returned. Then, he collected himself and moved on but his concentration was shot. He looked again at the road and there, surely, it *was* Marie Louise's car. This time the car was on his side of the road crawling until stalled by red lights at the intersection ahead. She was almost at his side. The left front window was down. Sure enough: it was Marie Louise.

"Hi! Luke! Are you enjoying the sunny weather after all that rain over the weekend?"

"Sure thing, Marie Louise."

The traffic lights must have changed.

"See you soon. 'Bye."

Once again, as had happened in her office, Luke had the same sinking feeling that he was becoming some sort of target. But the lightning impact of what Luke was to learn was that Marie Louise's latest obsession was not going to restore his sight, although it would sharpen his perception.

When Luke got home, there was a letter from the state waiting for him. Successful with the application for a federal pension, it seemed that Luke had been unsuccessful in his application for state financial aid in the five months before the pension started.

"Just think," said Steve Sharp who was with Hermione in the kitchen. "You're now eligible for handicap parking. You could get the blue badge and give it to me since you won't be driving anywhere."

It seemed that in Luke's new status there was something for everyone.

Marie Louise now found herself between her undependable black lover, the bird-in-the-hand who exploited her vulnerable generosity and whom she could lull herself into thinking of as "my man," and this whey-faced bird-in-the-bush. Realistically, Luke was out of reach. As a client, he should have been out of bounds. She knew that. But, as a catch, he represented her mother's compromise of genteel, pliant disability with a refined, educated mind. Marie Louise mused on this.

However, her mother's example was also never to make a choice and abide with it. Choice of a man was choice of the best available for the present. You could always find a new partner later. That was the American way. Or that was how Marie Louise interpreted it.

Luke's third visitor at home was none other than Marie Louise herself. He was tapping away at his keyboard when Hermione called up the stairs, "Luke, you have a visitor."

He sensed from Hermione's tone that this visitor was unwelcome but her tone also suggested concern for him rather than irritation at the intruder. When he went to the door of his bedroom, Marie Louise was stumping her way up the crook in the steps as the stairs turned a corner. He sensed she was apprehensive.

"I expect you're surprised to see me here," she began.

"Not really," he answered.

"No?"

Now she was taken by surprise, first by his not being surprised and then by the room, the rickety shelves bulging with box files, the windows that had perhaps not being cleaned for twenty years, and the scattered crumpled clothes. It was a dusty, dusty house and no mistake, and she, Marie Louise, must rescue her darling from it. Then she noticed on the wall, between the windows, museum reproductions of pictures of women: elegant aristos with capes, inviting bartenders before bottles of hard stuff; soft-focus gazelle-like creatures in poppy fields; and harder-lined, distorted faces that she knew were from Cubist paintings.

Distracted, she said, "You like art? This art?"

"Well, you know, I was working as a picture gofer for publishers just before the latest eye crisis."

"Yeah, you said. Great!"

Without seeing, Luke knew where her gaze had alighted and lingered.

"It's called *Las Meninas*—the ladies in waiting. The painter is Velazquez. He's looking at the king and queen as he paints their double portrait. You can see them reflected in the mirror on the far wall. In the right forefront are the king's daughter—the Infanta or princess—with her ladies-in-waiting and," he hesitated, "two playmates." He hesitated again. "Dwarves."

For once, Marie Louise said nothing. Luke went on with his little lecture.

"The painting hangs in the Prado, the art museum in Madrid. There used to be a large mirror in front of the painting. If you looked at it via the mirror, the entire painting was in pure 3D—absolute three-dimensional. But, when the Prado got a new director who wanted to set his stamp on the collection, things were rearranged. The mirror was taken away and, with it, the 3D effect. Pouf! Invisible!"

"So, everything became flatter?" asked Marie Louise.

"I'm afraid, so: dwindled into still life."

With that, Marie Louise reverted to her written script.

"Yesterday, I received these documents at work. They're for you to complete and sign in order to appeal against the state's rejection of financial aid until you start the federal pension. I was shopping in the neighborhood and I thought it best to bring them right over."

Luke sat on the bed and she sat on the bedside chair, shuffled in it and indicated a large envelope with papers. As he bent over the cabinet for the papers, Marie Louise grazed his forearm with a sheet of paper like a feather of desire. She quivered. Luke started. Then he realized he needed her.

"Can you—?" he began.

"Help you fill in the papers? Sure."

They toddled downstairs to the large dining room table through the arch. Marie Louise held her hand aloft for him to guide her. Luke hoisted her onto an old high chair, and put on the overhead light. They began to work through the questions and answers of the appeal papers methodically, according to Marie Louise's instructions.

When they finished, Luke realized that Marie Louise was waiting for something—a token. He went upstairs, peeled the *Las Meninas* reproduction from its moorings on his bedroom wall and brought it down for her. To seal the bargain of her helping him with a kiss, as she left the house, Marie Louise swung on his arm in the front doorway. Instead of a peck on the cheek, she poked her tongue in Luke's mouth. Marie Louise followed her parting gift with a crackled peal of laughter so intense that she had to hold her legs together to stop her wetting herself.

As Hermione appraised this quaint scene from her chair, she reflected that Marie Louise, wizened though she was, could have been any age. Yet her flagrantly expressed desire to be openly voluptuous was even more shocking to Hermione than it was to Luke. But, as she cautioned him, Hermione could not resist her natural impulse to put herself in Marie Louise's tiny shoes and to express her frustration at having to deny herself natural pleasure and fulfillment.

"Just think for a second about the extra load this tiny woman has to bear on top of her physical misshapenness, sensory problems, and bouts of ill health. Society expects her to play—no, to conform—to three parts. One is the spotless girl, sexually chaste. At the same time, she is expected to endure rebuffs passively, despite the fact that she has no realistic expectation of getting married. Think of the mental frustration there must be inside her."

Young Dennis called out from his scrabble game, "If I add an 'F', it turns 'rigid' into 'frigid' but I don't know what it means."

Neither Luke nor Hermione wanted to enlighten him.

"Then, society insists that she remains an old maid, compelled to eke out her life as a mental cripple as well as a physical one, wholly deprived of any sex life. Because she has grasped at whatever straws of sexual comfort she can get, her co-workers probably look on her as no better than a whore. It's almost as if she has no better status than one of her stray cats. But it shouldn't be your problem and she shouldn't try and make it yours."

15 Graspit Street

Luke thought he must be living through some cognitive dissonance—the sort of thing he had read about in college books and academic reviews. Here he was, three weeks later, with Marie Louise in a rundown social-security office in a slum neighborhood. Since the state denied Luke further benefit until his federal pension began and he had appealed the decision, the two of them were awaiting a hearing and a final ruling.

The dilapidated clapboard houses, many designed in Dutch-Colonial style as two-family houses for the rising bourgeoisie of the early twentieth century, had seen far better days. The original palette of colors—farmhouse vermilion, sky-gray Colonial, and all-purpose magnolia—still carried some residue of off-white trim for the eaves, window frames, and doors. But the baking sun of many summers and the lashings of winter rain and snow had done their work remorselessly without remedy of repair so that the paint had peeled, edgings had buckled, and clapboards had snapped.

The whole environment stank of dereliction from the ragged, overgrown grass verges to the uncollected garbage cans, overflowing with scattered rubbish. In addition, the sporadic street signs, many bent part sideways—everything bespoke dilapidation. This was a neighborhood rank with economic deprivation.

The people there—for it was the middle of the day and the thoroughfare was busy with grocery shoppers moving to and from a local convenience store and many others, including welfare clients, were wending their soulless way to the Graspit Street Social Services office—moved like shells of human beings.

The unofficial guards of the Graspit Street building, set back inside a small gated compound of ragamuffin wire meshing, adorned with a spiraling crown of barbed wire, were men loitering—hanging out—looking for a casual handout, partly by a show of servile begging, partly by latent intimidation with a patter that began with, "Can I ask you a question?"

It seemed to Luke that he was moving in a stagnant fantasy fiction, living in three parallel universes at once. One, rapidly fading, was the world according to government records, official histories, and newspaper accounts of political and economic news. For here in that poverty-stricken universe was a stereotypical broken-down neighborhood with, at its center, a government office processing benefit applications according to rules.

Another parallel universe translated this scene into something like the imaginative paintings of Romare Beardon in which the regular subjects of a painting had exchanged roles. For middle-class patrons of art, it was human beings who ran society. They owned the world and were possessors of its art. But no, in this alternate version, it was the buildings and the environment that controlled their lives. When it came to animal life, instead of humankind determining the way the world ran, in Romare Beardon's paintings it was cats and dogs, birds and insects, around whom everything else moved.

A third parallel universe was yet more surreal for, in it, the first two collided, merging and dissolving. In this universe, it was random chance—accidents of timing and location—that shaped results. In government-speak, it was "outcomes" that determined what happened. However, human choice and assertiveness, human courage and secretiveness, also interrupted, cajoled, and threatened the order of the first world and jolted the inanimate objects of the second.

Luke's own way of interpreting all this was determined partly by his experiences and his response to them; partly by his education; and partly by the special insights of his distorted visual field. His visual field was now restricted to a roundel of central vision but splintered by the damage to his retina, and multiplied by the overlapping of his double vision.

The entrance hall to the Graspit Street building was capacious with a low counter running opposite the door, and divided into portions by half screens, with chairs for clients at the front and chairs on the far side for the benefits officers. There was a second chamber to the right, hidden from view in part by an arched opening. In front of the main counter were metal chairs divided into two blocks. The gray walls and dark lighting could not completely obscure the peeling walls, and the sporadic stabs of illegible graffiti on the wall alongside official notices. It was as if the very décor, with its muted, dirty colors, was describing despair.

The low level of conversational buzz, punctuated by crying babies, toddlers tumbling about, and pseudo-threats of discipline by rattled parents—all these spoke about disorder and benefit dependency, as did the stench of unwashed human odor.

Clients were meant to take a numbered ticket from a machine on a wall, then sit and wait for their number to be called. Only regular attendees understood the system. They would contribute to the sullen conversation buzz by barking out advice to embarrassed newcomers, who entered timidly through the front swing doors. Once someone called your number, you showed your ID and explained your business to the benefit clerk. You were then apportioned a metal chair to await a summons for detailed discussion. As to the outcome, it was a lottery as to whether your benefits clerk was knowledgeable or ignorant, friendly or hostile.

As they waited for the summons, Marie Louise explained to Luke in her tiniest whisper, "You've got to understand that these clerks are poorly educated and on low salaries— perhaps only thirteen thousand dollars a year. So, in the end, they may be worse off than some of their clients. That's one reason why they're so gloomy."

Marie Louise's explanation gave Luke a glimmering of the public face and the behind-the-scenes culture of the social-services office. The workers were trapped in a dilapidated environment, crammed into tiny workboxes with co-workers they probably would not have chosen and clients they certainly would have preferred to avoid at all costs outside. However, faced with the necessity of having to make a living, their nine-to-five world was an unrelieved purgatory of physical discomfort. The dulling pressure of time remorseless drained their energy. Their world was unsettling territory. There was no point in questions about the meaning of life when everything proclaimed the emptiness of human existence.

Luke was abruptly summoned by a huge, menacing woman. She simply called him by his last name, "Reader!" As there was no response, she called out again, "Reader! Reader, I mandate you right now!"

Luke embarked on a yet more surreal twist to his journey. Holding hands, Luke and Marie Louise advanced, she needing his hand for physical support, he holding hers for psychological reassurance. They proceeded behind the huge shady form of the clerk to the hidden, second chamber. Motioned to sit in another gray room, the three of them faced not one another across a desk but towards an outsize flat television monitor hoisted in a corner. The large woman, Bertha, switched it on. Her outfit was as dreary as the setting, except for her bolero jacket, an iridescent concoction with sparkling thread so luminous as to concentrate Luke's eyes on this unexpected splash of haut couture.

Luke Reader had expected that he and Marie Louise would meet his benefits adversary together with an adjudicator. Marie Louise knew better. The adjudicator was but a face and voice on TV.

This latter-day incarnation of the Wizard of Oz skulking in his palace was an elderly man with gray hair, gray jacket, and gray face against a medley of trash-television colors, mainly pink, gray, and yellow. He opened proceedings. Here was an upright judge of impartiality according to state rules. The juxtaposition of high-tech communication in this tawdry side office with shabby furniture and equipment was, to Luke, the most bizarre element in this surreal world.

The moderator explained he was adjudicating the case from the state capitol. Bertha, the benefits adversary, began producing from nowhere, like a magician's assistant, sheaves of documents. Among them was Luke's file, which, of course, he had not seen.

Luke then put his case. Luke's argument was that he needed state aid to be able to survive until he received his promised federal pension in five months' time. The state's rebuttal was that it had to abide by regulations.

The state and its officials knew the rules. Part of its method of control was by not communicating them. Thus, it took advantage of clients' ignorance. What Big Bertha produced by way of figures and statistics, Luke mused, was like mass production. There were figures to show Luke's supposed income; figures to show his alleged expenses; state-determined estimates of what Luke should be paying for clothing and shelter, fuel and food.

Bertha positively quivered with indignation that a stripling would question her financial probity. When she moved, her flesh rustled the folds of her dress like the wind blowing to suggest devilish possession.

"Obey the rules," the rustle seemed to say, "You are destitute; grovel for cake."

The very sight of this clerk took Marie Louise back to her favorite childhood story of the cunning little vixen. From her tiny perspective, she was like a little fox cub before a forester's humungous wife in the childhood story. The clerk's aggressive behavior signaled to Marie Louise that she was a working mother trapped in a big dipper of a hated career hurtling ever downwards while work papers cascaded all around. Luke switched his mind to Alice in Wonderland seemingly about to be buried alive by the playing cards cascading at the end of the book.

As Bertha's tirade continued its *basso-cantante* rumble, Luke meandered into his memory of the world of daytime TV repeats. Hermione had squealed with laughter when she told him of a British comedy show wherein unfortunate victims found themselves confronted by nightmares of torture and responded with, "I wasn't expecting the Spanish Inquisition."

Marie Louise piped up about human need but faltered in the face of judgment by CCTV, itself a parody of the restricted parameters of partial hearing, partial viewing, and willing incomprehension by the state.

The adjudicator cleared his throat and began:

"You might want solace from the heart but the Congress wasn't established to instigate social legislation. Nor does it exist to support legislation on the grounds of compassion. Mrs. Rochester, your caseworker over there, knows this and so do I. Social programs exist to promote the economic survival of society. Our best legislation exists to support values of achievement and accumulation."

Having pretended in advance that this would be an evenly balanced decision, during the hearing itself Marie Louise needed to recover her status as savior in Luke's eyes. At the end, when the guillotine fell on Luke's hopes as the adjudicator confirmed state denial of aid, Marie Louise fumbled for words, now more to prop up her status than to console Luke. While the process of client degradation droned on, Marie Louise recalled again that, as her clients were processed with their applications for disability benefits, disability certification, and Medicare, the system operated via a series of double standards. It encouraged mean streaks in officials whenever it was convenient politically and acceptable socially.

"S'pose it's always difficult to know what will happen in such a close call," she began.

"It wasn't a close call at all," Luke replied. "It was curtains."

Hermione had her own scheme to jolt Luke out of depression and—just maybe—the possibility of part-time work.

When he came into the dining room, after his unsuccessful brush with the state, she was sifting through Luke's portfolio of illustrations for past publishing projects and laying out the photos of Hollywood stars on the dining room table, arranging them as if they were Tarot cards telling fate.

Steve Sharp was standing behind her.

Hermione explained, "Steve is going to run a TV feature on women's fashions in makeup and clothes in Hollywood movies and Madison Avenue magazines. I told him about your publishing projects and I thought you wouldn't mind me letting him see how far you had got and the range you had unearthed just before you came to live here."

Luke shrugged. He realized Hermione was trying to do him a favor by peddling his wares before someone who might—just possibly—help him.

Steve said, "All this is great. From the university museums and libraries nearby, it's easy to find illustrations of paintings by artists like John Singer Sargent of American aristos in England before World War I and of drawings by John Held, Jr., of flappers teaching old dogs new tricks right across the U. S. of A., in the 1920s. But we've been stumped to find anything other than dowdy images in the film stills of panda-eyes Theda Bara and the vacuous IT girl Clara Bow. Show these broad-beamed hearties on TV and the viewers will switch channels."

Luke knew Hermione was damned clever. Now he wondered if Hermione was also staging all this to goad him out of depression so that he might impress Steve Sharp? Who was she helping? Steve or him? But he rose to the bait.

"If I may advise you, you need to work with what TV does best and use its limitations—2D rather than 3D, line rather than flesh impact in the round."

Once he started, Luke could not stop.

"What it comes down to is this. What fashion advertisements need to sell clothes was—and remains—image. What that image was, turned out to be the best possible two-dimensional image on the printed page in fashion magazines and newspaper color magazines. It was not how women looked in three dimensions in real life that mattered but how their images looked in two dimensions. It was not

135

how they looked in the flesh but how their clothes hung on their skeletal frames."

What surprised Steve Sharp was that Luke with his quirky legally blind double vision had guessed at and interpreted something that the fully sighted Steve Sharp had never thought about until now. He became absorbed in the photos, setting them in apposition one to another in chronological order.

Luke went into the kitchen to help Hermione with coffee and she told him quietly, "Here's one way you could stay in the workplace while you're waiting for your federal pension and be in an environment sympathetic to, and supportive of, disabled people."

Back in the dining room, Luke said to Steve who was all ears, "Television commercials, which did, and do, show people moving and were, therefore, in the round, might show off makeup and beauty products. But they've never made a central feature of commercials for fashionable clothes. Well, that's just my opinion."

"And it's local news, too," said Hermione. "Luke has an unerring ability to find what's essential from what comes to hand. By chance, he found this coffee-table book of Vogue models at a street vendor's stall in Greenwich Village."

She produced the book.

"And look who we have here. Here's the former Juno Foster wearing a Dior gown."

"The wife of Abe Ripemoff, the head of VIPS?"

"Yip. And the sister of Bella Guerra, the police chief's wife."

"That's what I call big-time local human interest."

Plucking a half-thought out of mid air, he asked, "Have you any idea of an image we might use to promote the story—a single still from a movie, maybe—even a painting that would sum up the feature—not just some conventional Hollywood beauties. Find a single image that might make the TV Guide browser say 'Wow!'—like the Botticelli Venus being born out of an outsize shell for the soft cover of Betty Friedan's *Feminine Mystique*?"

"Well, why not use one of Wilhelm de Kooning pictures in his Woman series? Abstract expressionism."

Steve looked blank. Hermione knew what was coming and she was not sure she liked Luke queering his own pitch. Nevertheless, she showed a reproduction to Steve in another art book and watched him grimace.

Luke was baiting them both and she knew it, even if Steve did not.

"You know," added Luke, "woman as part siren, part gorgon, part landscape—that sums up the story of fashion and Hollywood. I even have a title for you: *Spoiled Darlings*. If you see this, you don't even need to watch the program: it's all there in the painting."

Hermione quashed the notion.

"Surely, isn't that the point of your program on women's fashions being changed by advertising—the dismemberment and re-assembling of idealized feminist women—icons made erotic by men for male consumption—women as consumer products?"

With no sense of humor, Steve said, "Trouble is the permissions for these pix will be too high. The viewing figures couldn't possibly justify our using them."

He went back to the collection on the dining table.

"These sure are lovely pictures of the stars in their full glory—Rita Hayworth as Gilda—her best role, don't you think?"

"But," said Luke once again showing off his hard-won technical expertise, "this one of Joan Crawford is spoilt by a stray feather gliding across her face. This one of Vivien Leigh from the sixties' badly cropped reissue of *Gone with the Wind* is so bright that it highlights her mustache."

Luke could imagine a smirk flitting across Mickey Garnier's face at that remark. He continued.

"If you use this shot of Vivien Leigh, it will be as subversive as if you were reproducing Marcel Duchamp's surrealistic rendering of the Mona Lisa with a deliberate mustache on her upper lip to ridicule Leonardo's homosexuality."

Sensation.

Steve Sharp knew he had been taken for a ride by an ungrateful, uppity ex-college kid, still wet behind the ears.

"Your preferred pictures emphasize line and angle, cutting-edge fashion, and what our viewers—mainly older people at home for daytime TV—want are soft-focus studies in which women positively glow."

"Like Sigourney Weaver in the last *Alien* film?" cut in Luke determined to exact some fun from everyone's discomfiture.

Steve left, his bubbly manner quashed.

"You'll be lucky if he gives you any crumb after that performance," said Hermione.

She was not in a good mood.

However, as the time of learning to be blind stretched from weeks into months, Luke began to sense a different world, of opportunities coming from the chaos of nothingness. Within the vacuum of his career, he sensed there might be all sorts of possibilities. This eased his sense of depression. It also increased his compassion for others when he decided to help Louis Cans.

16 The New Musketeers

When it came to affairs of the heart, Marie Louise was still in her fantasy world of jam today and tomorrow. Men had wives and girlfriends on the side. She determined to enjoy men as men enjoyed women. Yet she craved tangible proof of having conquered and kept a man: a ring. She had heard her mother hum a song that the ring must not be on the telephone; nor did she expect the ring to arrive with Santa Claus. Her chance of getting one free ahead of Christmas came when she went with Luke and her other current, preferred client, Louis Cans, to the university museum of natural history.

Luke wanted to do something for Louis for his help the night he was attacked. Marie Louise wanted to help herself to Luke. When Luke asked Marie Louise for a suggestion about Louis, she told Luke that Louis's chance of a better life would be increased if he had more opportunities to socialize, to stimulate his mind. Luke took the bait. Together, they planned education disguised as a day trip.

With spare money that Hermione had given him, Luke paid for three tickets to the museum at the discounted, disabled rate. They moved into the sequence of burnt-sienna inner caverns that housed the museum's treasure trove. They wandered round the huge dinosaur skeleton. They were struck by a primitively presented scene from Colonial New England, a mix of humanoid waxworks, stuffed fauna, dried flora, and painted cyclorama. Three Puritans armed with muskets seemed to present arms to a posse of American Indians before a powwow for peace.

"It's like the three mu-mu-musketeers," said Louis, colliding France and America.

"That's us," added Marie Louise.

The new musketeers next marveled at the several

dioramas, mixing more stuffed animals and birds from locations around the Americas with boulders and sand, twigs and scrub grass—all set in exquisitely painted semi-circular landscapes. They were such miracles of scenic work that time seemed to stand still.

All three visitors had the advantage and disadvantage of their different perspectives. Louis could see everything but place nothing in context for he had next to no history, geography, or science.

Despite years of substance abuse, Louis Cans still had a bulky, muscular upper body that dwarfed his short legs. With ease, he raised Marie Louise for minutes on end to espy the pleasures of desert and seashore, mountain and forest. Unaided, Marie Louise could only see the wall beneath the lighted windowpane; hoisted aloft, she squinted at the loveliness and saw everything as it would be for her on the ground, the same viewpoint as a cunning lady fox.

As she surveyed the scene through its glass, curved inwards to suggest there was no glass at all, it seemed that this world was so like the world of the cunning little vixen that it conjured up the characters: Sharp Ears and her lover, Golden Mane, their human predators, and the fields and forests of Ostrava nearby. Humankind and the insects and animals in the story and in real life were all part of the greater world. With this diorama Marie Louise could enter a gentler, more seductive age. The glass disappeared. In her mind, she could enter it unharmed and unharmable because it was preserved in art. She simply stood inside it.

Luke was of the right height and had enough knowledge to interpret what was before him, but he saw both more and less—more because he saw most things twice, less because the beauty was distorted by his damaged retinas.

Yet the beautiful tints and shades before the new muske-teers fused the natural with the artificially created panoramas with such exquisite balance that all three were held spellbound by the seven fixed scenes: they were at one with the world, not disabled people but humankind in Eden.

When their senses were sated, the three visitors went to the museum shop. Here you could buy souvenirs of what you had seen or previews of events elsewhere. The colored postcards reduced the quality of the dioramas but they enhanced the attractions of smaller objects whose details they seemed to enlarge: native jewelry, Paleolithic stones, and stuffed birds.

The shop had a selection of books and souvenir treasures from museums across the world. Louis hoisted Marie Louise up to the roundel carousels of postcards. One from the museum in Cairo caught her eye and captured her heart. It was a photo of a painted statue of two figures in ancient Egypt. One was a conventional, white-shifted matron with resplendent curled black wig, who stood next to her seated husband. He was a dwarf, apparently a court official, and clearly in control of the marriage to his trophy wife. Marie Louise took the postcard and became fixated, then emboldened in her quest to ensnare her bird-in-the-bush.

A little later she suggested, oh-so-casually, to Louis that they scrutinize souvenir rings with diminutive semi-precious stones in simple settings. They were arrayed in racks from shoulder- to knee-height. As Marie Louise and Louis became absorbed in trying them on to one another's fingers, they, somehow, ended up rolling around the floor in squeals of laughter. They were giggling like children at a private joke so obscure that only they had the key to it. Since the racks were partly hidden from the sales staff, their innocent merriment was entirely private.

Choosing her favored ring, Marie Louise said coquettishly to Louis, "If I wait for a man, I'll never get an engagement ring. Guess I'll just have to buy my own."

A museum bell sounded the tocsin for closing. Louis went to make sure Luke had not lost his way. After they all met in the lobby, they went together for a snack in the diner two blocks down from the museum. Over their meager repast, French fries for Louis, a milk shake for Luke, and a hot dog for Marie Louise (half of which she took home), they shared views about what they had seen.

Luke went to the cash desk to settle the check. Marie Louise opened her pocketbook. She took out the postcard of the Egyptian couple, kissed it, and put it back. Then she reached out to Louis's coat, lying by her side in the booth, took from it her delightful museum ring. She put it on her finger, winked at Louis, and said with mock humor, "Never take this ring from my finger."

Louis pondered this as he and Luke walked to the green to catch their buses home. There was a spare block of wood lying on the sidewalk at the curb.

"Going fr-fr-free?" asked Louis.

"S'pose so," answered Luke. "I think it got thrown out with trash from a store and the garbage men left it. Rosewood, d'ye think?"

"Naw. It's mahogany."

"Perhaps from a piano?"

"Yeah."

Louis tucked it into his jacket pocket. When he said goodbye to Luke by the bus stop, he added, "Y'know, somehow, I don't think Marie Louise paid for that ring."

On her way home in her car, Marie Louise tooted the horn as she thought of the magic power of her newly acquired ring.

Traveling home along White Water Avenue on the Beta bus, Luke reviewed his day. The way he had seen that the museum arranged and rearranged its treasures for exhibition rotation stimulated Luke's unease at being inside and outside society.

Just before he got off the bus, Luke noticed a folded up copy of the *National Enquirer* on an adjacent seat. He knew Hermione enjoyed tittle-tattle and he took the paper with him. Back at Hermione's house, he realized there was a wad of papers inside, including a copy of the *New York Daily Post,* presumably left by the same traveler. But it was thicker still for, folded inside, was a blue file. And inside the file, with help from his magnifying glass, he read haltingly the first of several typed pages:

Memo to Police Chief Leo Guerra:
1. Transparent Brush. This illuminating foam will give your face that certain glow. Foam all over.
2. The concealer will smooth out facial bumps and blemishes. Use under the eyes, for dimples, and for creases. Just blend in.

Looking it over later, Hermione said, "It's a simpleton's map for applying concentrated makeup."

"Well," said Luke. "This discovery will cause discomfort to the police chief because he paints himself"—he paused to see if she would appreciate his choice of words—"as a regular man's man."

There were other documents that Luke and Hermione found harder to understand: a memo on how to handle and mold press treatment of the campaign against the drug lords; a schedule for internal meetings and press conferences; and a few words scrawled, almost illegible, on "Baby."

Luke asked Hermione what he should do.

"Rather than go to the police, which might expose you to hostility because it's doubly embarrassing to the police chief, partly because it was left by someone—and that's a minor security breach—and partly because makeup is still a feminine subject, why don't we simply give it to Steve when he's over for dinner? In this way the TV studio can say an anonymous passenger handled it to them responsibly. And Network News Norse Hoven will then hand it responsibly to the police."

"After the studio makes its own use of the typed notes."

"Exactly. But that's not your responsibility."

When Steve was told, he was positively brimming with excitement.

"Great news. Thanks a heap. This story sure has legs. Public interest on the macro level—minor security breach—and the micro level—human interest. What does a man's man have to do to stay butch in modern America? Great."

Steve gulped down his dinner and, with young Dennis in tow, was gone.

When Hermione switched on the local news next day, the news anchorman was saying, "The PC is not the first male public figure to use makeup. He is scrutinized regularly in front of cameras. These beauty tips should help him lighten his recent exhausted look."

The commentator turned to his confrere.

"What do you think, Maisie?"

"The advice was spot-on, with a perfect base of loose mineral powder. But it seems the PC ignored the advice. He was pictured looking pale last week and could have done with a little bronzer."

In conjunction with the local *Courier*, the TV channel ran a phone-in competition for readers to win a makeup kit just like the police chief's emergency makeup kit and worth $100. There were ten kits to be won. Entries could be via e-mail or by phoning an 800 number but the calls had to be made by midnight that day.

Luke lost interest. By now he had other things on his mind. As he was going upstairs, suddenly, he felt dizzy. The sensation was overpowering. Then, he felt himself get hotter; then, more dizzy. Luke got to his room but he did not know how. He had heard that, sometimes, people about to have strokes or heart attacks got some sort of warning just before. Was this a warning? Luke lay down on the bed. Perfectly still. After a time, the giddying sensation passed away. He checked his speaking watch. He realized twenty minutes had passed. He decided to say nothing to Hermione.

The three musketeers met again for a day trip to New York. So as not to tire out Marie Louise and Louis, they decided to restrict themselves to two places: Grand Central Station and its Oyster Bar and the Museum of Modern Art—MoMA. Luke knew that MoMA was due for closure for massive renovations and expansion. He wanted Marie Louise to sample the harbingers of modernism and new ways of seeing the world while MoMA was still—if only just—of manageable proportions for her and while he—if only just—had enough eyesight to appreciate this himself.

As they waited on Track Fourteen in Norse Hoven for the closed train to open its doors, Luke began to feel dizzy. He leaned against the track Coca Cola machine. He knew his eyesight was changing but he had not expected what happened next. When he looked straight ahead, there was the cold, metallic gray of the darkened commuter train. But when he turned to the left where other travelers stood patiently waiting for the train doors to open for them to board, all of a sudden, they were not entirely there. Luke could see them, as it were, from the waist down—trousers and skirts, boots and shoes—but above there was nothing and his eyes filled in the background of the stationary train. When he turned to the center, everything was there, fuzzy to be sure, but all present and indistinctly correct. When he turned his head to the right, there were the people, heads and shoulders, torsos and upper halves. When he turned back to the left, their upper parts disappeared again. Just then, there was a recurring jolting sound. The train cars opened to invite the assembled passengers.

Luke knew he had to concentrate. "Pull yourself together!" He heard a voice inside him order him to attention like a disapproving schoolteacher of the old school. Marie Louise wondered why he was so quiet as he motioned them to corner seats, mumbling nothing more than, "Here."

They sat in the dun-colored upholstery of the dun-colored carriage flecked with steel frames for doors, windows, and seat partitions. It was pretty hot and stuffy there. Marie Louise felt she was being enveloped in veal like the inner filling of an escalope.

For Luke, the journey was a picture perfect fantasy of vistas merging into one another while snatches of overheard conversations intruded on his thoughts.

Marie Louise was initially excited by the new perspective that rail travel—some of it elevated—afforded of towns en route she had already visited by car for meetings. She felt strangely moved that Bridgeport, with its profusion of shoddy clapboard houses seen from the train behind token attempts of urban renewal, was thrusting its decline into the gaze of passers-through, while Stamford could still dazzle travelers with its panorama of glass-wall skyscrapers of billion-dollar corporations just hinting at shanty poverty behind. But nothing had prepared her for the jolting train that gathered more and more passengers with every commuter stop like a giant industrial combine harvester of the bodies and souls of men. She ticked off the various stops en route, one by one, like an excited child in grade school.

When they reached the third stop, it was clear that the train was filling up fast. Soon, all the seats would be taken. Two elderly women, each frail but upright and with gray hair tied back in an untidy chignon, got on. They took a quick look at the three musketeers. They moved ahead as swiftly as elderly limbs on a crowded train would allow.

Louis looked enquiringly at his mentor. Marie Louise mouthed, "WASPs—no lipstick, no blue rinse," by way of explanation. But this left Louis more, not less, perplexed.

Marie Louise started to speak aloud but got no further than "WA—" before the elderly women reappeared at their side, having had no luck finding seats farther down the carriage. The women sat on the neighboring seats across the aisle.

One gasped and quickly averted her eyes; the other looked on disapprovingly and set her face hard. Their instinct was to talk and to talk loudly in clipped New England tones without any concession to other passengers. Everything was in its place and everybody else must know his or hers, which, in this instance, was to listen. The conversation amounted to a running commentary on the demerits of the passing cities. Stamford was remarkable for meeting the criteria of being among the wealthiest and most impoverished of the cities—wealthy because of the abundance of billionaire companies just over the state line from New York, poverty-stricken because of the deprivation of its underclass. Bridgeport fared worst.

"They could drop an atom bomb on Bridgeport," announced the more senior ranking of the two travelers, "and no one would miss it."

"We'd all be better without it," chimed in her companion. "Done and dusted."

This was news to Louis.

"Drop a b-b-bomb?" he asked Marie Louise, his brandy-soaked voice at odds with the querulous nature of his tone. "Blanket bombing? Can they do that? My auntie Mo lives there. Will she su-su-survive?"

"Hush, Louis," replied Marie Louise soothingly—no small feat considering her irritation at the loudmouths.

"Are they gonna bomb Br-Br-Bridgeport? Is it war?" he asked three times till Luke told him to change the tape.

From time to time the Wasp ladies exchanged furtive glances about the three musketeers, a disdain lost on Luke and Louis but not on Marie Louise who started to stare back, fixing her eyes on them like a hostile owl. Then, all of a sudden, she said, "You think this is the nineteenth century and we should be travelling in the freight car or along with the coal."

"Nonsense, my good girl," answered the senior Wasp. "Speaking of coals, your face reminds me of someone with that sort of name. It eludes me. But I'll get there. I'm watching you. And keeping a tight grip on my purse."

The two Wasp ladies rose to leave at Greenwich. There was a pause as the train manager called out, "The first two and the last two cars will not open at Greenwich. If you're in one of these cars, move forward or back to the center cars on the train."

Then he added, also over the system, "Al, are we set?"

There was a pause during which the junior Wasp acknowledged Marie Louise and her friends for the first time.

"Such lovely, luxurious hair, my dear," she began. "And decked out with such pretty pink bows around the ringlets. So, so striking."

"That's it," came from the senior Wasp. "I knew it would come to me. You're just like Pamela Barker Cowles."

"Camilla Parker Bowles? Well, I never," said an Indian accent from the seat behind.

Marie Louise rose to the double bait.

"You park your own balls. I've never been drunk in my life."

A ripple of dwarf laughter followed from other attentive passengers as the senior Wasp smiled and moved almost seamlessly out of the now-open doors.

Luke did not dare laugh but he interpreted all this in the context of his history reading. Despite what seemed to be open-and-shut boundaries between these pseudo-refined descendants of Colonial America and Marie Louise, Louis, and himself as unwelcome musketeers—as savage and deformed slaves—the mini confrontation had thrown up uncertainties. Marie Louise and Louis's vigorous response—so typical of their feisty natures—showed how they could re-present their identities and confront their stigmatizers.

The train now passed small towns enveloped in large marinas; large towns with corporation offices enfolded in glass curtain walls; outskirts choked in industrial detritus; and dotted suburbs with picturesque wooden houses, cream and gray, dove-blue and lavender, all with white trim. In Luke's imperfect sight, they looked, for the entire world, like houses out of Hansel and Gretel, picturesque cottages inviting enough to eat but harboring suspicious secrets inside.

To Louis, the estuary at Greenwich with its little marina curling round the bay represented a sort of paradise postponed. It was the illusion of an American Dream of plenty. It would always be at the far end of a desert of hope that would always lead ever upwards and would always disappoint.

He wondered why he, himself, was travelling with these two curious people, one he owed much—not liberty or happiness but a semblance of life lived as if there would be a future—the other was his unlikely friend although he talked with words Louis did not understand. But the way they spoke to one another was like aliens from another world, sharing experiences and confidences beyond him. Yet the evenness of the journey, the absence of bickering in the halfway house, and the other-worldly experience of familiar types of homes, factories, and highways—all seen from the different vantage points of raised tracks and consistent speed—made everything seem like the comforting, peeled wallpaper of a children's picture book. For once, Louis could inhabit his world while moving in harmony with two other people.

By New Canaan the carriage was so crowded that the new musketeers sensed they should move closer together with Marie Louise sitting on Luke's lap next to the window while Louis sat by their side, guarding them from prying eyes. Luke could not see accurately but he and Louis sensed that they were being stared at, scrutinized, and disparaged since people knew there must be something strange about Louis with his bent head and slightly dribbling mouth and Marie Louise with her puckered and wrinkled face atop her little girl's body. Luke wondered if this day trip had been a good idea and if he could find enough stamina to endure what lay ahead.

They neared the great city with its outer tentacles of scrambling highways, giant warehouses, and anonymous stories that Luke knew hid elongated car parks. These muddy pink and muted ochre building blocks heralded the staccato appearances of soaring tower blocks of apartment buildings broken briefly by the silver-gray swathe of the Harlem River between the mainland and Manhattan Island.

Marie Louise now marveled at the train-bound activities of their fellow passengers—for this was an early morning commuter train. About half an hour before they were due to arrive in Grand Central, people sitting beside them, to left, right, front, and aft, suddenly changed. Earlier, they had chatted to neighbors, or scrutinized newspapers, or dozed—even while sitting bolt upright. Now, their dexterity knew no bounds. While confined to the due cubic space each seat allocation allowed them, their manipulation of space seemed as dexterous as the Chinese Circus. Women opened their pocketbooks and produced lipstick, eyeliner, compacts, mirrors, and combs and prepared themselves for their presentation of self in everyday life in New York. The train conductor might as well have announced "Makeup" as the local station names of Fordham and New Rochelle, so promptly did travelers use their time for beautification.

In the musketeers' bank of seats two men took out electric razors and began to shave, each confining his movement of arms and hands to his due space. Other male travelers opened wallets or delved into pockets whence they produced rings and earrings and bracelets with which, again without touching their immediate neighbors, they also adorned themselves, ready to face their New York public.

"This is the grooming stage of the journey," explained Luke. "Add and subtract that to your list of stages, Marie Louise."

"125th Street next," came the announcement, "and then straight on to our final destination, Grand Central Station, in about ten minutes' time."

Many people got off at the newly restored green metal structure of 125th Street station and bustled unconcerned on their way. Then the train ran smoothly into the blackness of the tunnel under Park Avenue to 42nd Street.

When the three musketeers left the train at Grand Central Station, Marie Louise thought she really was in a coal truck, so dark and cavernous was the track corridor. Luke made them wait outside the carriage until the track was relatively clear before they made their way to the gate behind a jumbled, straggling corridor of weary travelers, moving like a gray slowworm in an underground cavern as if this was some sort of underclass conveyor belt of almost-human beings, propelled forward solely by its numbers.

But when they clambered up the stairs from the lower level to the upper and moved into the main concourse, Marie Louise and Louis marveled at the array of bookshops and boutiques, bakers and pastry vendors, and the ubiquitous presence of soft drink stands. The activities were no different from a mall in any suburban strip. But the combination of the ceaseless flow of thousands of voyagers, spotlit by hundreds of un-shaded light bulbs, seemed to acquire vivid importance. It was if this collective surge of unbridled commerce really was a single organic entity. This was subterranean Manhattan showing off its wares of conspicuous consumption equal to 5th Avenue.

"Look, Marie Louise—you, too, Louis—at the barrel domed ceiling," said Luke, stopping them by the central information desk with its focal meeting-place clock.

"It's been cleaned, renovated, repainted, and relit over the past two years. The turquoise is the sky and the dwarf lights are the stars and their constellations."

"You mean, it's like the way we see the stars at night when there's no cloud?" asked Marie Louise.

"Not exactly," said Luke. "Here's the thing. When they built Grand Central, they had a draft map, a sort of rendering of the heavens. But, instead of making it as we see, looking from the ground upwards, they did it upside down. It's the sky as seen from above—like the gods might have seen the heavens in ancient Greece. But this time we're the gods looking down. Why, Marie Louise, at the front entrance, the sculptures on the façade have Roman gods dancing cheek-to-cheek with the American eagle."

Louis did not understand or, if he did, he did not let on. But what Luke told them began to change the way Marie Louise interpreted what she saw. Or, perhaps, it brought something in the back of her mind right into her foremost consciousness and it troubled her. People as ants or as cogs in a machine she knew as well as anyone in social work. But this time it was being presented and maintained by designers, architects, and businessmen as if they were their own creators above the Earth, above the stars.

"That's it," thought Marie Louise as she and Luke stood by the central clock waiting for Louis to come back from the men's lavatory.

"The heads of Rehabilitation Services and VIPS are like these old gods—spoilt, capricious, and vindictive. Probably, the police chief for all I know."

When Louis did come back, all he said was, "Made it. I was sick."

"Where were you sick, Louis?"

"In my m-m-mouth."

Luke sensed that Marie Louise was already tired and he wondered if he should have listened to Hermione's cautionary advice. But there was nothing for it now but to press ahead. So, Luke had Louis hoist Marie Louise in his arms and onto his shoulders up the stairs to the exit and taxi rank at Vanderbilt Avenue.

After leaving the taxi at 59th Street, they bore the stares of the line at MoMA and passed through cash desk, barriers, and offers of assistance from museum staff. Luke tried to get his shambling duo through at least a portion of the sequence of galleries.

"Hermione read me some of an article in the *New York Times* about art museums becoming the popular way for families to enjoy a day out and broaden their cultural horizons. It's because, unlike a theater where you sit in set seats and you are confined for the duration of the show, in a museum you can start, stop, finish, or break for lunch—anything you want. By your very presence with your family, you interact with the space. And it lasts for as long or as little time as you want."

On the exhibit floors, Luke wanted to explain the breakthrough from the later impressionists and first cubists to the tangled history of modern art movements through to abstract expressionism. Ever the student, he had prepared in his mind what he would say about Picasso's *Les*

Demoiselles d'Avignon. He knew what Marie Louise wanted was to see different sorts of women. Luke waxed lyrical about cubism, separating and dividing the planes of subjects and objects in the round into flat geometric shapes. He pointed out Picasso's fascination with the harsh geometric lines of African masks. Then he moved furtively to the subject matter: prostitutes hailing prospective clients in Barcelona and the ambiguity of the figure entering on the left. Was it a salacious sailor on the lookout or Death from the wages of sin?

Marie Louise did not know what to make of it all but she recognized in the painting the dis-assembling of conventional woman, being fractured into explosive shapes.

What Luke Reader did not detect was that Marie Louise and Louis Cans were fascinated by the same part of the painting: the African masks. To Marie Louise the masks represented sexual arousal and the sexual aggression that she expected from her black lovers. Louis was spellbound by the sharp ridges and aquiline curves of the African faces.

Jostling New Yorkers milled around them—canoodling couples, grad students thinking of papers, families with different generations in tow. While Louis and Marie Louise were absorbed in the painting, Luke noticed a young black construction worker pointing at one of the female figures and whispering something in his white girl's ear to which she replied out loud, "Sometimes, Frank, you say the sweetest things." Pointing at another, male, figure, she added, "And I can return the compliment."

But it was a different painting altogether that took hold of Marie Louise more deeply. Here was representational art she could appreciate and rendered with correct lifelike and historical detail of the figure and her surroundings: *Christina's World* by Andrew Wyeth. Luke said the artist was a realistic painter—not always fashionable in art circles but always liked by the public.

"The model, Christina, had had polio and was lame."

The figure of the girl lying on the breast of a hill below a house with one leg extended behind her struck Marie Louise forcefully. The painting was well placed for her, being low on the wall by a doorway. Christina's isolation, partly by her solitariness and her position in the lower right of the picture, and partly by what Marie Louise now knew of her being disabled, moved her. The mood was heightened by the painter's choice of colors: the greens, browns, and yellows were all tarnished—almost discolored—creating a murky environment.

"At the bottom of the hill we never climb up, our lives trapped in a murky pea soup of disappointment," said Luke.

"It's how we all feel," replied Marie Louise plaintively.

She was downcast. Luke, who had brought her here, did not know what to say.

Marie Louise was silent for the rest of the tour. They went through several rooms mechanically until she said, "I've had enough. I want it over with now."

Without asking, Louis bent down and scooped her up and carried her half slung over his shoulders as they made their way down in the elevator. Luke felt that everyone they passed must be staring at them, noting their perceived deficiencies from Luke's red-and-white cane to Louis's slobber, but principally at the extraordinary little child-woman without being aware of the charm she could exert or the fierce strength of her determination.

Outside, Luke stopped them at a curbside vendor selling hot dogs and Coca Cola because he thought Marie Louise needed to drink something fizzy and sweet. While Luke was buying three cans, Louis strolled over to the next sidewalk stall that had all sorts of artifacts: leather pocketbooks, polished stones, carved figures and African masks. Louis asked the vendor, adorned in a red kerchief and a cream kaftan, if he could hold a mask. He ran his fingers longingly over the sides, caressed the detail of the eyes and mouth, and joked about the ear lobes distended with elaborate earrings—all exquisitely carved.

"You like?" asked the vendor. "Very good price for Nigerian art: $20."

"Is that where they're from—Nigeria?" asked Luke, who wanted to help Louis out.

"You interested?" asked the vendor with a generous smile. "They come from all over Africa. Broad, dark faces from the northwest, like Upper Egypt and Sudan; decorated with paint from the east; leather camels and figurines from central Africa."

The vendor sensed Louis wanted to buy something but had next to no money.

"We make good price."

After tactful negotiation so as not to embarrass either party, and due to Luke's diplomacy, they settled on a diminutive dark figure, a stark statuette with elaborate headdress for $8. Louis had three dollars and Luke supplied a five-dollar bill. Marie Louise offered to place it in her pocketbook.

This little purchase meant much more to Louis than it would have done to either Luke or Marie Louise. It was a token participation in consumer society. It was something to be cherished, because, without purchasing power, you were an incomplete person.

For their afternoon snack, Luke had chosen the Oyster Bar in Grand Central Station, partly for convenience before the evening rush hour on the commuter trains but also because it was an astonishing place on account of its gigantic hurly burly, its mix of New York traders, lower grade clerks, and Madison Avenue executives among the clients. Then there was the breezy, whip-snap humor of the staff, almost as if they were parodying New Yorkers of the twenties and thirties.

Even safely slotted on a white bar seat at the counter, Marie Louise was more intimidated by the bustle than energized by it. At first, they downed their New England clam chowder in silence. Then Luke spoke.

"I was born in the suburbs and the very air of New York excites me, the pulse of high energy on the Midtown sidewalks. If you're like me, then the city is in your blood. New York will always call you. Its thousands of voices invite us to shops bulging with merchandise."

Toward the end of the little meal, Louis asked to see his present. Marie Louise opened her pocketbook and took it out for him, still wrapped in the toilet paper supplied by the street vendor. Louis carefully unwound its Lazarus-like shroud and examined it closely from every angle. He did so longingly as if it were not his.

As he had previously agreed with Hermione, Luke bought four helpings of the famed chowder for himself, Hermione, Steve Sharp, and Dennis to have for their evening meal. The server poured the helpings into a handsome paper carton. But when Luke went to the cash desk to pay for it, it was already leaking over his hands and dripping onto the floor. There was no apology, no top-up from the staff who simply forced the first container with the chowder into a second as buttress.

"The business of New York is business," remarked the server.

As they walked to their track, Marie Louise remarked, "Even when you're lost in a magical world, there's always something to remind you that you're disabled, second class."

Midsummer

---

17 Incubators

In the rickety house in Louvre Ville Candice was alone and apprehensive in her room. She peeped through the window blinds. She tried, but could not find, words to express her feelings. The stumps of the trees on the street, after men had come to lop off some overhanging branches, had sharp jagged outlines and seemed to be accusing her of she did not know what. She still missed the big guy's burning kiss and his adoring gaze at her beauty. She wanted to see him again. Now there was no one to draw her soul up, up, and out of her body into the fire of his mouth.

"It's always the same," Carrie told her. "They have the pleasure and you have the pain. Don't fret. There's no shame. Don't peer out so. It will make your heart beat too fast if you think he's coming back."

Information drip by information drip, all the way from the way she was referred to in the house, to his predatory black looks, made Candy realize that her coming baby was under threat from CJ.

Candy sat on the bed in her surprisingly chilly room and pulled the ragged duvet around her. She had just overheard CJ in the next room tell Carrie, "It's now or never. The cops will raid us soon. We're a target. After all these times with people knocking at the front door all hours, everyone thinks this is a crack house."

When her time came, CJ had everything in hand. Candy was young and pliant. This birth would be straightforward.

He would go with her to the hospital. No matter that their names were different. He would present himself as the supportive grandfather whose son, supposedly the baby's father, was among the self-disappeared young men of never-a-fixed abode, never on the electoral register, guys who never answered letters from the state, let alone stayed around until a child was born.

CJ could certainly play the caring grandfather. It was a role he had long been preparing. Everything went like clockwork, although CJ knew that there was a good chance Social Services would soon get to know about the little baby boy and might well intervene.

He cooed and gurgled in the baby's ear and kissed him on his forehead.

"Love him, tender," he told Candice when she was drowsy.

She half heard CJ and thought he was telling her to name her son, "Tender."

The baby nestled so tightly to her that Candy simply wanted to hold him and, somehow, to have this precious moment frozen in time.

One day when Louis appeared at her office, Marie Louise was in her all-guarded, strictly-business-only, we're-super-professional-here mode that Louis found so comical. Louis listened to Marie Louise's latest diatribe against him. It was the same story and he was the usual suspect of wrongdoing as she ran down the catalog of his drinking, his getting high, and his general unreliability. Marie Louise knew that what she said was going in one ear and out the other.

"You done?" Louis asked at the end, as matter-of-factly as if she had just given him another form to sign.

She stared back with bottled-up indignation. Then Marie Louise remembered another college lecture about a philosopher who had explained how despondent people were never at hand for themselves, how they just existed—no more than that. It was as if they were waiting for something better in the future. But, because there never was an improvement, they were always abstracted from the present, always looking at themselves from the outside.

Then Louis surprised her.

"I br-br-brought you this."

He took a red handkerchief from his side jacket pocket. There was a surprise. Marie Louise knew the handkerchief was not for wiping his nose—he had the back of his hand for that. Louis undid the handkerchief on the desk.

There it was: another carving. This time it was a delicate, larger copy of the African figurine Luke had helped him buy on the sidewalks of New York. Marie Louise did not want to, but she could not help it. She melted.

"Thank you, Louis," she said.

"You're welcome, Marie Louise."

His voice still had that under-educated drawl and brandy-soaked tone she found so affectionate.

"Louis, there's a chance opportunity that will suit you better than Fast Track Sports. A picture and ornament restorer is looking for an extra hand. They need someone who can fix things artistically. Also, to be creative with moldings and carvings."

"You want me to go for interview next w-w-week?"

"No. No delay. You're going with me now in the Marie Louise taxi. No time like the present. I'll also arrange what we call vocational training to help you about how to behave in the workplace, any workplace. I'll try and get you some specialized speech therapy; it will help you with what my people call social communication skills."

All this was lost on Louis.

"Let's rock and roll."

With that, Marie Louise slithered down her high chair and

held out her arm for Louis to help her down and to escort her out of the office.

"Grab your coat—and mine."

"I dunno w-w-what to say."

She did.

"If it wasn't for me, where would you be? If it wasn't for Marie Louise Garden, Louis Cans would still be starvin'."

ART'S ATELIER ran the sign over the door and across the picture frame window. The shop floor was an Aladdin's Cave of furniture and bric-a-brac: giant mirrors with gilded frames propped up against the walls; mahogany tables with buckling bow legs; wooden statuettes holding aloft candelabras; children's rocking horses that had seen better days; and woebegone cases of grandfather clocks. Although there were glass and silver and gold plate aplenty, the commonest element was wood—dark and pale, red and brown.

Marie Louise, who had been to the atelier several times to place clients there, now saw the shop floor differently from before. The boss, with curly dark brown hair and a goatee beard, like the leftover 1970s protester he was, carried his wad of notes attached to a clipboard and his large soft marker like an artist's easel and brush. Before him, his little girl, no more than seven or eight, with fair hair and an outsize smock, was curtseying playfully with three women workers, giggling away to the smallest, one of the little people Gina had always told Marie Louise to avoid. There were massive theater flats from some community theater propped up against the wall.

In a flash it all brought back Luke's bedroom reproduction poster of the Spanish painting, *Las Meninas*. It was a make-believe world of safety for disabled people. Marie Louise felt—as she had felt before the dioramas in the university museum—that, by her simple presence, she completed this picture-from-life and gave it meaning.

As Louis waited with Marie Louise and nervously studied the objects, he realized that they all had the same thing in common: they were broken.

Almost as an afterthought in the atelier, there were several chandeliers. Four were lit and dangling from the ceiling but hanging lop-sided as if they were soft and fluffy instead of metallic and crystalline. On ground level two more were unlit and hanging from rods between sizeable cases. The boss saw Louis fascinated by the shimmering glass and acknowledged his glance. Art also noticed Louis inspecting a table with some gilt edging.

"It's a mock eighteenth-century French occasional table— probably Louis Quinze."

"Like you, Louis," said Marie Louise.

The shop's mission was to repair, renovate, and restore furniture and ornaments generally for sale in the city. Within this scheme, Louis's tasks would be to repair carved artifacts, either by gluing and matching, by reproduction of a missing or broken chair leg or of a missing or broken piece of statuary from a set. On the desk before Art was his last present to Marie Louise, the pseudo African figure.

"Kid, it's great," said the comfortable Art with his 3D abdomen pushing his shirt out to flop bulbously over his fraying jeans. He had bulging eyes, one of which squinted.

"Marie Louise has told me about you. We want to give you a try this week. See how it goes. Fran will show you the ropes. Here's two projects for you. Carve an imitation Queen Anne leg missing from this mahogany breakfast table. Use rosewood; we can dye it later. After that, study this wooden deer with antlers, copy it as near as you can—or get the spirit of it—in this leftover pine. It doesn't have to be exactly the same. You can have the head rearing in a different way.

"They're all damaged goods—like the rest of us," he said aloud. Immediately, he regretted his words.

At the sound of a bell, Marie Louis led Louis to an inner

workroom and he met his co-workers—all male. Fran and Lee were little people. Dana had Down's syndrome. These people with their physical problems seemed so mobile that Louis was suddenly embarrassed at his own clumsy limp.

Art was giving instructions.

"Right, well, it's a matter of taste, but a building with a Chicago-style façade that's being converted into loft apartments, well, the yuppies want a touch of class—that means fin-de-siecle-style ornaments. We can give them that from whatever bric-a-brac would otherwise be jettisoned."

"Hi! I'm Fifi," said a slender man of startlingly fine ebony features. "I'll show you the carving tools," he continued.

Louis noticed he had one complete arm and the other, the left, ended in an imperfectly formed hand that Fifi used with nimblest dexterity to sort papers, carry coffee mugs, and punch in security codes through chamber doors.

"Fifi?" questioned Marie Louise.

"I'm from Nigeria—Lagos."

Louis was none the wiser.

"Can I make a st-st-start on the deer rather than the chair leg?"

Louis was half way through without noticing the passing hours. He was so tired, as well as absorbed, that, when he got back to Lancaster House that night, he was too exhausted even to think about doing drugs.

At the end of the first week, Art asked Fifi, "How's the new kid doing?"

Fifi produced two objects: one looked like an outsize carrot that had lost its way.

"Boss, he hasn't the control of machines to do furniture repair. He'll have an accident worse than he's gone through already."

Art paused. Fifi then unfurled a cloth over a proud, finely chiseled deer.

"But—and here's the good news, his carving is first-rate.

Amazing. Whatever you want he can make, but he has to take his time."

Art paused a second time.

"Well, we'll give him half time at minimum wage. Four days of five hours each."

When Marie Louise broke the news to Louis, she added, wanting to make the glass of his troubled life half full, "Half a loaf is better than no bread."

Louis shrugged. He was not that sorry.

Yet, despite her platitude, Marie Louise was not satisfied. She wondered if this half-full glass with its haphazard routine would exacerbate Louis's anxiety disorder that might flare up if he were placed in a situation where he was not supervised.

Police Chief Leo Guerra planned to confiscate his little boy during the forthcoming raids on the drugs cartel but he could not risk exposure. He had to signal to his officers that they must proceed carefully in the tarnished neighborhood. There must be other people, so he told his staff—innocent people—living perfectly decent lives there. There might be children and they must be protected somehow.

He remembered what a bent cop had told him years ago when he was a rookie, "If at first you don't succeed, destroy all the evidence that you ever tried."

Slowly, an idea germinated in his mind. If the police discovered an uncared-for infant, could he demonstrate his civic responsibility, his pastoral care, by offering to raise the tender child himself? How would he persuade Bella? By sponsoring the child's upbringing at the Children's Center? After all, his oldest, Magdalena, was planning to move into Social Services with an internship at RRS. His family had the right sort of form. Would he get away with it?

But this time he could not do what he most liked to do when faced with an awkward challenge, talk it through with his seconds. So, there was no balancing reason, no back-and-forth discussion of devil's advocacy for clarification: nothing to support his fledgling plan. Leo Guerra was frozen into inaction by an emotion new to him—fear. The threat of discovery was stultifying.

At work his team now found him more prickly than usual.

"He's always like this before a raid. It's understandable," said Carter.

"This time it's different, somehow," answered McSweeny. "He usually gets excited, fired up by the chaos of expectation. This time, it's as if he half dreads the outcome."

18 Working Girls

Everyone heard the crack. It seemed to ricochet across the college auditorium. Luke had edged his way forward to the microphone. Then he touched the sides of the podium to steady himself when he stubbed his left foot in its chamois moccasin on the wooden base. And it hurt. Damn bad. Everyone heard it. Pro that he still wanted to be, Luke was not going to show pain, let alone curse himself, but only deliver his speech without hesitation.

He began.

"Successive stages of the Industrial Revolution and consecutive advances in medicine led to more and more ways of categorizing people—not only by height and weight but also by ethnicity—and disability. Increased mechanization in the workplace accelerated this trend. The upshot was that disabled people found themselves first isolated and then eliminated from the workplace."

To Luke, the swooping, curling mass of bobbing heads

before him looked like a college of tropical birds. He was not sure if his voice carried. He needed to get a better grip. Images of past masters of the microphone flitted across his eyes.

It was a late weekend in the stifling heat of a damp day in May. Babel City University was hosting a symposium on social services. The university had folded into the symposium a competition for students in public speaking, all well primed from social-science texts. Marie Louise, Rod Fortune, and their boss were among the panelists representing social services for disabled people. Marie Louise had arranged for Luke to speak because she thought that sensory-impaired people were under-represented in such forums and she was tired of the tyranny of the wheelchair.

Luke knew Marie Louise would be in the front row, still with her own romantic agenda but rooting for him, nevertheless.

"Society considers those of us who are dwarves, or blind, or people with mental illnesses undesirable deviants from its norms whom it doesn't want and will reject. And I'm in the box for people who are not quite normal; my friend, Louis, is in the box for people who are not quite human. We get called names: 'mongo,' 'cripple,' and 'moron.'"

When Luke had finished and let his hands that had been gripping the podium fall to his side, the audience erupted with hooping cheers as if he had hit a winning home run in baseball. Thoroughly embarrassed, Luke did not know if the applause was for his message, his delivery, or that old standby, audience approval of a disabled person's victory over colossal odds. Or was it simply because everyone had heard him stub his toe and yet he had continued as if nothing had happened?

As he came offstage the full shock of the pain hit him. He thought he would faint.

"Careful son," said a man who caught him and moved him into a chair. "That was great. Is the pain bad?"

Marie Louise was now backstage. With her was this

matinee idol type of guy, a heartthrob whose dark curly hair, flecked with becoming silver streaks, framed a handsome chiseled face atop an expensively suited athletic body.

"Luke, this is my brother, Todd Carter Fox. Todd is quite the hotshot TV executive, here from New York to settle a business incorporation of our local station in their regional network."

They got no further in the introductions because of an announcement from the stage.

"Folks, please give a big hand to our next speaker, a savvy girl with a big future, Magdalena Guerra."

Luke knew immediately who it was.

Ellie was not yet twenty although she was now a junior at the campus. As Magdalena Guerra, she was a hot favorite to take a highly recommended student certificate at the conference.

Ellie started. However, as a speaker, she was not yet a flower opening its petals.

"It's not difficult to see why society is cruel, you know. It's institutionalized by our culture, you know."

Ellie faltered.

"Society encourages competition and greed in our schools, you know, and in sports on all levels—school, college, even professional sports—ya'see what I mean? Society also perpetuates competitive cruelty through discipline in the work place, you know."

Marie Louise caught a hint that her favorite sociologists must have prised open some dark shutters inside this smart girl's as yet unknown family troubles. For Magdalena seemed to understand the bleakness of society—its instinct to degrade the old and the poor, the weak and the disabled.

Despite the girl's fumbles, Marie Louise was transfixed. She thought this Magdalena was a potentially good public speaker and one whom she might train to be an advocate for disabled people.

When they met face to face during a mid morning break for coffee and sticky buns, Ellie said, "Please call me Lena—everyone does, ya'know."

This was news to Luke whom she ignored.

"Well, congratulations again, Lena, on a terrific speech," said Marie Louise.

"I'm sorry I was so nervous, ya'know. I really can do better. I would appreciate it if you would advise me how to be as effective as you are on stage. If you help me, I'll owe you big."

Marie Louise was flattered. No one had ever sought her out as a role model.

Todd brought Luke into the conversation.

"Marie Louise, I've suggested to Luke that he applies to the studio for work as a backup reporter. With this coming takeover at NNNH, there will be more jobs, not less, and we need to bolster our disabled personnel."

"I can't thank you enough, Marie Louise, for this introduction," said Luke. "You certainly do go the extra mile for your clients."

"Such an auspicious event."

That last remark from a person unseen nearby prompted Luke out of his reverie at the table with its flagons of coffee and plates of pastries. Faces and figures—everything—now merged and collided together in Luke's particular sight. But Luke sensed that Marie Louise was fixated, pondering an Italian-American sisterhood: besides, it would be useful to make friends with the well-heeled daughter of the famous police chief.

Marie Louise had always idealized Italy but her knowledge was limited to what she had seen on television. Then, she had recently received treasured postcards of the Ca d'Oro in Venice and the Pantheon in Rome from her co-worker and girl friend, Carmine, who was there on vacation.

She and Lena, aka Ellie, met several times over the two

days of the conference. Lena asked Marie Louise all sorts of questions. She seemed to drink in every drop of wisdom as if it were vintage champagne. Marie Louise advised Lena as to which courses she should take at college in the next semester to build a strong foundation for a career in social services. Marie Louise also passed on to Lena points about speaking in public that had been drilled into her at school.

Marie Louise was amazed how well and how quickly Lena grasped what she was taught. It was almost as if she knew it all already. One of Lena's girl friends lent her an Alice-blue, single-strap evening gown for the final reception where she won a special mention from the moderator. Then, her uncle, Abe Ripemoff, the big noise in disability politics in the county, had her called onto the platform to take an individual bow.

Lena's father was also proud. Although he had come to the last session without fanfare, everyone who was anyone knew this was the high and mighty police chief. Leo Guerra said to the moderator when he shook his hand, "Did well, didn't she? Still, I don't agree with all this left-wing support for delinquent single mothers—encourages unlicensed sex and imposes unwanted children on the benefits system."

"Gee, Marie Louise," said her boss. "You've found a real gem in Lena. She's an unusually mature youngster: great possibilities in social work."

No Cheshire cat grinned more broadly from ear to ear than did Marie Louise.

"Imagine," continued the boss, "When I asked her what was her all-time favorite film, she didn't go for last year's hit but a Hollywood classic—*All About Eve*."

Marie Louise looked blank.

"You know, the Broadway tale with Bette Davis and Anne Baxter."

Marie Louise was nonplussed.

"You remember. Marilyn Monroe was in it, too."

Later, Marie Louise told her newly discovered disciple, "You made a big hit, kid. Can I ask you? Tell me, honestly, is my hair like Marilyn Monroe's?"

Lena had watched *All About Eve* sure enough when her mother, Bella, had borrowed a DVD from the video store. The first time she had only seen the last twenty minutes while she was waiting for her date to collect her. She disliked the black-and-white, found the dialog corny and the movie plodding. But she was transfixed at the very end by the images of the predatory fan bowing and scraping to her multiple selves in the closet-door mirrors.

When Lena's date honked his horn, she called out "'Bye Artie," to the parrot as her mother wrapped the blanket round his cage for the night.

When she came back after her date had dropped her off much later, Lena caught sight of the DVD case left on the piano stool. She opened it and popped it into the DVD player. Now she was absorbed by the sweet manipulation of anti-heroine Anne Baxter and her even sweeter success as she rose on the broken backs of those she betrayed.

"That's the way to do it," came the voice of the parrot from inside the cage.

"You bet," Lena answered him. "Thank you, Artie."

"You're welcome," clucked her captive little friend.

In fact, the African Gray said nothing. The words simply resounded in Ellie's head. She had always wanted her parents to have a parrot that talked. Her imaginary instructions emanating from Artie were really her mis-conscience, always reminding her to do what she wanted without asking. As a habitual sinner, she knew it was easier to get forgiveness afterwards from her parents for wrongdoing than permission beforehand.

While she was acknowledging imaginary applause, Ellie thought she heard a tinkle from the chime bells in the porch—something that happened when the postman left mail in the metal box by the front door or there was a rustle of wind. She paid it no heed.

"It's the night time breeze."

She went back to pondering optimum forms of her name: "Magdalena" or "Ella" or "Lena" but no longer "Ellie." Which would be best for a rising star of state politics? She could use and discard each in turn as stepping-stones as she rose politically.

"Can I have a glass of water?"

Ellie turned round. There was her younger sister, Lizzie, at the top of the stairs in her nightclothes.

The next morning, Bella Guerra discovered a trove of misplaced treasures in the porch of their fine house behind the tumbledown garden on Rigid Road. There was a plastic bottle of milk with a blue cap and something underneath it: a Hershey chocolate bar. These were everyday objects but, clearly, they were not gifts. They were malicious darts but she could not fathom why.

When she asked Leo that night, he simply said, "Yes, anonymous mail, sickly sweet tokens of malice—it's one of the cruelest crimes in the whole criminal spectrum. I'm the police chief. We're sometimes targets of malice. But I can't stop the world to sort out this tiny, domestic misfortune. Bella, we're on the brink of a major gang bust. Hold tight for now. After next week, we can get this sorted. But it has to be done without publicity or there'll be awkward questions about the hoods, police procedures, everything. Just hang on. You can do it. As the police chief's wife, you've always been a pro. You've done it before. Stay true."

Using a handkerchief over his fingers, Leo put the Hershey chocolate bar and little bottle of milk into two plastic bags with zips that Bella used for the kids' sandwiches. Then he put them in the fridge, and next day, he took them away when he went to work.

Leo fairly sped out of the house that morning, leaving Bella to check for any early mail. When she opened the front door to collect the daily papers, there was a grubby pink envelope in the mailbox with two words cut from some Italian paper and pasted on the front to make her names "Bella" and "Guerra." The envelope had not been stuck down. Bella flipped it open. She was already apprehensive. An anonymous note? A threat? On yellow, lined paper ran the message:

Mrs. Guerra
It's my bounden duty, honey, to tell you your husband now has the little baby son he always wanted.
Signed
Your well-meaning friend Hershey

Bella started to heave. She steadied herself and slumped on a chair. She read the letter and thought, based on the bits and pieces of police detection she had learned over the years from Leo, that two hands had written the letter. Although there was pretence at a child-like script, she sensed someone or two older people had written this. Ashen-faced, she rose and went to the bar and made herself a whisky sour. That day she did her household chores like an automaton.

When Leo got home earlier than usual, clearly agitated, she was sufficiently agitated herself to confront him.

"I'm the police chief. No one has more enemies, especially a chief who's leading a big bust-up of crime. Whoever sent this is an enemy to both of us. I'll have it analyzed."

Something about the way he had first blanched, then got excited under the surface made Bella suspicious. No matter how persuasive were his reasoned words of experience, she had developed an instinct for knowing when he was not on the level. God knows she had had enough experience with his years of political flannel. All she could do was wait. But it was hard. Better not to say anything to Juno and hold tight onto her emotions so as not to trouble the kids.

That evening, when the kids were out at a sleepover, Bella rounded on Leo, who had been taciturn through dinner.

"Well?" was all she said.

"Well," he answered. "Nothing. I'll give it to Forensics. It may be some time before they can find any sort of hand-writing match. If ever. My investigators agree with my basic instinct about the Hershey bar—ignore this till after the raid. To do anything else will give comfort to our enemies."

Bella had long ceased to trust him. She was glad she had used a photocopier at the supermarket during her groceries round.

Leo was disturbed all right, furious at himself for becoming open to blackmail; in inner turmoil in case he would forfeit his career; delirious at the prospect of his longed-for son.

At work, Leo felt his remorse would stifle him. But he said to the small mirror in his desktop drawer, "Pull yourself together. Imagine that this is *Boot Camp*, another Reality TV show. Just keep going and stamina and nerve alone will get you through. Think positive."

Luke could just see well enough to realize that the TV studio was an adapted, re-used Gothic church, its steeple lopped off just above its fledgling tower base. Its mix of yellow stone and red brick had been burnished by cleaning-by-blasting. Its stained-glass windows of Jesus in his many acts were illuminated by concealed strip lighting to provide picturesque creationist detail. Inside, segments of serrated church carvings had become staircase banisters. The entire restoration was a masterpiece of turning the disused into the recycled.

He had come after Marie Louise's brother, Todd, chief executive at Network News Norse Hoven, had suggested he apply for a job there.

"Luke, this time, please don't mess up. Don't try and be too clever," were Hermione's parting words when she dropped him off.

While he waited sulkily in the Human Resources Office for his interview, on the wall above him Luke could just make out a large notice on a yellow board with bold black letters:

"At Network News Norse Hoven we rejoice in diversity and encourage everyone to give of their best. We support applications from right across the community, regardless of gender, race, sexual orientation, and disability. We are dedicated to equality of opportunity for all."

The candidate on the next chair said, "Job adverts at the studio always include that sort of promotional announcement."

To Luke's imperfect glance, this girl with the sequined turban seemed a wan waif. Her skin had a white pallor. But Luke surmised from her sense of style and natural command that she was not only experienced but also resourceful.

"My name's Opal Pearl. I'm here for a secretary's job. And you?"

"News, I think—research, support, back-up. I'm Luke Reader."

Then Opal added, "Someone in the studio told me that last year studio chiefs were forced to waive their bonuses after failing to recruit more disabled and ethnic minority people. You'd think familiarity with disabled people would lead to more understanding but that's not always the case. If you get the job, you'll learn fast enough," she finished.

When the interview was over, the human resources manager, said, abruptly, "Luke, welcome aboard," as if his appointment had been a foregone conclusion.

Never was there a surer career predator than the lovely Magdalena, aka Lena Guerra. After the symposium, Lena had stayed in touch, first sending Marie Louise a delightful thank-you note and, then, a best-wishes card for summer. Rather than spending Memorial Day in summer vacation shopping, Lena called Marie Louise to suggest that she and Marie Louise did lunch.

Over lunch, she had no difficulty in persuading Marie Louise that she was already training Lena as her protégée for glory in rehabilitation services. Over the next weeks, Lena skillfully fashioned Marie Louise's pliant friendship so that Marie Louise, delighted to be on the outer fringe of the beautiful people who came from luxurious houses, was eager to use her connections—social workers, administrators, and so on—to get Lena into Remedial Recuperation Services, first as an intern, and then as an aide. This would be while she was still in her senior year in college.

Offstage in RRS, Rod Fortune warned Marie Louise.

"Kid, for you it's risky. If this white girl fails, it doesn't matter much to her. She has plenty of time and lots of connections. And she's very young. But if she makes a hash of the paperwork, it will tarnish you because you've staked your reputation on her. Everyone knows you've been grooming her. You put your job on the line to get her into RRS—ya'know."

"But Rod, if she went through all the hurdles but the higher-ups wanted to eliminate her, they could do that easily enough. She's got the mind and the commitment. If we lose her, we lose someone with great potential."

"Well, I guess the other youngsters—her rivals in social science in college and our own trainees—haven't had time to come to their senses as to what's been pulled over them, ya'know."

Neither had Marie Louise.

Marie Louise's mind was always turning over new

projects, new ways to advance the cause of disabled people. She thought one of the causes of so many disabled people being mired in dependency was not only poverty but also lack of educational opportunities at an early age. Marie Louise was well seasoned in hearing people like Louis expressing deep dissatisfaction with their restricted chances.

To put that right, she thought the state should first hear from, and then react to, such young people themselves. Thus she proposed a Commission of Young Disabled People, young people from seventeen to twenty-four from all ethnic backgrounds, whose brief would be to meet, discuss, and prepare a draft paper on the problems of disabled people from their perspective. The state assembly could then consider their arguments and, perhaps, improve its disabled provisions—education, opportunities, and benefit awards.

"What a wonderful idea. You're so clever as well as compassionate, you know," said Magdalena as if she had been Marie Louise's inspiration all along.

At college, Lena had observed lesser people ensure they earned recognition by how successfully they played student politics. By massaging the egos of those upwards and concealing the contributions of those below, Lena knew she could earn enough political girl-scout points to ensure her own promotion.

Lena did not in the least mind working as an office gofer at RRS or answering the phones in reception when Carmine was at lunch or on one of her breaks. Lena had learned from her mother that reception work gave her a vantage point of seeing everyone, being acknowledged in return, and allowing her time to appraise who really was a mover and shaker in this little self-regarding community—not merely those who had the best titles. She would study everyone while they thought she was just that bright young girl whose special talent that crafty little Marie Louise had espied.

Behind the scenes, as part of her scheme to supplant her, Lena criticized Marie Louise's project on the grounds that the young people's forum was somehow impractical and too expensive. Besides, it would need a more photogenic front woman, a more acceptable face of disability—in fact someone who was not disabled at all.

One night, Lena told the parrot, Artie, "If Julia Roberts wasn't considered photogenic enough for her body to be on the posters of *Pretty Woman*, then the state deserves a better body and face for its face of disability than that little lick-spittle lump of deformity. And you and I know just who we mean, don't we?"

Whatever the temperature outside, the room in the house on Cherry Street was still slate cold. Carrie was minding Tender Little Fella next door. But Candice sensed that CJ had some plan. She felt, although she could not explain it, that her son was in some sort of danger. It was Candy's growing sense of unease that she was some sort of pawn— although she would not have understood that word. Yet she knew she was being used. Worse, Tender Little Fella was being used.

She knew what she had to do. She lay down on the bed. She decided to pretend to be asleep just as she had pretended years ago when she used to hide under the bed to escape being sent to church on Sundays.

As the Delta bus turned a corner, with Dickon having given all the right signals, a kid on a bike—no more than fourteen or fifteen—swerved diagonally across the bus path. It was like a Spanish matador swirling his cape at a mad bull—the bus—in the ring.

"Crazy kid," said an assertive woman passenger. "If they don't want to get killed one way, it's another."

Farther back on the bus a lithe girl said in the ear of a guy who seemed to be dozing, "Mister, I know you're Carrie's friend."

Louis had been daydreaming. He looked up.

"Please take my little boy. Give him Social Services. Quick. Better for him."

Louis had not seen her for months but he knew who it was.

"Candy, why, what's wr-wr-wrong?"

"Can't stop. Was gonna leave him at the end of the run."

Louis noticed that above her halter-top, Candice was wearing a red tie with a crest. He had always found photos of print models wearing men's shirts attractive and provocative but this tie seemed, for no reason, out of place. He remembered that when Candice had given Luke a rose he had been attacked. Coincidence? Was he safe during the day on a public bus?

Louis looked at the seat behind him. A little mite was asleep.

"I'm not a mom who don't care. Can't cope."

At the next stop, while Louis was looking at the baby, Candy got off unnoticed.

"Funny," thought Dickon, as he caught sight of her in the mirror leaving by the middle door. "I thought she had a baby with her when she got on."

Louis bent forward. There was something brown on the baby's foot. It was a luggage label. Then, by its side, a rose.

The woman on the seat across from him was leaning over.

"Lemme look see."

She read the label.

Please take tender little child to social at grasspit

"What do I d-d-do, Chief?" Louis asked of the driver when he had got to the front of the bus. Dickon was surprised at his drawn-out brandy-soaked utterances.

"Lookee, it's a tiny baby," called out Louis's new friend.

"Where's your mommy, little one?" she said to the child.

"Better call Social Services," said another woman at the front.

"Social Services are at Graspit Street. One stop away," said Dickon. "I'll call Control."

While Dickon was on his phone to Control, the woman started to cradle the baby, cooing maternal noises.

"I'll go with you, son," she said as the bus edged to the sidewalk at Graspit Street.

"My name's Rose," she said when they had stepped onto the sidewalk.

"I'm Louis."

"Ro-Ro-Rose?"

Louis noted the connection. They started walking to the left.

"Been here before, have you, son?"

"Yup, I have," came back the response.

The Social Services Office at Graspit Street never improved. The baby was awake. He seemed to sense that the gloom of the interior spelled doom and started to whimper.

"Shush you," said a man in the row in front of them.

"We've found an abandoned baby," said Rose. "He needs help—and a change—fast."

All the conversation among waiting attendees ceased abruptly, as if someone had switched off surround-sound effects on TV, then, just as quickly, it started again. Heads turned. Some people sitting nearby came over to take a peek. It was as if these many astonished faces adorned with plumed hairstyles were penguins, upset that they had survived some stampede and yet lost their own chicks but were fast scrutinizing this spare fledgling to see if they could take it as a replacement.

After a delay, all of them gave statements to the police. Louis's was minimal. For years Louis had relied upon being one of the self-disappeared—young guys with no fixed address, no electoral registration, and no traceable ties to discarded families—to avoid trouble with the state. He was not going to admit that he knew the mother. Let the cops work that out for themselves. They had never done him any favors. He would repay them in kind. He and Rose had done their duty. Candy wanted "privacy." And what was Marie Louise's word—closure? That's what it was.

Candy's reception from CJ was predictable when she owned up to giving her baby away to Social Services through one of Carrie's friends.

"You stupid, stupid little shit. I told you I got cojones. That's my name. That's my nature. But you are something else. You give away your bargaining chip for a better life, being kept, being pampered, which is the only thing you understand. You think I keep you and supply you out of the goodness of my heart? My heart is black. Give me a good reason why I shouldn't raise my hand to you."

Candy cowered.

"Well, are you that stupid, too? If I do you over, then what good are you to me for working on your back—which is all you're good for? You're gonna work that much harder from now on. I'll have your johns in-out-in-out till your fanny is blue with strain. Dy'hear me? Hear it loud and clear."

CJ lurched over her, his face leering with hard resolve. He clutched her chin and moved her face to one side and then to the other until Candy was sore beyond crying.

"She gets the message, CJ. Leave her be," said Carrie from the doorway. "Besides, we couldn't ever prevent what happened to her first born happening to this second child. Sooner or later, Social Services would have claimed Tender Little Child."

"You make me livid. Don't cross me. D'ya hear? As for

that white motherfucker who took the kid, he'd better watch his back. The cops ever come to my house and he'll get it fair and square."

19 La Lolla Day

Marie Louise's observation of the world of men from her vantage point had made her an astute judge of social systems and social behavior—except where her own emotions were concerned. She saw that men took, used, discarded, and changed their women. In her heart of hearts, this was what she wanted to do to men, for the pulse of sexual need was often overpowering.

But she also craved social acceptance and status—not simply that of a tiny cog in the churning wheels of the state's sluggish social services but also the high-status role of a trophy wife of a young executive on the way up. Caged by her frame, her big heart beating for escape, trapped by the conflict between desire and status, and with her mother's rampant sex life as her role model, she sat down to arbitrate her affairs, as usual by a conference with her kitties.

If she stayed with Dickon, sex would come with ever-decreasing satisfaction. Her social humiliation at his deepening alcoholism and economic distress would end with them both in the gutter. If she made a play for Luke and caught him, she would try and get him to satisfy her physically. If not, she would keep Dickon for dessert.

"Well, that is what men do with women. Momma over-lapped her husbands and lovers," she told tiger-marked Lemel, the best hunter of her brood. "Why not me?"

It all coalesced in her mind when she met her mother for

lunch at a downtown diner. Marie Louise was agog to introduce the subject of her new beau. She had rehearsed her production speech in front of the cats. She was word perfect and never faltered even when she reached several points where wish-fulfillment elided the truth.

"How did you two meet?"

"I was at a reception for a co-worker's leaving presentation. Luke was there. He's recently had sight loss. VIPS is training him for promotional duties. Someone at the party introduced us and we hit it off."

"What's he like?" Gina asked encouragingly.

"Tall, dark, and handsome," answered Marie Louise coquettishly as she handed current husband Harry his ice cream dessert from as far across the table as she could reach.

"Tall, dark, and handsome?" repeated Gina with ironic questioning.

Marie Louise sensed Gina's incredulity was laced with puzzled pleasure. Thus emboldened, she continued, "Well, sort of tall, sort of dark—no, being honest, dark blonde, really—sort of ginger; sort of handsome—presentable, at least."

Gina was grateful for Marie Louise's injection of reality.

"Am I hearing this right, Marie Louise? Are you and this Luke—"

"Yeah, momma, we're not officially an item—trying to take things slowly—but that's where we're heading."

And again, oh-so-casually, she folded her napkin stylishly in order to have her hands above the table in order to flash her mother and stepfather the ring.

Mother and stepfather exchanged glances. Gina did not know if she wanted Marie Louise to have a blind swain. But at least this Luke sounded respectable and solvent. While Gina pondered this, her shift in expression from caution to optimism was evident in her tone and the way her face relaxed.

Then came the special invitation to the as-yet-unasked question.

"Sure, invite him over for the Fourth of July," piped up complaisant fourth husband Harry.

"But, Marie Louise," added Gina. "Don't explain the other significance of the invitation. It'll save a lot of embarrassment. No presents."

"Sure thing, momma."

Gina hoped to show this Luke that, although Marie Louise was palpably different, she was, also, just the same as everyone else and certainly marriage material—especially for someone who was visually impaired.

All Marie Louise now had to do was persuade Luke to come over. Here her courage almost failed her. But Luke's circumstances played into Marie Louise's hand. Screwing up her courage and trying hard to sound casual, the next time Luke was in her office to complete yet more forms for VIPS, she popped the question with all the surface daring of a skilled, sexual predator.

"My mom, Gina, knowing you're likely to be by yourself on the holiday, has invited us over for lunch at the farmhouse. I'll drive us, of course." Faltering, she added, "It's likely one of my brothers and his wife will come over— maybe with their teenage kids—so it'll be a fun family day. No pressure."

Before she had time to add, "Whadda you say?" Luke was ready.

"Thank you, Marie Louise. Please tell your mother I appreciate her nice offer. I'd be delighted to come."

Luke could not see Marie Louise at all clearly but he sensed that her eyes must have been widening with genuine astonishment.

"You mean you want to? Come? You really mean it?"

"Yes, I'd be delighted."

Marie Louise was now not at all sure she wanted to follow

her own scenario. Without fully understanding why, she had the undermining feeling that she had somehow overplayed her hand. Had she had the same insight into Luke's mind as she had into Dickon's, she might have better considered a strategy of wait-and-see before she made her feline pounce—especially when it came to Luke's coda request.

"Marie Louise, there's just one thing. Sometimes, when people become friendly, one of them invites the other for a meal. Sometimes there's chocolate cake for dessert."

"Yes," said Marie Louise, wondering where this was leading.

"Well, I'm somewhat allergic to chocolate, especially if it's mixed with flour, as in a cake, a cookie, or a decorated mousse. It started with school lunches years ago. If I try to eat chocolate—this isn't polite—it will all come back up."

"Well I never," said Marie Louise. "Chocolate? As in chocolate-chip cookies? Do you miss it?"

"Yes, yes, and I'm not even tempted to try. So, if you could advise your mother—to spare embarrassment. I'm okay with other people sitting beside me eating chocolate cake." And, helpfully, "Perhaps I can have an apple or an orange? If that's all right?"

"Sure, Luke. I'm so excited."

Her heart pounded so much that she reached for a glass of water.

When Luke arrived home for dinner that day, Hermione detected a slight spring in his loping, cane-assisted gait. While they ate their supermarket corn-on-the-cob with butter and tomatoes from the front garden on the side, Luke relayed the story of the invitation.

"I'm relieved it's come to this. If I go, it helps us in two ways. First, it takes me away on the Fourth of July. So, you and Steve will have the house and garden all to yourselves without me—and Dennis, of course."

"You don't have to do that," said Hermione.

"It's for the best. Number Two: it will bring the Marie Louise problem to a head. Because I'm in the hands of the state, our paths are bound to cross. And, if this doesn't happen naturally, she'll be sure to make it happen. I'll never be free of her obsession. You've been concerned for me, with all this unwelcome pressure.

"Given what she's told me, Marie Louise's own family are very loving. Since, sooner or later, I have to tell her straight that she has no chance with me—not now, not next year, not ever—she's going to be hurt. If I tell her when she's with her family, she'll have her mother to comfort her."

"Are you sure?"

"Pretty sure. The only thing is that, when it comes to explaining things, to make sure I don't chicken out. Stick to my guns. I hope there'll be something to drink."

"Dutch courage?"

"Right."

Chez Gina, the matron checked the day before lunch when she phoned Marie Louise to see that everything was all right.

"Yes, momma, it's fine: everything's on."

"Does he see differences in dark and light, shadows—that sort of thing?"

"More than that: he can tell people and see things close by but it's jumbled up 'cos of problems inside his eyes. He'll be able to move once he's adjusted to a room. And eat okay."

"Does this Luke have any dietary requirements—religious, taste preferences—anything he doesn't like?"

"No, momma. He's easy. Eats like a horse."

"Marie Louise, you say that because you eat like a bird. Remember, not a word about whose celebration this is. See you. 'Bye."

For Marie Louise, collecting Luke the next day, driving to the farmhouse along not-so-busy roads was fine.

En route, she explained to Luke, "In order to wangle this invitation, and to show you off as a good friend, I told momma that we met socially. She mustn't think you were a client at Remedial Recuperation Services. Are you okay with that?"

Luke nodded grimly.

When they arrived, the family reception went like a dream. To cap it all for Marie Louise, it was a perfect summer day: sunny with a slight breeze and no hint yet of the intense humidity that exhausted people when they ventured outside air-conditioned homes in a humid New England summer. When she squinted up to the azure skies, Marie Louise thought of the exhilaration of white-wine spritzers: she was in seventh heaven.

Once they had settled in that bourgeois conceit, the faux cottage, Luke, like all city dwellers, professed delight at pretend-country living in a vermilion farmhouse adorned with white picket fence, gracious overhanging trees, and an extension to the house prodding into the garden. Inside the extension, decorated window screens and easy lacquered chairs provided exquisite comfort in a tempting hothouse of semi-tropical plants.

The hosts seemed to want to extend the hand of friendship, always trying to put Luke at ease but always making him aware he was an outsider. Luke quickly grasped how attentive Harry was to Gina's every need, moving chairs for the guests, serving him bourbon and ginger ale with pickled herrings, propping up any conversational lull.

As he sat in the little conservatory among the bushes with their myriad shoots and sprinklings of exotic flowers, Luke with his special sight fancifully imagined Harry's large head with its shock of white hair as yet another large flower and Gina with her stunning presence as a special iridescent acacia bush. For, Broadway star or not, faded was hardly the expression for Gina. Here she was, a gossamer-like creation whose natural beauty, consummate sense of self-presentation, and sympathetic personality had almost made time stand still. But not quite.

Her simple low-cut off-white blouse hinting at, but not revealing, shapely breasts, her tight navy-blue skirt, modest shoes, and flecks of gold jewelry, showed off a perfect figure to perfection. What most took Luke by surprise were her flashing Mediterranean eyes, luxurious reddened hair, and inviting smile. This was doubly so for Luke because his double vision was acute that day and he saw Gina twice. Her merging into two shapely, overlapping forms made her even lovelier.

He knew he had seen her before, but where?

The fleck on Gina's timelessness was neither wrinkles nor age but worry. Her disappointment at her own life, her guilt over Marie Louise—both were etched on her face.

"Please call me Gina—everyone does—especially on my birthday."

"It's your birthday?"

"Sure. I'm so glad Marie Louise didn't mention it. No fuss. We're not an Italian family—at least not exclusively—more Czech really. But my parents called me Gina. Then, when I was in my teens, there was a popular Italian film star—Gina Lollobrigida—incredibly attractive. Anyway, my mom read in some film magazine that her birthday is also July 4th, like mine. From then on, although we're ultra patriotic, in our family July 4th is always Gina Lollobrigida day—our excuse for a party away from Uncle Sam."

Marie Louise was silent though all of this but it sent shivers of unhappy memories down her spine. She remembered her grandmother being so stifled of emotion that they could only touch her on such ceremonial occasions as family get-togethers at Labor Day and Thanksgiving. Gina's voice brought her back to the present.

"Is your birthday also in the summer, Luke?"

"No, October, October 13th."

"That makes you Libra doesn't it? Anyone famous born that day?"

"Giuseppe Verdi, the opera composer."

"Anyone more modern born that day?" asked Harry, anxious to keep the conversation light.

"Margaret Thatcher—the former English prime minister."

This sent Gina into a paroxysm of pleasure. She waxed lyrical about power women, during which everyone else fell silent. Luke realized that there would follow a confusion of scenarios: Marie Louise's presentation of him as her intended to her family; his determination to set relations with her back on a professional footing; and Gina's presentation of herself as a birthday countess whose every morning was a leisurely levee before ersatz aristos.

"How did you and Marie Louise first meet?" asked the elegant contessa in benign mode.

Cautioned by Marie Louise, Luke gave an evasive reply.

"We were introduced by people we both know in Remedial Recuperation Services. She's a tireless champion of disabled people in the workplace."

"Because this is our special day for our special birthday girl," said Harry, to ensure there was no pause, "we have to have a special dessert, ordered from the confectioners. While Marie Louise and I go to collect it—would you like to stay here so you and Gina can get better acquainted?"

"Of course," replied Luke, who guessed where this was leading and thought the opportunity might help him pave the way for the disappointment in store.

As soon as she heard the car disappear down the country lane, Gina opened up to Luke.

"I know what you're thinking. Marie Louise says you have residual vision, and you're wondering how very different we look, Marie Louise and me."

It was true. Luke *was* thinking how could Gina, with her

perfect face and figure and whom so many men had desired, have produced a severely disabled child?

Gina was thinking there was no point in concealing anything. Past experiences had taught her it was better to talk and let her emotions out.

"When she was born, the shock was overpowering. Here she was—an angelic tot already with a mop of fair curls. But the medical staff in Pittsburgh—that's where she was born—soon discovered that Marie Louise, seemingly so perfect at birth in size, weight, and disposition, would never grow fully—that she would be lame. Her breath was so enchanting—lovely, sweet—like sweet flowers in an early Easter."

Luke could tell Gina had said the same thing so often it had become a script learnt by rote, albeit with sculpted words.

"Did they know the cause?"

"The doctors thought it was that my womb got infected from industrial pollution in Pittsburgh.

"'The worst of it is,' I told Walt later—he was my husband then—'There's no way we can cover up her abnormality— it will become more obvious with every passing year. There's no exit.'

"Shortly after, when Marie Louise was still in the hospital for tests, I went to collect Todd—that's my eldest—from a birthday party for Todd's little friend, Drew—cute as a button. Drew's mother's eyes were red with crying.

"'Oh, Gina, forgive me,' she said when she answered the door. 'This afternoon, I banged my new car coming out of the drive. It's badly dented.'

"I was choked up with my own problems," Gina continued.

"I said, 'But you've got a healthy little boy. It's his party and you're crying your eyes out over an automobile!'

"By the looks the other parents gave me at the party, I felt

I was being stigmatized. It was as if Marie Louise's condition was my fault.

"My parents insisted on separating us, mother and child. My own mother, Lucy, told me over and over again, 'It will be for the best. Not only will Marie Louise be properly cared for, professionally—which none of us is able to do—but the institution will also teach her the sort of discipline she will need to get ahead as best she can.'"

Luke sensed that Gina's eyes were moist.

"So it was. Lucy had Marie Louise placed in what we always called a home for crippled children. Our desire to safeguard Marie Louise by isolation had the effect of reinforcing her exclusion from any regular social life with other children."

Gina thought Luke was moved by compassion. He probably belonged to the modern school of thought that special education was bound to be inferior and that it contributed to the further disabling of impaired children, partly because of a narrower curriculum where disabled children's achievements were further compromised by teachers' lower expectations.

Luke was beginning to feel like a heel. He had come to Gina's home to break it off with Marie Louise, to end her current obsession, to stop her puny attempts at stalking him and now he was being drawn into this cavern of sympathy.

"But, surely, there was a positive side to Marie Louise's experience in school? She gained a sense of self-worth, by being together with other disabled children."

"Yes, but it was also like having her sleep in a warm batch—like raising chickens. With the way my parents took over and made all the big decisions about Marie Louise and also in the way they allocated money, this was Lucy exercising her power. And I regret it. My parents worked on me, finding compulsive reasons to persuade me not to bring Marie Louise up myself.

"You know, I never accepted that Marie Louise was disabled. For a start, as you must know, there's absolutely nothing wrong with her mind. And she isn't a dwarf. Her smallness is caused by a skeletal malfunction. There are very few cases around the world. That's why we always resisted calls for her to join the Little People. Imagine."

Gina shuddered.

"Although Marie Louise was away most of the year, she was ever-present in my mind. When Marie Louise's healthy younger brothers were small and I tucked them up in bed and kissed them goodnight, I always felt I was also drawing the bedclothes over her even if she was absent."

Luke was more than a little interested and wanted to keep Gina talking, if only to postpone doing what he had come to do.

"When she was young, the one person who was always there for Marie Louise, the one who could always loosen her tension, was her older half-brother, Todd. It was Todd who made himself available to Marie Louise as much as possible. You've heard about Todd, I'm sure, Todd Carter Fox, the New York TV executive."

When Gina went into the kitchen to toss the salad, but still taking about Todd, Luke stayed silent. He began to draw his own conclusions: if Marie Louise's little body would not grow, not only would Gina try and ensure that Marie Louise's mind must excel but she also insisted that eldest born Todd must triumph in both mind and body. It seemed that, whereas Gina had been coerced into handing Marie Louise over to the "school for crippled children," she involved herself in every facet of Todd's life: school homework, sports activities, and piano lessons. Thus Gina made Todd work to dissolve everything that had gone wrong for Marie Louise.

Luke's reverie was brought to an abrupt end by the return of Marie Louise and her stepfather with the precious dessert held in its specially decorated box. It was closed but Luke caught a scintilla of a smell that made him uneasy.

Owing to Harry's seamless management of things, without any guest realizing it, they were now all at table on the first course of the meal. Luke also realized there was not present, nor would there be, any brother with family in tow. This was Meet the Family, Tie the Knot Day in capital letters—or face Capital Punishment, Death at Dawn. Luke knew he must not falter or lose the chance to let Marie Louise down as gently as possible without betraying her.

He began: "I'm very grateful for everything Marie Louise has made possible for me."

"Made possible?" queried her serene highness.

"Connections, advice, help with the forms."

Luke was faltering but he sensed the tigress in Marie Louise and that she could fight her corner and show Luke he had in the past, and still had, need of her, besides owing her much.

Where had he seen Gina before?

Luke took a sip from his first glass of wine. "Very nice," he said.

"You're so accomplished," said Gina. "You take your own food just like anyone else, and drink, too."

"Like a fish, sometimes," said Luke, trying to lighten things.

There was a sharp intake of breath on the other side of the table. Luke realized he had strayed into some troubled part of the collective family memory. Abruptly, Luke changed the subject back to his mission statement.

"Marie Louise gives good professional advice and has guided me to start a new career, helping other disabled people in VIPS."

"Yes, Marie Louise is dedicated."

But Gina did not then follow this with, "We're so proud of her," as Luke had expected. Instead, she shifted the conversation.

"We're so very alike. When Marie Louise was young, as I told you, we used to get invitations from organizations like the Little People who asked us to join. But my parents and I knew we—she"—Gina corrected herself—"was better than that."

The gracious lady's eyes brimmed with tears. Harry stepped in.

"What Gina means is that we're behind Marie Louise one-hundred-and-ten percent. Yes, sir. Marie Louise has striven to overcome the crippling problems of her disability. Yes, sir. We want the best for our little girl."

La duchessa, now recovered, took over.

"Luke, we're so delighted Marie Louise has found you and you, her. We'll always be supportive of you and your disability. With me standing beside you at parties, people won't even notice you're there."

Now Gina *was* in full vocal flight. Having played the heroine-mother ennobled by suffering, Luke was disturbed that Gina seemed to be reverting to the conventional, brittle role of faded but always self-obsessed star.

"I was always the center of attention—at school, at the prom, in my early career—and I never had to think of others. But now you're here before me, I think it's amazing how you've coped. No one just meeting you would ever know. And you're so refined, so educated and—so different—from Marie Louise's other friends—even her co-workers."

"You mean so white," thought Luke.

"It's just been so difficult," said Gina, reverting to her role of troubled heroine.

This time Luke sensed a steely determination not to break down again. He downed a second glass of wine.

"Marie Louise's always been so special—through school and college always bright, so deserving. D'you know, even through sixth grade, she was so angelic that she always played Jesus at Christmas? Lovely golden hair, she had." Gina paused. "Still does."

Luke realized that Marie Louise had been silent for some time, possibly in awe of her mother, but he could feel her squirming beside him. Trapped in an alcoholic haze, blinkered by his double vision, Luke tried to make some sense of a commonplace family scenario: girl introduces boy to her family and thus loses him. It was all like a parody of the boy David Copperfield dining with bookkeeper Uriah Heep and his mother in which the hosts manipulated the conversation, tossing questions and answers to one another like a ball, rendering the guest an object for strategic advance.

For every time Luke tried to steer the conversation round to Marie Louise, his regard for her professional services, his disregard for her as a romantic partner, he was blocked by Gina's self-obsession, Harry's platitudes, and the silent Marie Louise's own determination to ensure her social prize never eluded her grasp. This was not a family with psychological tension simmering under the pleasant formalities of a family get-together. This was a family with a collective mission. Luke was unsure if the announcement of his engagement to Marie Louise would come with a peck described as a kiss and "Congratulations, we're engaged!" or simply by his very attendance at the family sanctuary on Gina Lollobrigida day.

The mechanisms of serving the courses proceeded between desultory picking at the food, punctuated by Harry's adept joking, and then silence with everyone diving in at the food so fast it was as if the ingredients were still alive and might escape from the plates.

The *piece-de-resistance* came with the dessert.

By now, Luke was intensely frustrated by never being able to open up his planned subject without Gina turning the conversation round to her own shimmering presence or to Marie Louise's prodigious skills. Luke's repeated swigs at

Dutch courage, *aka* house red, had neither increased his control nor sweetened his temper. Then, there it was, in the center of the table: a colossal chocolate cake adorned by fruits of the forest. Whatever Luke's limited sight, there was no mistaking the chocolate mass, its color and smell and its ceremonial importance. The blackberries, blueberries, and raspberries that adorned it were like blinking red and mauve lights mocking his revulsion.

"Damn Marie Louise," he thought. "She didn't tell them."

Then Luke remembered where: Gina was the unknown beauty from Pennsylvania, the eternal feminine lovely.

Gina trumpeted the splendors of the dessert.

"On my special Gina Lollobrigida day, we always keep things low key—absolutely no presents—because I'm modest. But the exception is this dessert. Chocolate cake is my once-a-year weakness to compensate for twelve months of abstinence. Now I'm over twenty-one, you didn't think I maintain this figure with junk food, did you?"

With self-deprecating whimsy, she chuckled at her own aside.

"But, Luke, you're my—our—special guest, so you go first. I'll serve."

As he stared at the dessert it seemed to have acquired Gina's face carved on it in bas-relief. Luke gripped the sides of the dining chair for something he could use on which to clench his fists. He could not see but sensed a secret smile flit across Marie Louise's face. Across his own face there flickered a determination to be as expert as she was: take the medicine, grin and bear it, and evade her control by disappearing at the end of the day. So, he would have to try and control his aversion.

As he took a fork-and-spoonful of the dreaded cake, it seemed to him that a stray berry turned into Gina's right eye and winked maliciously at him. He closed his eyes, swallowed, and breathed again. Somehow, he would get through this damnable meal. Gina asked Harry to bring in some extra paper napkins from the kitchen. Luke took a defiant swig of his wine glass. Then he took another mouthful of cake. Disaster.

Luke knew everything was coming up roses and no mistake. He rose, gulped, put his hand over his mouth and rushed clumsily to the open rear door that led to the deck. There were calls of, "What's wrong, Luke?" and "Can we help?"

Luke did not take them in. He tripped over the slide rod for the glass door and collapsed half upright on the deck rail that separated upper deck from lower lawn. He bent over. Then, he well and truly vomited.

The contents of his upper stomach, Gina's precious birthday meal, spewed out over the manicured lawn. Fuzzy though his sight was, he could see the flotsam and jetsam, the detritus of the Gina Lollobrigida meal, and confused speckles of red, brown, and yellow. In his acute embarrassment, it was as if the mangled colors were all day-glow. Everything had an unpardonable stench of downtown Saturday night fever after the bars closed. In a flash, all the garbage sediment of his hatred of becoming a creature of Remedial Recuperation Services and VIPS passed like lightning in his inner eyes.

As Luke tried to stand upright, there to guide him to a garden seat was dependable Harry. He heard Gina say, "Luke, we're so sorry. Marie Louise's just explained. Why didn't you say?"

Luke gasped, "Sorry."

"You're as white as a sheet. Sip this cool water. It'll settle you."

Gina was beside him. Luke sensed that Marie Louise was helping Harry douse down the deck and lawn to purge it of its telltale smears.

"Just stay quiet, dear boy," said Gina now from inside, where she had started to clear the table.

The hosts left Luke to himself and spoke *sotto voce* from inside. He heard Harry say, "Very nervous occasion, new surroundings, meeting the parents, can't see properly, too much wine—that's all."

Luke nodded off. When he awoke, he was inside. Harry was still talking, asking Marie Louise, "Why does he slump like that?"

Marie Louise answered, "It's something blind people do—slouch—it's because they don't have a sense of how they appear to others. You'd be surprised how difficult it can be to train them out of it for job interviews."

She padded over to Luke. Her stumpy, scrawny legs filled him with revulsion and he wanted to mash her face.

"Luke dearest, it's around six thirty. We need to move now to avoid the worst of the homeward-bound traffic."

Luke made futile gestures as if dusting himself down, though there was nothing to dust. Gina collected his cane and case.

"Luke, it's been so nice to meet you at last. We look forward to receiving you again."

Suddenly, Gina looked more than her age, game enough for her hairdresser and her sheath-tight clothes but old in the sense of being weary of life. Yet Gina was indomitable, refusing to give way to tiredness, or to forget her darling daughter's romantic interests.

As Marie Louise and Luke moved off with the windows of the car down, Luke was only too glad of the breeze created by the rush of air around the automobile as it revived him. As they sped along, where the route ahead was clear, Marie Louise started to talk about her family and their pleasure at meeting a new man. Because of the rush of air and the noise of the road, Luke could only partially grasp what she was trying to say—something again about her mother and her African-American boyfriends.

"My mother pretends she is liberated and tolerant—that

she isn't capable of hate toward black people. But, it's like in the Old South, where contempt of African-Americans is layered with honeyed words—love for blacks, if only they would stay in their place and stay off-limits—all that sort of thing. So, Gina and Harry really wanted to meet you."

Weak though he felt, sorry for Marie Louise though he was, Luke knew it was now or never. His main reason for accepting the invitation was to foreclose Marie Louise's unrealistic expectations. Delay had been fatal. The setting was far from ideal. Dusk was settling. The highway was perceptibly busier—even to him. With the windows open, the thunder of the traffic was oppressive. And Marie Louise, with all her sensory impairments, had to concentrate hard to drive them home safely. But she, herself, had raised the subject of boyfriends. Luke now prised it wide open.

"Marie Louise, you are my rehabilitation officer. I owe you a debt of gratitude for opening doors—career, social, rehabilitation—and for freeing me from incapacity—the desolation of isolation, really."

He paused.

"I've learned a lot from you."

"I sense a 'but,'" she said, half-choking more with apprehension than fumes.

Luke realized they were both shouting.

"Yes, there's a 'but.' My sensory problems came to a head and it's caused much emotional upset. I can't commit myself to anyone romantically. Besides, I may need friends and companions socially but I'm a solitary kinda guy."

As he spoke, Luke thought how fluent he was because he had practiced this hard. But he was not at all sure that he was hitting the mark.

"At present, I've almost no money. My prospects, if I have any, are way in the future. If I've learnt anything from you, it's that I have to rely on myself and not expend money on other people—at last until I'm more settled on a future life path."

Now he thought he was being pompous. Nevertheless, he finished with his prearranged flourish.

"I'm sorry but I can't respond to you romantically."

"Is that all? Nothing else?"

"I'm sorry. No."

Marie Louise tried to concentrate on driving through the ever-more crowded highway. It was odd, she felt. She was losing him and, as the process of Remedial Recuperation Services handing him over to VIPS continued, she knew her prized control would ebb away.

Now it was Marie Louise who thought the day would never end. The trees astride the highway were bursting with new leaves as if it were still June. Yet, to her, they were as lifeless as winter. At long last they were up the breast of the hill towards Hermione's house. Luke got out. As he lent over the seat to collect his case and cane, Marie Louise nuzzled her face in his. As he knew she would, she thrust her tongue through his lips.

When Luke added the tired old cliché, "We can still be friends," she said to herself under her breath, "He thinks I'm ugly. When he says, 'I've learned a lot from you,' what he means is 'Next girl, come on!' You bet we'll stay friends."

When Luke opened the screen door of the porch, he heard Hermione from her armchair rustle the newspaper she was reading.

"How did it go?" asked Hermione.

"Not as well as it might have. I did it but—"

"But, when you try and explain things to clear the air, you find that all that you do is leave litter. Luke, she'll claim it was just a misunderstanding and start to milk it—no, to mine it—to exploit hurt feelings."

"You may well be right."

"Hermione's always right," piped up Steve's now ten-year-old from the kitchen table where he was drawing.

By now Hermione and Luke could hear the Fourth of July

fireworks a mile away from the park behind the town hall.

"More sound than light," added Hermione.

When Gina called Marie Louise next day to see if she had got home safely, Marie Louise was ready with her cover story about Luke:

"We decided to postpone the engagement. It was a relief, really because Reader—well, he's not really my type."

Gina was not deceived. She said to Harry, "He won't sleep with her."

Harry answered, "Another try—but no cigar."

20 Night Games

Two days after the Fourth of July, Louis decided he would celebrate by getting high one last time. Then he would throw away his drug paraphernalia. He knew that the local product would not be good because it was a holiday weekend but—what the hell.

There were fireworks aplenty that night.

Louis was not afraid of police cars but, as he dragged his way up Sizewell Street, he noticed darkened cars one after the other in the quieter side streets. They were jutting their snouts out just behind the intersections, lurking, he thought, like so many of the teenage mutant Ninja turtles he had loved as a kid. So, he knew he had to proceed cautiously, stump forward ten paces, fall back two or three, peer left and right. Come to think of it, he was surprised the streets were so deserted.

But when he got to Cherry Street, all hell erupted.

Suddenly, there were all sorts of police about: bright white police cars with sirens snoring away, and flashing lights like spots at a rock concert. There were cop cries to one another and coarse orders to men they were arresting: "Get the fuck inside; stop yelling; you're under arrest; you can yell to high heaven but save it for the judge."

All this was punctuated by the *son et lumiere* of stray neighborhood fireworks. There were two snappy bursts of firework flame in the maroon sky, followed by a hissing noise like an outsize snake. Louis dived for cover.

Amidst the chaos of alternate dark and light caused by the periodic fireworks, the relentless cars racing back and forth along the highway a few blocks away, there he was, dripping mud from a little hollow where he had fallen, perspiring great globules of sweat. Then, he heard loud and clear, "I'll get you, motherfucker. Asshole. This is for you."

Suddenly scared, he did not know if he would burn to death or be crushed by what seemed a plastic garbage can that had fallen on him. He knew he had been hit. It was like the whinnying pain when the car had hit him months ago. Yet it was also a singing pain. Then there was utter silence. He had never felt so alone.

When the raid took place, Leo Guerra was in the forefront. He assigned two officers to target two separate rundown duplex houses to see if there were, just possibly, any children inside who needed special protection, while he would play the same part in a third house. This last was one he knew well, of course—his designated house where he expected to find his son.

The door was open. Nothing unusual there. He went in cautiously with his driver. Everything was dark. He could not stop himself.

"Candy, Candice, are you there?"

Silence.

The blaring noise of the raid outside was punctuated by police cries: "It's payback time."

He moved forward from room to room while his driver guarded the door. The house was empty. Concern overcame fear even though his heart seemed to have dived into his stomach. Amid the tumult he started to do something new for him. He began to reflect. He was thinking, "Hell must be like this. Hideous noises outside. Toxic fear inside as retribution summons me to exposure. Nightmare."

Bella Guerra did not know whether she tossed and turned more in the daytime or at night. Nasty, vicious even though the anonymous letter and poisonous gifts were, they were about more than jealousy of a well-heeled police chief's wife. She had not been in the least worried about Leo and his raid. He was well protected and enjoyed what were, to her, childish displays skirting danger. Besides, her heart was closed to him. If it had not been for his serial affairs, the daily routine of home management, child rearing, and, not least, the petty tribulations of grocery shopping and food preparation would have stifled any residual embers of love.

Then, it came to her in the middle of the night so sharp that she sat up and almost cracked her head on the jutting curls of the William-and-Mary gated headboard of their unhappy bed.

"This time he has had a child with someone else. He has a son and it's with a black woman. He'll never admit it. Whoever it is, is trying to blackmail him and, somehow, this is connected to his precious drug raid. But he has always wanted a son, been disappointed with our girls. Now it's a boy who cannot have his name. It's war all right. I'll give him hell."

When Ellie came back from her heavy-petting date later than her curfew, it was just past One AM and her folks were having an almighty row.

"You've had a black bastard with a black prostitute. Love

child? Talk sense man. You're the real bastard. What do you know about love? Like Bill Clinton, couldn't keep your dwarf dick zipped? So fat round the middle now your pants just drop at every opportunity?"

Ellie could hear her mother raining blows on her father's head and shoulders left and right. When she peeped through their open bedroom door, she saw her mother hit him with a dress shoe, its stiletto heel dangling off but inflicting wounds like the vicious pecks of a trapped hen against an unprepared fox.

Despite the row, they had heard Ellie on the landing halfway up the stairs, looked round, and stopped.

"Ellie, girl, it's not what it looks like."

"Not what it looks like? It's exactly what it looks like. Forget your kids, your promises after the last time. Well, I will show you. You're scum of the lowest order. Whatever you do, wherever you go, my hatred will follow you night and day, not in public—don't you fret—but in the pit of your guilty heart."

Ellie froze.

Her dad said, as lamely as she had ever heard him, "We don't really know if it's mine—even if it's true."

Ellie went into her kid sister's room and found her sobbing silently. She climbed onto the bed and held her in her arms.

"Have a heart—he is my flesh and blood. He's not black—he's mixed race, part Italian, part Dutch, part Creole."

"Yeah? But it's the nigger that shows."

That was it. Leo pushed her and Bella fell onto the bed. But not helplessly.

"That's it, asshole. Now I'll have you. I'll screw you for every last red cent you've got."

21 Makeup

Early in the morning, Ellie found her father in the kitchen applying makeup to his face but leaving the stab wounds. He answered her unasked question.

"I got these last night in the call of duty—fights around the druggies. Nothing to do with your mom and me. Today more than ever, remember you are the police chief's daughter. Keep your mouth buttoned with your girl friends."

Ellie edged warily round her father to make her kid sister breakfast. She took it up on a tray.

After they had all gone, Bella left her room. It was with grim willpower that she waited, showered, dressed, and applied her own makeup. More than ever she would act her part of serene composure behind her mask, applied with scrupulous determination. Leo was right. She had been round the same marital block before and might have to travel that way again. All she now cared for was her position, the money, and to see her daughters through college and following her into a status marriage. Bella deliberately did not look at herself in a mirror. She felt her facemask tightening around her soul as a protective visor for whatever joust lay ahead. She would show them. Use style to face down the opposition.

Yet within the bravado she proposed lurked the nagging fear that, at forty-eight, she was no more experienced than she had been at eighteen. Could she manage a performance as the police chief's loving consort worthy of an Academy award? Could she even manage a performance just worthy of a nomination?

Then she saw them. There was no need to check the mailbox that morning. The unknown well-wishing Hershey had left other tokens of affection. Bella gasped involuntarily. Hanging across the windows at the back of the house and fluttering gaily in the wind were streamers of little dark brown roundels. They were strewn together by translucent Scotch tape. Bella realized that they were cookies. When she went out gingerly to inspect them, she realized they were Oreo cookies—black on the outside and white on the inside. They were small, half-sized, children's cookies. Their meaning was unmistakable.

The fox terrier was whining.

After her second whiskey sour, Bella set her mind as firm as her face.

"I'll make him pay, Artie," she said aloud to the African gray. "I'll make him pay big time."

Struck by her own word, "make," she added, "Pay through his makeup."

She went upstairs to their bedroom to his side table and mirror. Then she went into the bathroom and took one of her disposable lady-shave razors from the cabinet. From her sewing box in the bedroom she extracted her most vicious-looking scissors. She hacked the razor to pieces. Using two Kleenex tissues together, she took shards of the broken-up razor.

Lapak padded in the corridor to drink water from his bowl in the bathroom. She felt the fox terrier's eyes were following her.

In addition to pots and pads of foundation, Leo's makeup box included some sticks of stage makeup left over from the high school musical in which Ellie had appeared—albeit only in the chorus—two years previously. The makeup sticks had been the Guerra family's contribution to production costs. Bella had kept them for Leo to use to touch up his police makeup as necessary, something he had done ever since.

Bella selected a makeup stick from the box. Then, she embedded the razor shards in it and smoothed over the insertions with similar colored makeup paste.

"That'll teach him to use his makeup and deliberately leave scars from our fight so that they looked like honorable wounds of battle in his drug gang bust. I hope when he gets to this precious stick, it shreds his face good and proper."

That was what Bella thought. She tidied up the makeup sticks and pads and reset them in Leo's box. She discarded the debris in the trashcan downstairs. Then, she tidied herself and steadied herself to drive to—to drive anywhere—to a breakfast of an ice-cream sundae in any diner where no one knew her.

Later, when Ellie collected Lizzie from a friend's home, she found her kid sister ashen faced, looking as uncomfortable and bereft as she knew both of them felt. Back home, she made Lizzie a peanut butter sandwich with jello and asked her if there was anything she would like to do.

"I'd feel better in momma's room, you know, the cushions and toys by the pillows smell so good, so nice and fresh and lemony."

They went upstairs and Lizzie lay down on their parents' bed by the cuddly toys and laundered bedclothes. Ellie cradled Lizzie for a while but the young girl soon fell asleep, exhausted by her anxieties, her sleepless night, and the never-ending day with her rowdy friends.

Ellie made sure that Lizzie was comfortably settled and went to her room. She knew she had to re-read Marie Louise's draft proposal for the young disabled people's forum if she was going to skewer it well and truly. Besides, concentrated reading might blot out the family pain.

She did not know when she drifted off but there was some commotion that woke her up—a fall of something next door. Lizzie was crying. With one shoe off and one shoe on, Lizzie was bawling her eyes out, crying as badly as any toddler deprived of a favorite toy. She was wearing one of their father's formal white shirts. It looked like an outsize Victorian nightdress. Ellie did not need to ask what was wrong.

Lizzie's face was cut across both cheeks and bleeding; her little right hand was cut, too, smeared with blood and makeup.

Instinctively, Ellie put her arms round her little sister.

"Whatever's wrong, we'll fix it."

But Lizzie's cheeks were gashed and no mistake.

In between sobs, Lizzie gulped, "I thought I'd play with your stage makeup, like a change from playing with mommy's makeup."

Ellie continued to hold Lizzie with her left arm while using her right hand to wipe away the blood with bedside tissues. There was no mistaking the torn fissures in Lizzie's fair cheeks.

When Ellie turned momentarily to the open door, there was her mother, not entirely steady. However hung over she was, Bella was sober enough to survey the misfired pattern of her intended butchery. Lapak was woofing away.

"Own up. Be honest for once in your life. You tried to get your own back on me. You shafted the makeup and you've scarred Lizzie."

"No, it wasn't like that. It was a horrible accident. There must've been something wrong with the school makeup."

"Accident, my eye! How could there be? If there'd been problems, they would've come out during the school show, not two years later. You just don't get it. Own up."

This was the mother of all their rows. Leo had Bella pinioned to the bed.

"The debris from your little prank is in the trash can. You've no realistic idea of the world of work. All you care about is stuffing your face. Now, you and you alone are responsible for scarring Lizzie. God knows what psychological damage you've caused. Not me. You. This isn't a quick fix. Not one operation. Several. Thank God for our insurance to cover the medical costs.

"All you have to offer a man is tricks and lies. I've been onto you for three years now—nicey-nicey phone calls to Juno; innuendo to the kids about not being able to satisfy daddy. Getting ready for a rich divorce settlement, are we? Wanting the judge to be able to ask your lawyer if you're an investment banker? I should take the strap to you, Miss Dainty Spread."

In her room, Ellie held Lizzie tight.

"When they take the bandages off, will it hurt?"

"No, baby."

"Will it hurt much when they cut into my face?"

"No, Lizzie. In time, everything'll be fine."

"What will I look like?"

With all this tumult, and the cause of them simmering away from home somewhere, Magdalena Guerra steadied herself for her rise. She understood that resolve might not be enough. She might crack and make a mistake.

Louis knew where he was all right. He was trapped in his body. Just beyond his paper-thin skin there were drips and tubes, men and women in green and in white.

Yes, this must be it: the house of the dead. Not like Marie Louise's Egyptian postcard pictures of burial preparations but a cold prison somewhere in Luke's imaginary tales set in Asia.

Louis was back in his hometown jail. A jailbird brought a wounded American eagle into the yard. It had damaged its wing. The other prisoners admired the eagle. But they teased it for having got caught, just like them.

Was that Luke, offering to teach him to read and write properly? A jealous prisoner, Speedy the Vampire, broke a jug of water over his head. It must have been this assault that had given Louis his fever. Marie Louise was also there, attending him on his sick bed, much to the livid fury of his stepfather dying on the next bed. When Marie Louise admitted that she loved Louis, his stepfather, now speech-less with rage, blotted her out.

Louis knew what was coming but not the word for it. Marie Louise and Luke would know. Nothing mattered now.

Just before oblivion, one last thought. As Louis escaped his hometown jail, the other inmates were about to release the eagle. Louis was climbing murky spiral stairs upwards and upwards. Eventually, there was nothing but bright blue sky and he was in it, ready to fly. The eagle was ahead of him, willing him to follow. Just before he did, he recognized his surroundings. He was standing in the high torch of the Statue of Liberty. He flew. Oblivion.

Ever since their fateful Fourth, Luke dreaded Marie Louise calling again. When she did, Hermione tried to protect him, parrying the call.

Hermione mouthed, "Sorry," to Luke. Then she said aloud, "Marie Louise really does need to speak to you. There's been an accident."

"Has she been hurt? Or her folks?"

"No. It's not her—you'd better speak to her."

Luke felt his stomach crease with dismay. But he was taken by surprise, deepened by Marie Louise's audible sobs.

"It's so unfair. He never had a chance. Not then. Not in life from the beginning. Programmed for failure. Then, this end."

Now Luke knew whom she was talking about.

"How did it happen?"

"It was during the police raid on the Sizewell Gang. They say Louis was caught in crossfire but they also said the police didn't fire anything. He did not die immediately. Went into a coma. Died all alone. I'd gone to the hospital but left for the night. He died alone."

Luke could read the *Courier*'s banner headline on the front page in Hermione's lap.

Sizewell Gang Cracked

Without really stopping to look up, Hermione started to read to him. "It says, 'Norse Hoven is a safer place this week after the county's most infamous drug gang was shattered with the multiple arrest and arraignment on the night of July 6th of nine merciless hoods. This followed the county's biggest-ever organized crime investigation, codenamed Crackdown. Unusually, most of those arraigned have chosen to confess via plea bargaining.

"'It took a battalion of 50 officers to seize the nine arrested men. The alleged drug lynch pins are brothers Rafael Purgatori, 31, and Anton Purgatori, 29. A senior cop described them as psychopaths, hoods "who are so ill mentally that they shoot people for the sheer fun of it."

"'Police officers worked through a hi-tech maze of thousands of cell phone calls between the gangsters. They have also built a case from evidence supplied by former gang insiders.

"'The gang is considered unusual by criminologists because leading members are drawn from across the ethnic spectrum—African-American, Hispanic, Italian, Wasp. In this respect, the gang echoes the mixed ethnicity of Chicago bootleggers of the Prohibition Era.

"'Active members have been known to sell hard drugs and commit robberies, using guns to protect themselves and their interests, enforce their reputations and settle scores. The most senior are organized career criminals who control the gang's arsenals and funds. They also authorized attacks on rivals in other gangs.

"'Police estimate that the Sizewell Gang's main drug dealers, led by Taurus O'Neal, 32, a career criminal with several previous drug convictions, made up to $3,000 a day from selling hard drugs on the streets. The dealers bought heroin and cocaine in New York, Bridgeport, and Hartford. They packaged the drugs in $20 wraps, and then distributed them to drug dealers. Street dealers were paid $100 to $200 a day.'"

Hermione added, "Here it is: the paper mentions that there was one personal tragedy.

"'Although the police operation went smoothly enough without having to use guns, Louis Cans, 27, an innocent bystander, was shot by members of the Sizewell Gang during the raid. He died of his wounds later in hospital. Police are treating his killing as a revenge murder for something unknown.'"

"I remember what you said the night I got here from New York," said Luke, "whether our lives were in three acts or five, in this city, the backdrop was drug warfare. Well, it's certainly enfolded poor Louis, smothered the life out of him."

It was some time before Louis's funeral because there were various formalities prior to the authorities being able to release his body. His death was part of the case the police were handing to the state prosecutors for getting heavy sentences imposed on the Louvre Ville gang. There was also the issue of a separate charge—Louis's murder.

Marie Louise and Luke were chastened by the modest state funeral farewell to their friend. Luke was surprised to see Rose and her husband among the scant mourners. After it was over, however, Luke soon realized Marie Louise would use the opportunity to renew her marriage campaign. As he turned to leave the tiny Colonial-style church with its white walls, pilasters, and columns, Marie Louise, already simmering with rage, burst forth.

"Luke Reader, why do you treat me like this? Why do you make my suffering worse? I have a body, too, with a face, like yours: it's my most personal part—just like yours, with eyes and nose and mouth and ears. My body may be tiny but my heart is big. I have all this love inside me, bursting to be shared with you. And I have physical needs—to kiss and be kissed back; to hold my guy and to have him hold me; and in my most private parts, this urge to make passionate physical love. And, if someone wrongs me, I feel the same burning need for revenge as everyone, to hurt that someone in return—just like you."

Luke did not like to be lost for words but he almost was.

"Marie Louise, this is Louis's funeral. I don't think this is the time or place."

She continued as if he had never spoken.

"It's like, in our heart of hearts, we have an inner cloak that conceals happiness and sorrow. We hide these things deep inside so that we can face the world with our outer selves intact. Well, I want everything out in the open—to break free and get my share, like everyone else."

Afterwards, Luke had no illusions. He realized that, upset by Louis's passing or not, Marie Louise Garden was not to be trifled with. Her unspoken rule for her imagined court of admirers was their craven obedience.

Later, Luke realized that now Marie Louise pretended that theirs had always been a strictly professional relationship. She started calling him by his last name. It was "Reader, do this," "Reader, do that," and "I told you, Reader." He fully expected her to sing the praises of her present lover, concluding with, "Look, Reader, I married him."

Out of nowhere, as it seemed, medical bills for Luke arrived at Hermione's house for Luke to pay: bills for eye examinations at the university hospital, bills that Marie Louise had said she would arrange for Remedial Recuperation Services to pay. They included a bill for the Goldman test to determine his legally blind status. He did not have the necessary thousand dollars.

"That's her payback," Hermione advised him.

When Luke called her office, they told him Marie Louise was not available. After he put the phone down, he went upstairs. At the apex of the staircase, he seemed to hear her say in his ear, "I won't you let pass me by with a quick look over your shoulder—difficult to do in your case."

Later, when he was downtown, going to work at NNNH, once again he felt dizzy. He had now had several of these little episodes. But this time it seemed worse because he was crossing the street. The lights were with him and he could hear the buzzing, twanging sound to signal pedestrians that it was okay to cross straight ahead or diagonally to the kitty corner. What was it? Was this a panic attack? When he reached the far side at the bottom of the sloping green, he grasped the wrought-iron base of an ornamental streetlight.

Fall

22 If I Persist in Gazing, Myself I Shall Adore

There was more than one fall in downtown Norse Hoven that year. The golden leaves in suburbia were as lovely as ever, the bitter November wind as biting, and the gales as forceful. But with their jobs on the line, it was their professional tumble that most exercised Leo Guerra and his brother-in-law, Democratic Party yes-man and county supremo for blind and visually impaired people at VIPS, Abe Ripemoff. Abe thought he was a hell-of-a-fellow. He was the sort of extrovert who did not need a drink to be loud in a bar, an office, or his mistress's chamber. His voice was always at bugle strength.

He swanned into work at 10:30 AM and swaggered home to his trophy wife, the former Juno Foster, by 8:30 PM. During the day, Abe feasted on the adoration of his sycophantic staff. They responded to his barked orders as if they were not really his toads at all but the best of buddies, off together to buy drinks in some western saloon: "Sure thing, Abe," and "You bet, Abe."

When they passed on Abe's orders to subordinates with a smile of sincere intimidation, they would say, "Abe wants us to—" meaning—"You'd better get on with it, pronto."

Abe cared nothing for the scowls of his deputy, Tia Schulberg, who hated his little court. She wanted his job—he could see that. But all she did was sit on her butt: "No flair, no brains, no guts," he assured himself.

Abe's swaggering home actually began about 5:30 and usually took a detour for business with his pretty secretary. She had not begun work as a secretary but as an intern from a local community college. Pretty young filly she seemed to the office guys and dolls. Cute as a button were her shanks in thigh-hugging jeans, her tight tops, and beach-blonde hair, drawn up for work and tossed down for salad days of liquid lunches and alluring afternoons. And allure she did.

"Never mind Viagra," said honest Abe to himself. "Seize the day, seize the moment," as he fondled her bubbling breasts.

In days gone by, when Abe was a simple party regular volunteer, he had worked in a bank. Of course, he had no head for figures—that was too much like work—but he appreciated profits and the lifestyle they offered. When a co-worker left, he asked to be sidetracked from accounts to personnel as it was then called. He embraced the 1980s transformation of Personnel to Human Resources and with it, a beguiling fast track to promotion.

When a new manager came who wore a hearing aid, Abe completed his metamorphosis by becoming an authority on disabled access. His much-younger brother, Stuart, worked as a sound technician for a hi-fi store across the state. Stu also worked part-time—one night mid week and two at weekends—at different discos downtown. Stuart quickly learned about sound loops. He fitted them in the local branch. This was the making of Abe's career as an expert on disabled access. The beauty of it, from his point of view, was that he had not had to do anything—just move the people around at work until they helped him rise without trace.

His next lucky break came from inside the Beltway. After former Hollywood B picture star Ronald Reagan became the ever-popular fortieth president of the United States, both Congress and the National Institutes of Health in Bethesda,

Maryland, turned one chink in Reagan's physical armor—his deafness—into yet another political asset: compassion for the deserving poor—in this case deaf people. They carved a separate new institute out of the existing platter of the old—to serve deaf and speech-impaired people. An augmented battery of experts in speech pathology, and ear and throat medicine, found themselves first moved sideways and then raised on a fast track to accelerated promotion.

In New England a tiny state took the hint.

By this time, Abe had a reputation for getting things done. The fact that he could employ men better and more agile than he, himself, was gave him greater credibility. That was what Human Resources was all about: playing with the cards you had, moving the chess pieces around until you had taken the king. Moreover, Abe had always retained his banking connections, always been able to deliver generous donations from sponsors, his as well as his disabled clients' organizations.

Abe's conceit was so profound that he believed he had become a gift to women and that his lucrative position was all down to his managerial prowess and charisma. When it came to role models, Abe still hedged his bets. In his mind, he styled himself on Bill Clinton: "He's not called 'Slick-Willy,' the 'Teflon Kid,' for nothing," he would tell his colleagues. On weekends, he retreated into his fantasy of being *Playboy* entrepreneur Hugh Hefner. Before dates, he would preen himself like a peacock. He could not pass by a store window on the street, or a mirror inside office or home, without approving his reflection.

Yet, as Abe Ripemoff continued his path of conquests, if more imagined than real, he detected unwelcome signs of aging in his figure and face. He would ask his casual conquests with unconvincing indifference what they knew about nose jobs, Botox injections, and so on. He asked his hairdresser what he knew about hair implants. Was this in order to be more attractive to his supposed admirers or to bolster his nagging inner insecurity?

About one self-improvement he was less coy. He asked his physician straightforwardly to arrange for the deepening bags under his eyes to be removed by plastic surgery:

"You see, doc, it's like this: there's no doubt when you're before the public—like all of us who lead political teams—making TV appearances, meeting journalists, and so forth—it's important to look your best. There's no hiding from media spotlight or pretending that how you look doesn't matter."

The doctor looked at him quizzically as if sculpted beauty was for nymphets and mature ladies but not necessary for men-about-town whose wallets were fat with credit cards.

Sensing this, Abe added, "It's not just how I look but how I feel inwardly. The camera will pick up anything hesitant. If I don't exhale confidence, then, politically speaking, I'm dead in the water. Besides, unless top executives look their best, their teams, their clients, and the public don't have confidence in them."

Realizing he was gaining ground, Abe concluded with a flourish: "Unless I stay in control, people won't have confidence about my youthful vigor; so, refer me to a good New Yorker for some discrete nip-and-tuck under the eyes. Money no object."

So he commanded; so it was done.

23 Blind Seer

After a hard day at Network News Norse Hoven, Luke was finding it hard to concentrate. He thought that Candice Quint had been trying to tell Louis something without putting it into words. She may have had learning difficulties but she had enough native wit to seek protection for her little boy. Why? Who was his father? Was that the key?

When he got home, Steve Sharp's son, Dennis, was over for his evening meal and was going to stay until his father returned home later from work. At the dining table, Hermione was teaching young Dennis Solitaire, explaining to him how to stack the cards from kings downwards in an alternate red-black-red-black formation and then re-form the suites upwards from their aces.

As he tried to concentrate on Hermione's nimble fingers as she moved Dennis's little hands to regroup the cards, this game jolted Luke's mind. While Hermione was showing Dennis how to spread the cards, they seemed to make a clickety-click rhythm like a train on the railroad: "Connect-it-up, connect-it-up."

Luke thought of Mickey Garnier at the publishers laying out illustrations and setting them in apposition one against another to compare and contrast the images and then make the best selection.

In his frame of mind, Luke wanted to assign card designations to his friends and acquaintances. Marie Louise as queen of hearts—or should that be Hermione? If, however, the queen of diamonds was Candy and the jack of diamonds was her son, who was the king? And was the king red or black?

He knew that at the side of the table was the day's copy of the local paper with yet another story involving the police chief.

Hermoine answered Luke's unasked question. "Yes, it's

him again. Leo Guerra has been photographed in front of a rowdy bar in Louvre Ville, named the Clubs."

Luke could make out the caption: "King of Clubs closes liquor joint."

Hermione continued Luke's thoughts.

"Once again the police chief is sporting his red tie. It looks damn close to the tie Candice wore at Mistress's party, from what you told me. Surely not?"

Hermione went on to explain to Dennis the significance of some cards beyond card games; that the king of hearts was the only card king without a beard; that the queen of diamonds faced in a different direction from the others; that the king, queen, and jack of hearts were characters in *Alice in Wonderland*; and that the ace of spades signified death. She told Dennis how spitfire gypsy Carmen foresaw death for herself and her discarded lover, Don Jose, no matter how often and how differently she shuffled the cards.

"Wicked."

Dennis was intrigued. But Luke Reader was in another world.

In another of his eureka moments, it was as if Candice Quint, then his experiences and those of Louis Cans and Marie Louise flashed before his eyes: the inner turmoil of becoming different; the outward signs of stigma. He felt for the injustice of Candice being thrown into the urban cocktail of poor education, no job prospects, and a downward spiral of drugs and prostitution. There were the two police officers at the hospital talking about Randy Quint, Candy's brother, and about a kid on the way. Then, there was Tender Little Child, born into poverty, and becoming as surely pro-grammed for failure as his mother before him.

The little boy must be the son of the police chief!

And he was in care, being paid for by the state!

How could Luke prove it and help Candice? He felt, somehow, that he owed it to Louis.

When Hermione paused to let Dennis shuffle the cards and play Solitaire by himself, Luke said, "You could say it was Louis's fault that he was in that neighborhood on that night of nights. But I think that his death was more than a tragic accident when he got caught, allegedly, in crossfire. The gang leaders would've hated him for taking away their precious bargaining tool. We've read how they used murder as a political tool."

"Exactly. This was pure revenge—that simple, cut, and dried."

Chance dealt Luke the ace of spades.

Magdalena, aka Lena or Ellie, Guerra came to Network News Norse Hoven next day to record a pilot commentary for a program on Marie Louise Garden's pet project, the Young Disabled People's Forum. She eyed Luke warily, as he did her. He thought Ella was not on the level and that she intended mischief to Marie Louise's project even while she was speaking for it. Whatever his emotional problems with Marie Louise, he knew she had opened doors for him that no one else would have attempted.

Luke fired a surprise opener.

"Hi, Lena—I can still call you Lena, can't I? You're looking great. I hear you're a born natural on camera. The pros here really rate you as a TV presenter."

Cunning or not, Ellie was disarmed.

"Thanks, Luke."

"How're things at home?"

"My folks work so hard. You know what they say when they pass like ships in the night? 'Long time, no see.'"

"How's your kid sister—brother, too?"

"They're fine, ya'know."

She paused. Something was not right.

"Must be hard with a new baby at home. Up all night. Joy, of course. But very tiring."

"The kid's not there, ya'know. Their rows—I tell you—it's like a war zone. It wasn't as if the child was white. Dad's affairs have always been discreet—until now. Now, it's with this black crack head, ya'know. We don't even know where the little critter is. Mom's distraught. Dad's always wanted a son but it's not one he can acknowledge. Takes it out on all of us."

Luke knew he had to conceal his little triumph, not to give as skilled a career predator as Ella Guerra any more unease till he had acted.

Candy Quint had gone to Louis for help. And for that Louis had been shot. How could Luke expose the police chief, get help for Candy, and make the child's paternal identity work for the little boy—give him a proper family and a proper start in life?

"Gee, Magdalena, I'm sorry. But I know your family will work this out. It may make your parents stronger as a couple. Good luck with the shoot."

When Magdalena Guerra was in the studio, she could feel fury at her father and tears for her mother rise like sap and choke in her mouth. She sensed her eyes must be red and that her—oh-so-crucial—performance might be marred. Indeed, the disappointment was evident on the faces of the director.

"Something's wrong with the kid," said Steve Sharp.

"She's normally so radiant on camera. D'ye think she had a row with a jealous boyfriend who upset her so her eyes would read firehouse red on camera—something like that? Whatever the reason, we'll have to use the footage—just cut it down, use some of Lena's comments as voiceover over cityscape views instead of concentrating on her face."

"And cut her down to size," Luke thought when he heard Ellie had not measured up.

In his break, Luke made three phone calls—to Marie Louise, to Rose, and to Carrie Behan.

He met with them next day at the car repair lot run by Rose's husband.

Rose told Marie Louise the story about going with Louis and taking the baby to Social Services and that the rose was a signal to her to help Candy's baby. Carrie Behan told her story about Candice getting pregnant by an older client with the power ties and how CJ planned to use the little boy as a bargaining chip to escape prosecution. He also planned blackmail since the guy had done drugs with Candy. She explained how Candice had become terrified of CJ, and frightened for the future of Tender Little Child; that she wanted him in care where he would be safe from CJ and from his father's family. When she returned, having handed over the child on the bus, CJ had threatened to beat her fair and square so she was now too afraid to come out herself.

The four of them knew what they had to do. Rose's husband took Rose and Carrie to Graspit Street; Marie Louise ferried Luke Reader there in her adapted car.

The skeptical Social Services manager listened in astonishment at a hastily convened meeting.

"These are serious allegations. They come out of the blue. Where's the evidence? If you are right, and it's a big 'if,' it will come down to one backward girl's word against the police chief who has done more to tackle drug dealing than any of his predecessors. Who would the public—or a jury—trust more?"

"There's DNA nowadays," replied Luke. "You could ask his older daughter. She will do much for her career. And Candy will testify."

"I'll see to that. But you've got to promise she'll get protection," injected Carrie. "And that CJ stays behind bars while she does."

"Anything else?" prompted the manager, suspecting this little group was holding something special in reserve and feeding them an opening.

"Oh, yeah," said Carrie. "Upstairs, there's a machine gun wrapped in cling foil stashed in the attic. The Louvre Ville gang keep it there in reserve."

The manager was so lost for words that he failed to notice the surprise Carrie's little announcement had had on Marie Louise, Luke, and Rose.

24 Blind People Are Ugly

Luke Reader felt his indignation rising. No matter how often it had got him into trouble before, he had to express it, and take action. When he broke the police chief's secret story to Steve Sharp, he was in full crusading mode, persuading his line manager to take the approach of high moral ground against disability discrimination—prejudice against Candice Quint.

"It's a lead story—no question—if everything you've found out is true. But it has to be cast-iron before we can run it. We know the little kid is in care, raised by the state, and whoever the daddy is, is in denial or avoiding his responsibility. The DNA evidence will be crucial. Once that's out, there won't be any scoop.

"It's a real tragedy for Leo Guerra given what he has achieved and then to be exposed in public for having feet of clay. Genuine Greek tragedy stuff—the big hero with the tragic flaw of hubris that takes him down to zero—no doubt about it. But what the public will want is the visceral excitement of exposure."

As agreed with Steve, Luke Reader was the duty reporter on the late shift at Network News Norse Hoven. He was excited at being able to report his scoop on the TV news where it would be the lead item. Accordingly, Steve Sharp told Luke to prepare his script for when they could break the story. Luke began to shape and to mold his story into an argument for disabled rights. He started to do so: "Hi! I'm Luke Reader. And this is Network News Norse Hoven."

When Luke was out of the way, Steve Sharp had his secretary call Magdalena Guerra. He invited her to meet in the downtown diner near the university museum.

For Lena, aka Ellie, the lure of media promotion was enough. Having for some time known the story and how it must inevitably break, Magdalena was ready to expose her father. She could act the injured daughter, the vessel of political probity, the guardian of her injured mother's interests, while, at the same time, supplying information in exchange for a clear, if understated, offer of future promotional work for the studio.

"Yes, they asked for a DNA sample, you know. Dad was cornered and admitted the kid was his—probably. Thinks he can get away with it."

Steve knew he had to move fast. He promised to confine the story to Leo Guerra's transgressions; that the studio and the press would not harass Magdalena Guerra and her sister; and, most importantly, they would safeguard her mother, who was to be presented as a selfless heroine ennobled by tragedy.

Luke had Sister Carrie's permission to give Candy's side of the story: an abused child lured and manipulated into prostitution by drug dealers. To reassure Joe Public, he would emphasize that the drug dealers had been apprehended and would go down. He also intended to make clear that, as a disabled girl herself, Candy had never had any productive career options.

Steve Sharp, editor of the Late Night News, still appreciated how big this story would become. However, he now had had second thoughts about Luke as presenter. Looking for some immoral support, he said to his temp secretary, Opal Pearl: "We can't use Luke—his face won't read well on screen. He squints. His eyes flutter upwards."

"Surely it's not that bad?" asked Opal.

"You bet it is on TV. The camera will magnify everything that's wrong with his face—which is plenty. It will distract viewers."

Steve reappraised his temp replacement. She was wan but chic with innate style all the way from her stylish teal turban down to her tailored emerald sleeveless shift dress and shoes. Tonight, however, she seemed troubled. But Steve Sharp continued his fast-paced political musings.

"Late at night and through the day tomorrow viewers grounded at home for whom local TV is their fondest companion will react against Luke. Our sponsors will be horrified. What viewers and clients want is not the news."

"But the story is tremendous: it must come first."

"You'd be forgiven for thinking that. Our viewers want stories with well-routed local gossip, sympathy stories about family accidents, or us harping on economic perennials, such as the price of gas. Here is a juicy scandal. But Luke on TV will shift the whole emphasis from the druggie police chief to his bizarre-looking self. Let's find Janis Reilly. Get her to present it from the steps of the police precinct."

The phone rang.

"Here, quick—this is the call I was expecting. I need you to hear this. It's part of your training for future reference."

Steve Sharp grabbed the phone and switched it onto speakerphone so the temp could hear the conversation. He began to show Todd Carter Fox, the top executive in New York, and the lowly temp before him how he had everything under control.

"Sure thing, Todd. I'm with you on this one hundred percent."

The other phone rang and temp Opal Pearl picked it up.

"He's here. Please hold," she answered.

As Steve Sharp continued with Todd, she mouthed silently to him, "It's Luke."

On the other line, Todd was saying, "This is a terrific scoop. Don't get it wrong. But we don't want Luke present-ing it. I got him a job as a favor to my sister until his federal pension kicks in but I don't want him seen. We want to keep our audience, make them concentrate on our cutting-edge."

Steve Sharp's impatience got the better of him. He made motions to Opal with one hand to indicate she was to keep Luke on hold while signaling with the other that he could not wait for his boss to wrap himself up while Todd Carter Fox continued as if they had all night.

"I'm sorry for Luke. It's not his fault, poor guy. He's okay as a background boy. Keep it that way."

"Got it, Todd; it's under wraps. I've thought it through. I'll let him down without hurting his feelings."

"How's the new temp working out?"

"Fine, Todd, just fine. She has remarkable assets."

"Big tits, huh?"

Steve Sharp winced toward Opal Pearl, who had heard the boss's description of her loud and clear. He mouthed "Sorry."

Then to his boss, "You think I mean those are her assets?"

Big Boy Todd simply said, "You're being coy all of a sudden.

"And there's another thing, I heard on the grapevine that you've got this smart-ass kid, police chief's daughter, who helped you break the story of the chief and his black girl-friend and their little boy. She's working as some kinda intern?"

"Correct."

"Well, it seems she'd sell her father for God-knows-what promises of fame and fortune. But she's not going to do it at the expense of Marie Louise—shove my sister out in the cold when she's done so much for those Goddamned disabled kids? Outrageous! Calling my sister all sorts of things behind her back. She'd better learn and fast that what goes around comes around. If the disabled project isn't working, can it; and can the interfering police chief's daughter as well. With her hypocrite father no longer a player, she's out of the picture, too. Do I make myself clear?

"Sure thing, Todd."

"'Bye."

"'Bye."

To Opal Pearl, Steve said, using his wrists to boast of his prowess, "Ambidextrous, or what? Multi-tasking—it's a synch. Learnt it as a bartender in grad school."

Opal did not know which astonished her more, the political skullduggery or Steve Sharp's insouciance.

Steve now turned his attention to the eager Luke, waiting on the other line.

"Luke, we really appreciate you breaking this story and giving it to us. But we can't use you to broadcast the story. Our bosses in the capital have ruled we need a proper—a duly accredited, experienced—political correspondent on screen."

Luke gasped, "But I broke it. Without me, the studio wouldn't have this."

"Luke, I'm sorry. It's just that we need someone more experienced. Janis Reilly will cover it. She's already outside the police precinct with a crew. Luke, I said 'I'm sorry.' Now, gotta go."

Steve lowered the mouthpiece and breathed a sigh of relief.

"Mr. Sharp," piped up Opal Pearl, suddenly timid, her eyes welling.

"I also said 'sorry' to you," answered Steve Sharp.

"It's not that. I'm still not completely familiar with your

phone set-up. I may have had Luke on line but without putting him on hold."

"You mean he may have heard what I was saying to Todd Carter?"

Steve Sharp could not understand why Opal was crying her eyes out over a tasteless, but to him, trivial remark.

"Yes, it's unfortunate but not life and death. Pull yourself together."

Opal broke down. When Steve Sharp was not looking, she left in the middle of her shift.

At the other end of the building, Luke was cursing his luck. He slumped in his chair, the posture he sometimes fell into when he was communing with his inner thoughts. However, he was wide-awake most of the shift, silently fuming. When he went home in the early hours, he could not sleep, waiting for a decent enough hour when he could disturb Marie Louise with the story.

Consummate pro, Janis Reilly did as she was bidden, hiding her hair, which was in rollers, under a gaudy scarf.

When Hermione collected the local newspaper from the front porch next day, the headline fairly leaped out at her:

THE JOB IS MINE AND I WILL STAY
Vows Police Chief

Before making her breakfast, she sat at the kitchen counter and scrutinized the story under a peculiar photo. It looked like a scuffle between the white police chief and some African-American bystander. Hermione started to read.

"'I will never leave the job I love,' declared Police Chief Leo Guerra, when he spoke to TV and press reporters on the front steps of the police precinct in downtown Norse Hoven.

"'My conscience is clear,' he concluded."

Hermione said to herself, "Well, that's it: another instance that a clear conscience is a sure sign of a bad memory."

She read on.

"This statement follows a political storm when news broke that Police Chief Guerra, 55, had fathered an illegitimate child upon Candice Quint, 18. Quint has previously been a sex worker in Norse Hoven's dangerous red light district. She also has a previous child by another man. Diagnosed with learning disabilities, Social Services had already declared her an unfit mother and placed both children in care of the state.

"In the presence of his attorney, Guerra read from a statement but declined to answer press questions. The statement said:

"'Although I have answered all questions about knowing Ms. Candice Quint, I have not, until now, answered them completely. I have known Ms. Quint for a few months. My relationship with her was not appropriate. I regret the suffering my friendship with Candice Quint has caused my loving wife, Bella, and our two beautiful daughters. I extend to them my deepest apologies. I do have a child by Ms. Quint. At present, he is in care. I will provide for my son. This is nobody's business but ours.

"'I am now concentrating on the work I have been selected to do—making the streets of Norse Hoven as safe as possible for all citizens in our war against the drug gangs. Even though the gang leaders have been apprehended, we must still remain vigilant. There is a power vacuum in the underworld that other young hoods may try and enter. As committed police, we have to continue our eternal cat-and-mouse observation of lowlifes. This is the job I love. Thank you.'"

The press story continued:

"There was a scuffle. An unknown man threw an egg that landed squarely on the police chief's lapel and splattered his jacket. The chief pulled away from his minders. He tried to land a punch on the man's face but policewomen whisked him up the steps.

"As Guerra withdrew into the police precinct, his attorney, Tom Grady, said, 'No individual questions. Thank you.'

"The man who threw the egg, later identified as Rob Burr, was folded into the police offices but subsequently released after being cautioned.

"The mayor of Norse Hoven, Maxine Thoroughbred, has ordered, as is her prerogative, Police Chief Leo Guerra to wear standard police uniform henceforth—no more power ties and fancy belts."

Hermione turned and said, "Luke, dear, there's no mention of you here—that you broke the story."

"What did you expect? In journalism, it's every dick for himself."

"Like politics, I suppose."

"I heard this old joke at the studio: politics is showbiz for ugly people."

"And Luke, there's nothing here about the police chief doing drugs."

"I suppose it couldn't be proved. The story's rich enough. And, if it included drugs, then the public outcry against the police would be too great. There would be widespread disgust at Leo Guerra since his mission was to eliminate drug gangs. It could undermine future attempts at law enforcement."

"That's terrible, Reader," Marie Louise said when she heard about his being denied the opportunity to break the story on TV, her political antennae swiftly attuned.

"It's obvious it happened because the TV bosses simply didn't want a blind guy presenting their lead story. You're the victim of discrimination, all right. Probably falls within the practices outlawed by the Americans with Disabilities legislation. But what you're going to do about it isn't so clear since you've already applied for a social-security disability pension.

"First, you must get the studio's answer. Go and see Steve Sharp and have your letter of enquiry ready."

Two days later, when young Dennis brought her the paper as she was toasting her mid-morning bagel, once again, Hermione stopped in her tracks to read the main story under the banner headline:

POLICE CHIEF RESIGNS
THE SHAME WILL LIVE WITH ME FOREVER

"After a week of mounting pressure upon him and febrile tension across public offices and in the Capitol building, embattled Police Chief Leo Guerra has resigned. A statement issued on his behalf by his attorney said:

"'The overwhelming attention given to my personal life has caused significant disruption across the precinct. Media scrutiny and speculation have made it increasingly difficult for all of us to continue with, and concentrate on, our principal task—that is police supervision of the City of Norse Hoven and our disruption of the drug gangs—a battle we are now winning.

"'With the interests of the public and my colleagues foremost in my mind, I have decided to resign with immediate effect and, thereby, allow the police to continue their operations under a new chief.

"'I thank all of my colleagues for their loyal support. I owe a debt of gratitude to my dear wife, Bella, and my beloved daughters for their understanding.'"

Before she could digress into the background of the story and the editorial, Hermione found that she had let the bagel get burned.

She read on:

"The chief prosecutor applauded Police Chief Leo Guerra for his lead in catching the Louvre Ville gang. He declared that their arraignment and plea bargaining has 'huge implications for public safety.'"

The story then quoted crime reporter Joe Flynn's findings that Guerra would receive his full salary for six months, during which his advisers would negotiate a final financial settlement.

"But what will happened to the little girl?" asked Hermione.

"Little boy," Luke corrected her. "Dunno, but if he has some problems like his mom, then he'll need state care for some time to come. I suppose when he was born, his father's name was unknown, so, the sole, official parent is the mother, and she's not able to look after him. And anything the father does will have intense public scrutiny, not least his substantial pension—which should mean he could afford to have his little boy looked after.

"What a mess! And no public sympathy for the two victims, mother and son."

"What about the wife?" asked Luke.

"She'll get a settlement. I don't mean to sound hardhearted but I bet she's used to it. To get along and enjoy being Mrs. Police Chief, she went along with infidelities. Saved her having to have sex with him. Big fat oaf. Then, look at this cartoon."

Hermione held up the paper and guided Luke's hand to a front-page cartoon with a drawing of a little old bag of a man and a little old bag of a woman. The old-bag man was reading the story of the police chief's political demise in the paper. Referring to the punch-throwing incident on the steps of the precinct, his wife was saying: "If it was me, I'd rather he hit me than took me to bed."

"My feelings exactly," concluded Hermione. "I'd rather

be locked in a police cell than I had to have sex with him. What a lout!"

Hermione was in full mode as wise woman of the suburbs, coffee cup in hand, insight to dispel over the breakfast table.

Young Dennis was in the dining area, playing scrabble with one of his little friends. He called out, "Reign or resign? The only difference is an S."

Two weeks later, Hermione read out to Luke a briefer inside story in the Norse Hoven Courier that Leo Guerra and his wife had separated and that his wife had filed for divorce.

Luke was determined to fight his corner about discrimination.

He found Steve Sharp was not available. Hermione discovered that she was no longer in the loop of Steve Sharp's little support circle when it came to young Dennis's after-school needs. The house opposite was suddenly dark and silent.

It seemed that NNNH could only find their newest administrator to accept Luke's letter of complaint. When Luke went into her office, she was looking out of a window at the police precinct across the street.

"Hi, I'm the new head of business. My name is Dolly Drum Dong. What seems to be the problem?"

She wore a dark gray women's business suit with the faintest hint of pinstripe, diminutive diamond studs in her ears, and a gold wedding band. In short, she was dressed for the then contemporary role of Manhattan office worker, not as a leading player. She was all business-like professionalism, behind a grim smile. Luke thought of feral African cats. He realized that when they bared their teeth, they were honest about their business of killing prey for food.

Dolly Drum Dong was still pondering the problem of her previous visitor. There was this girl, her ex-secretary, claiming sexist discrimination and she had clear evidence.

Now she resented Luke mumbling through his account of "the problem."

Dolly Drum Dong took his papers.

"I think there's just been a misunderstanding," she said matter-of-factly.

Then she parroted the studio's impeccable credentials in hiring disabled people. She rose as if to go and motioned as if Luke should also now depart.

"No. It's not a misunderstanding; it's disability discrimination. It's against the law."

"No, I don't think so. It's only a misunderstanding."

With that, she left the room. Luke realized she would not return. He also realized another attack of unsteadiness was upon him, and he sat down again. After another few minutes a security guard came in and, with a tight grip, moved him out of the building.

Two weeks later, he received a reply from the studio's chief of news broadcasts, based on an internal investigation.

"Our internal investigation has revealed that there was no discrimination. Unfortunately, when Ms. Dolly Drum Dong explained the procedures reasonably to you, you chose to insult her verbally. She was left shaken by the experience. The studio had to apologize to her about your behavior."

Luke was becoming livid but, as he handed her the letter, Hermione was ahead of him.

"Dolly Drum Dong? There's a name to conjure with. She's been around Norse Hoven for years—always trouble but she uses office politics to her advantage. What she said—it's an old trick. You complained about the studio's discrimination against a disabled employee. The response of the studio, *via* their head of business, is to queer the pitch by saying, 'You have insulted us,' and thereby shift the ground from disability discrimination to 'insult' and 'inappropriate manner.'"

Hermione continued, "I have an old college friend who's now a labor lawyer. His little boy has Down's syndrome so he's sympathetic to disabled issues. I've invited him over for dinner to discuss your case and your chances. He'll charge but, perhaps, not unless you win."

Over coffee, Ben Johnson, Hermione's lawyer friend, said, "I'll take it. The real issue is not whether the studio likes you or doesn't like you but whether it has fulfilled its obligations to a disabled employee and complied with the law. The evidence is against them. They're playing for time. It's something all third-rate institutions do when they're cornered."

"If you had been a studio employee of long standing, this case would be a sure-fire thing: experienced journalist breaks top story but gets kicked into the backroom because he's blind. However, you'd only just started work so they can play the experience card against you. Might any of your co-workers know anything that would help?"

"Well, there's Opal Pearl, the girl hired at the same time as me: she works as Steve Sharp's secretary. She seems to know everything. I think she's still there but I'm not sure."

"Get me her number and I'll call her."

Marie Louise was absorbed in her emotional turmoil. She did not realize that her brother had thought he was doing her a favor to pay Luke back for turning down her unstated offer of marriage. She raised the matter of Luke being bypassed with her line manager. He told her straightfor-wardly and brutally, "The job of Remedial Recuperation Services is rehabilitation, not law suits, not political protest, and not psychotherapy."

As usual, when she was in a quandary Marie Louise went to her trusted co-worker, Rod Fortune. After she gave him Luke's side of the story, Rod discussed the case the next time he was at a breakfast meeting with Abe Ripemoff, the county director of VIPS. He had to plunge into the conversation without preparation in order to make his point quickly because a TV crew was there setting up equipment for a live broadcast about bureaucratic reorganization in the Capitol.

"The thing is, Abe, no one could say Luke Reader isn't a good correspondent. Luke broke the story but he was not used to tell it. He was right there in the studio, on duty, and ready immediately. Yet someone who was off duty was called in specially, instead of him—made the broadcast with her hair in rollers."

Abe Ripemoff was present in body but not in mind, hung over and distracted because his current squeeze was not returning his phone calls.

"So, I've heard," he said absentmindedly. "I've heard about this guy. Pierre LaFarge mentioned him to me. Supposed to be as bright as a button. Well, maybe his mind is sharp but, from what I hear, he looks terrible. He uses a white cane like some badge of honor.

"I've heard that he squints badly when TV lights are on him and his eyes go into an upward flutter, showing their whites. It distracts the person he's talking to. Besides, it makes him look like a halfwit, or, so I've heard. But what can you expect?"

"Don't you think the case is embarrassing to the TV network because it takes pride in being politically correct—claiming how unbiased and generous it is on diversity issues?"

"The thing is Network News Norse Hoven has to do as it thinks best for its audience. They pay. They don't want VIPs in their face. Besides, all blind people are ugly. We should know. We look after them; protect them from society; and, in many cases, protect them from having to earn their living. They're better out of the way."

Abe was so absorbed in his own world of upwardly

mobile sexual pleasure that he was totally unaware of the impact his tirade had on those present.

Slowly but surely though, Abe Ripemoff found himself cut off when his colleagues bypassed him, no longer circulating him with memos, no longer sending him invitations to meetings. Behind his back, they demanded Abe's removal from VIPS immediately and without any pension.

25 Eye Witnesses

Vivien Petkoff, political secretary to the governor, found herself faced with a deputation of busybodies for the greater good, all with the highest motives and all wanting Abe axed. They included Rod Fortune, Marie Louise Garden, Pierre LaFarge, Eddie Carreras, and Tia Schulberg, Abe's discontented deputy. She posed the same question to each of them in turn.

"In your opinion, is he a bad director?"

The consensus was that Abe was a politically effective administrator who had been able to secure more resources for VIPS than had any of his predecessors.

"Well, what's your problem?"

Self-appointed spokesperson Tia Schulberg began: "What it comes down to is this: he said that blind people are ugly and no one wants anything to do with them."

Startled, Vivien Petkoff replied hesitantly, "I heard the rumor that he said something like that. But it was an off-the-cuff private remark—nothing prepared. Surely, you can't think he meant it."

"He meant it all right," chipped in Rod Fortune.

"I've heard him say similar things in the office—blind

people are boobies, they're hideous to look at, and best kept out of sight."

"Where's your proof? Independent proof? There's nothing in the public domain."

Tia Schulberg came to Rod's rescue.

"That's where you're mistaken. What he said about blind people being ugly was caught on camera when Network News Norse Hoven's news team were setting things up to record some material for a broadcast. The story's all over the television studio and, besides, there's his memo."

"Memo?"

Tia repeated the word. "Memo. He circulated a memo suggesting that we find ways of seating blind people and other disabled people right at the back of the conference hall for a meeting this summer—only one line of seats, with all the others secluded in a separate room where the party conference is to be broadcast on CCTV."

"Well, then, it's not so bad," argued Vivien Petkoff. "We can put a gloss on this."

"I don't think so. For one thing, there's this."

The spokesperson produced her trump card, the morning edition of the two major state papers, each carrying the story with banner headlines on page three. Such an ideal chance of eliminating Abe might never come again. She seized it.

The face of the governor's new political secretary was agape with dismay. Vivien Petkoff could no longer ignore the condemnation not least because, if she did, the complainants would go and see someone else. And this time, their accusations would envelop her—declaring that her lack of action showed that she sided against disabled people. Nevertheless, as she paused before committing herself, the governor's secretary sensed that, among the gallant accusers' motives, was payback for past slights, impure and simple.

Indeed, Abe was to find to his cost that the office-politics traditions of betrayal were alive and ready to kick aside anyone with a weakness. When he heard about the malcontents' meeting through an accidentally-on-purpose remark on the grapevine, Abe said to his wife, Juno, when he called her from the office, "I suppose I can understand Tia Schulberg hating me. During her thirteen years at VIPS, she's always been my second."

"Yes, and you've always kept her feeling like that. You've enjoyed the spotlight, kept her in the background. You flaunted your bimbo girlfriends in her face. It's inevitable she would loathe you."

As his car meandered along with the throb of homeward-bound traffic along Sizewell Avenue, in the distance, to the north, he could see the unmistakable outline of the three rolling hills known as the Sleeping Giant: the head, with its gentle slope of the brow and sharp jutting out of the chin to the west; the undulating torso in the center; and the expansive stomach to the east. The giant slept shrouded in forest, the thickets of trees swarming over him like the little people of Lilliput who ensnared the sleeping Gulliver with ropes and pegs. Abe wondered if this helpless, dormant giant was more, or less, supine than his own hollowed-out character.

Next day, when Abe Ripemoff was just through with his morning shower the phone rang. The caller said, without any ado, "Lucky I caught you. You know you were meant to travel to Maryland to the disability conference today—"

"Not meant to, we're about to leave for the airport."

"Don't leave. The state is sending your deputy instead."

"Why Tia? And who is this?"

"That's not important. We've never met. You can call me Olive Branch," added the man's voice.

Abe wanted to explode. His wife called from the bedroom, "It's not the time to get on your high horse."

The anonymous caller continued: "Someone from the governor's office will call you later."

With that, the phone went dead. Abe felt like someone had kicked his testicles.

"Now, what's all that about?" came from Juno in the bedroom. He told her.

"Call Oliver Swindle. Find out what's what."

"It's 8:30—too early."

"Too early?" she asked in surprise. "Not too early for him to start drinking. If you won't, then I'll do it."

Juno took the phone handset and dialed the number.

"Yes, Mrs. Ripemoff. Oliver Swindle is in already; I'm sure he can find time for you. Please hold."

The phone went silent for a moment.

"I'm sorry. Mr. Swindle is at a symposium. As soon as it's over, I'll be sure to ask him to call Abe. Sorry, but I have to take another call. Goodbye."

The dejected couple sat in silence at breakfast. Breakfast was liquid: bourbon—Wild Turkey.

"Why don't you set off for the office, just like normal?"

"No, I can't do that. It's being redecorated. It was all timed to happen when we were to be in Maryland—minimum disruption to the working schedule and so on. If I turn up, it will open me up to more scrutiny."

Two hours elapsed but not without much soul-searching by the crestfallen leader. Then, Abe called Oliver Swindle to try his luck again.

"No, unfortunately, Mr. Swindle isn't here. There was an unexpected call for him to go to the governor's office."

Two hours later, Abe called again.

"Mr. Swindle has had to speak on behalf of the governor at a press conference."

It was clear that the damn Swindle was hiding out. But Abe and his wife did not have to wait until the next day for their torture to peak. When Juno switched on the local TV news, it

240

was all over. Although he had not said anything more in public or private, Juno heard on TV that Abe deeply regretted his misstatement about blind people, withdrew his comments, and so on. Then a hitherto unknown spokesperson for the governor also apologized unreservedly.

Juno said quietly, "So, it's true: success is always private but failure arrives in full view."

The phone started ringing again.

"Don't answer, please; it's the press."

Juno was not sure which surprised her more, Abe's sudden resolution or his adding "please." It was not a token gesture of unexpected politeness. It was a declaration that he needed her help or they would both be sunk. He was now to be taken by surprise by constructive advice from his trophy wife.

"It's not all lost. Work through a plan now. Have it ready. Don't phone the lieutenant secretary. Use two intermediaries, say you're willing to resign from VIPS immediately—even apologize for a wrong-footed statement—yes, I know that will stick in your craw—on the understanding that they move you sideways to a comparable position and salary. That way you still have a job, we keep the house, survive financially, and the kids get through college. Brazen it out. In a couple of months, it'll all be forgotten."

"To whom should I ask to speak?"

"Two people who can't abide one another. In that way you'll be sure they will report much the same thing to the governor. Perhaps not personally, but through others, he will have to consider your suggestion, and reply to it."

"Do you think it will work?"

"Sure, you've been a good party regular. The state wants this crisis over and with as little damage to the party's reputation."

"What about Joan Winterland and Donny Dooley?"

"Perfect. Besides, I've always said, if Joannie doesn't like

241

Donny Dooley, she shouldn't have let her husband sleep with him. No wonder they can't abide one another—and, like Tia, they both want your job."

"It seems friends may come and friends may go but enemies not only go on forever but they also multiply."

Abe put his wife's plan into action. A skilled telephone flaneur, it was easier and less humiliating than he thought possible. After he had made his phone calls, he poured himself another bourbon. Feeling mellower, he wanted to reach out to Juno but felt clumsy.

"I just wanted to touch you," he simpered, like a green girl. He stopped short, looking over how ample Juno's figure had become through years of his neglect and, like her sister, her countless comfort breakfasts of hot dogs and ice cream. She read his mind.

"You wanted to reach out. And now I have so many places for you to touch me."

Abe and Juno were still ignoring the phone and the front door in case it was the press. But there was an e-mail from some new state functionary, asking them to expect a call at 3.00 PM precisely. When the phone rang, Abe was on top of it with feverish anxiety.

"That you, Abe? It's Vivien Petkoff, the governor's secretary. I'm sorry I was held up yesterday and could not reach you. When I did try, you were out," concluded Vivien Petkoff, not at all convincingly

"And?"

"Listen, Abe, we're in a fix and no mistake. Here's the thing: what can we do if our best players no longer want to work with you?"

"Why's that?"

"Your remark about blind people was most unfortunate— and it's on tape. Politically, you're in deep doo-doo—no integrity and the state simply can't entrust you with a socially responsible PC mission. Matters have gotten out of hand. The media is all over the story. You leave and we'll see about your suggestion for the future."

"Book me an appointment, make me an offer, and I'll go quietly. Otherwise, I'll fight this on the grounds of misrepresentation and unfair dismissal—and as a slight to disabled people—getting rid of the best advocate they've ever had in this state."

"You've got a brass neck, d'you know that?" was Vivien Petkoff's response. Then, "Can you be here in two hours' time? I'll clear the decks. We'll bring this little local difficulty to a head."

Juno was fast on the button.

"You have to use this once-only opportunity to show that you still have political momentum. That, by itself, means they have to give you an equivalent job in status and salary. Otherwise, you'll cause trouble, sniping from the side. Hone your farewell statement when you go for this interview and make it work for you. Don't let them think for a moment that your executive career is over for good. Bella mentioned when we spoke yesterday that the section head of primary education is leaving for a job in Massachusetts, so you could suggest that they move you sideways."

Abe now realized Juno's political acumen was sharper than his. They both fell silent as he scribbled away. Then he started to read his pearls of wisdom, inviting Juno's constructive comments.

"I have told the governor that I am resigning immediately as executive head of VIPS."

"Just before he could go ahead and fire you," came Juno's retort delivered with a snort.

"My humanitarian beliefs are grounded in my values as a born-again Christian. I believe that disabled people are capable of extraordinary achievements, provided they are given due support."

"What you mean is that you're originally from a blue-collar town and that you have a disabled younger brother (whom you've not bothered with for years) but snobs in the Capitol have always looked down on you."

Abe decided if he stopped at every sarcastic remark, they would get nowhere, so he continued.

"It is the duty of a progressive administration to empower disabled people along with all US citizens. I've never sought office for what I can get out of it, but for what I can achieve for disabled people whom I serve through my advocacy and fund-raising and organizing abilities. I did not go into disabled politics to make money out of blind people, despite the unfortunate row over my misunderstood remark."

"Good. Now get the governor and his crew to see that you mean business—that you mean to stay."

"In the next chapter of my career I will increase my efforts to promote the cause of disabled people—to give political voice for the dispossessed."

"In other words, you're saying, 'Get it through your fat, lazy heads that, in future, you won't be bound by mistaken tribal loyalty to collective responsibility. In fact, you're going to criticize the shortcomings of the present governor's administration openly and whenever you choose.'"

"In returning to the grassroots of disabled activism—where I began my political career—I am returning to the cut and thrust of political debate. Most of all, I want to help the Democratic party to renew its American obligation to disabled people, to remind them that their American dreams and aspirations are ours, too."

Using his trophy wife as dresser and chauffeuse, Abe was ready fifteen minutes after the appointed hour and had his two intermediaries, Joan Winterland and Donny Dooley, in tow. This proved his saving. Both the intermediaries did, indeed, covet his position as much as the disregarded deputy, Tia Schulberg. Therefore, the state found its collective hands tied.

Two weeks later, the *Courier* reported an announcement from the Capitol.

"Yesterday, the governor announced a new position for Abe Ripemoff as state director of primary education. Ripemoff, 53, formerly head of VIPS (Visually Impaired People's Services), was forced out of office after being caught on tape declaring that all blind people were ugly. He will now take office at a reduced salary of $55,000."

Three days later, the paper ran a story about protests by some disabled people's groups about the governor having moved Abe Ripemoff sideways. Through Freedom of Information legislation, they had found out that, whereas at VIPS, Ripemoff's salary had been $75,000, his new salary was not lower but higher, at $85,000.

But Juno's strategy did not work for everyone, not even her in-laws.

That autumn an unexpected, unseasonable brief fall of snow left her brother-in-law, Leo Guerra, feeling that the flakes were like morsels of passing time. His obsession with rank and position was as if he had a splinter of glass in his eye that prevented him from seeing the facts as everyone else saw them. Bored by inactivity, livid with his wife, and stymied by bureaucracy, almost every weekday, raddled Leo Guerra was on the phone to his attorney about his settlement.

"I want to be recognized for my achievements, to become an elder statesman and to be paid well for it."

But his lawyer, Tom Grady, while equally interested in the disgraced police chief's payoff, was not sympathetic to his hurt feelings.

"Elder statesmen, Leo? Sorry, my friend. Elder statesmen are politicians—politicians whose only achievement is to have survived despite their poor reputations. Abe Ripemoff's saving grace was his outstanding backslapping fundraising abilities with his banking friends.

"Don't even think of getting any sympathy. You chose to lead your life as a public figure. Surely by now you've learnt that the public arena is not the place to expect respect, approval, or understanding—let alone sympathy?"

The rhetorical question remained suspended in mid air and unanswered.

"And remember, Leo, no matter how bad things are between you and Bella, do not leave your house and go and live somewhere else. Lots of men who break up with their wives make that mistake. If you do, you'll never get back in—whatever the law says."

Leo's lawyer shifted gear: "You could consider working as a private eye—there's always a market of jealous spouses with more money than sense after errant partners. You've got the know-how."

"Yeah, yeah, yeah."

"I see you're ahead of me."

It was true. Leo Guerra looked up from his shabby brown desk through the opaque window panel of his shabby brown door where a sign painter was finishing the sign: "McGUFFIN PARTNERS: Private Detective Agency."

But before they finished the call, his lawyer said, "If you're looking for operatives and someone to mind the office, you could do worse than take on the preppy youngster who got to the bottom of your secret."

His attorney knew Leo would be fit to be tied at that suggestion.

"I know what you're thinking. But before you get on your high horse, think about it. Be practical. This guy is blind but he worked everything out. From what I hear, he can bend any lawyer's ear to see things his way and, because he's blind, people treat him as if he's the invisible man. He can pass through walls."

Candy sat cowering in Mistress's house, where she had

taken refuge with Sister Carrie Behan who was reading to her what the papers had to say about her. When Carrie finished, Candy pounced on what she read about herself, seized a newspaper, and stamped on it.

"Black prostitute? Black prostitute!"

"Well," said Mistress. "Someone had to tell you."

26 Pearls That Were His Eyes

The hospital had sent Luke an appointment to appraise his failing eyesight and to determine its impact on his other senses. Three days later, he found himself in a darkened sound booth, listening, first with one ear and then with the other, to high notes and acknowledging them with a klaxon button-pump.

"That's one test I'm sure of," he thought. "My hearing is acute."

Then he undertook another Goldman field test, first with one eye and then with the other, pressing another button in response to diminutive spots of light within a circle to plot his field of vision. Tired at the end of the tests, he almost nodded off before two doctors, one for eyes, one for ears, met him with Dr. Chicago.

"We don't want this to come over like a family intervention," said Dr. Chicago. "But my colleagues tell me that you have some hearing loss—definitely on high notes. It's not total. It may be what's sometimes termed SAD—severe auditory dysfunction. This means that your ears hear but your brain doesn't process correctly what you do hear. That, combined with the damage to your sight, is causing you these bouts of unsteadiness, dizzy spells, and loss of balance. In a word, you have vertigo. We can prescribe repeated eardrops that will heal periodic ear infections but vertigo will recur.

"We also have to get you to a designated clinic to see about digital hearing aids. You will hear better and your hearing better will help these problems of balance. There is a category of disability that is deaf-blind. You have problems with sight and sound: we have to monitor you."

Luke was stunned. Dr. Chicago could tell he was also worried about costs but Dr. Chicago was ready for him.

"The good news is that, because your case is interesting medically, we believe there is a way to pay for your appointments and treatment.

"There is a program at the National Institutes of Health in Bethesda, Maryland. Government scientists study special cases in all fields to help future patients. We would like to recommend you for one of their research programs. Travelling and attendance are supported by the federal government—paid for."

Luke had travelled so far without moving at all that he could respond in no other way than wordless resignation. He did not think he would have the energy to apply himself to the Labor Tribunal that afternoon.

Luke's lawyer, Ben Johnson, said as he drove him to the Labor Tribunal, "Don't be nervous. Justin Dashiell, the lawyer for the TV station—he's often been my adversary and every time I've won the case. We got a good break with Opal Pearl, as you'll see."

"Another thing—just so that you're aware: I know you have residual vision and that you make good use of it. Justin Dashiell—when he was younger—a German shepherd dog mauled his face. He didn't want plastic surgery. He's still scarred and he can look scary in the wrong light. Plus his manner leaves a lot to be desired."

This left Luke more, not less, apprehensive.

Luke's lawyer was addressing the tiny Labor Tribunal, held in the Department of Labor, adjacent to Art's Atelier, part of the same lengthy block built in World War II for the manufacture of extensive coils of war materiel wire. The interior design was bland with cream walls subdivided by a maze of five-feet-high gray cubicles circling out from the few floor-to-ceiling offices reserved for sensitive business: hearings and disputes.

"Network News Norse Hoven takes great pains to emphasize that it is an equal-opportunities employer, providing work for disabled people on the same terms as everyone else. But, in the sad experience of my client, Luke Reader, who is blind, NNNH fails to practice what it professes. Mr. Reader was prevented from presenting the story about the police chief's ill-fated liaison with a disabled girl on the Late Night News, although he, himself, had broken the crucial story and had been promised the segment."

The opposition was ready.

"The reality is more complex: Mr. Reader is a novice journalist and others with more experience were better suited to the story. An internal enquiry has concluded that there was no evidence of discrimination. Mr. Reader's response has been unreasonable—angry. The studio has sent employees on disability-awareness day courses—"

"—Only because adverse publicity over this case has made NNNH embarrassed at its shortcomings," interrupted Luke's lawyer.

"As to other journalists being more experienced, not one of them was able to detect this scoop, let alone break it, because none had the necessary skills and insight"—he savored the word—"even though the story was right under their noses. The police precinct is opposite the studio. Moreover, this important story has had wide-ranging political repercussions."

When the moderator asked Luke to speak, he was only able to do so with clarity because he had rehearsed what he would say. Instead of it coming out as if by rote, it sounded deeply personal. Instead of denying he had been ever been angry with Dolly Drum Dong (which was the truth) and rebutting her false written deposition, Luke took the opposition by surprise by seeming to agree with them. He turned this apparent liability into an unarguable plea for justice.

"Yes, sometimes, disabled people feel anger and their anger is righteous. When it comes to such idiotic ideas of my disability in the workplace and what I can and cannot do, of course I confront the injustice of it all. I had to work significantly harder than others at NNNH simply because I'm blind. The studio expects me to prove my worth each and every time."

Luke sensed that the moderator had relaxed when he spoke. It was as if Luke and his attorney were doing his job for him, making it easier for him to achieve a favorable decision.

Ben Johnson said, "I also put it to the tribunal that Network News Norse Hoven is rife with disability discrimination and other prejudices."

With the moderator's permission, he called Opal Pearl into the room. She had no turban. She had a buzz cut adorned with an indigo bandanna, the same color as her sleeveless dress.

Opal gave her evidence. Her temp agency had sent her to NNNH for a few months to replace Steve Sharp's secretary who was on maternity leave. It seemed Opal had considerable secretarial skills and had worked for several years as secretary to the senior partner in a law firm in downtown Norse Hoven.

"Why did you leave?"

"I was diagnosed with breast cancer and became too weak to continue work."

"What was the treatment?"

"After some chemotherapy the doctors told me that the only way to save my life was a double mastectomy."

The little tribunal fell completely silent—not that anyone else had been talking. Luke's lawyer wanted Opal's statement to sink in. Now the tight little room seemed drained of everything but shock and apprehension. Luke was jolted sure enough and came back to earth as Opal was telling the tribunal how difficult it was to find her courage and get back to work. She had started all over again as a temp and then applied to NNNH.

"How did Network News Norse Hoven accommodate you?"

"When they interviewed me, Human Resources assured me that the studio would appreciate my skills and experience—accommodate—your word—my circumstances—be understanding about my health—and so on."

"And did they?"

"No. Almost the reverse."

"What were the problems?"

"First, the new acting head of Business, Dolly Drum Dong, always insisted on extra work, long hours. Also, she appropriated me to do her work on top of my work for Steve so, overall, I simply had too much to do and I was always exhausted."

"Anything else?"

Luke's lawyer knew his adversary looked like thunder and he relished that discomfort.

"Yes, everything was sexist. The head honcho in New York—I think that's Todd Carter Fox—made lewd remarks on the phone about my breasts—and, of course, I don't have any.

"I heard my boss, Steve Sharp, and his boss, Todd Carter Fox, talking about Luke Reader. It was as if Luke was a commodity, an embarrassment, too disabled to be put on

251

camera. It was awful. Then, more jibes about my breasts. The conversation was on speaker phone so I heard both sides of it: Todd Carter Fox as well as Steve Sharp."

"Anything else?"

"Because I was working for Steve Sharp and Dolly Drum Dong, I was a target of jealousy from some secretaries who'd been there longer than me."

"What form did this jealousy take?"

"They sent me these in the internal mail."

She opened a large padded manila envelope. It contained two pouches like malleable chicken breasts; indeed, they were false breasts.

"Eventually, the pressure got so great. I couldn't take it—the insults—and I left in tears in the middle of my shift just after Steve's conversation with Todd Carter Fox about Luke."

Luke's lawyer said, "I rest my case about discrimination—sexist and disability—being endemic in the workplace of Network News Norse Hoven."

Justin Dashiell, looking even more furious, asked for a break and left the room. Nothing was said but Luke sensed his lawyer was winking at him. Then the studio's lawyer returned and asked Luke's lawyer to step outside.

Luke and the arbitrator looked blankly at one another.

"I think they may make you an offer," added the arbitrator *sotto voce* as he looked at the ceiling.

And, indeed, that was it. Luke's lawyer returned, and asked the arbitrator if they could both be excused momentarily.

Outside, he told Luke, "They've made an offer in exchange for your silence. They offered $40,000 for hurt feelings, unprofessional behavior by their human resources manager, etcetera. I told them to stuff it. Then, they upped the ante to $70,000. It's your call, of course, but I recommend you take it.

"You may not get TV work for some time but, since your federal pension starts soon and, when it does, it puts restraints on how you can work and how much you can earn, anyway—and all this comes just prior to that pension—this is probably your most practical option. The other price you pay is silence: no press interviews, no going into print on your own."

Luke's legal eagle thought that Luke would be delighted and could not understand his seeming absent-mindedness.

"Okay, I'll accept your advice."

The lawyer disappeared and then reappeared to say, "It's a deal."

The arbitrator looked relieved.

As Luke was getting into the lawyer's car outside to be driven home to Hermione, studio lawyer Justin Dashiell came right up and said with cold venom to Ben Johnson: "I hope you're satisfied with this. The studio director, Todd Carter Fox, and other top executives cannot take their expected bonuses—hundreds of thousands of dollars—for the second year running because their board has ruled that the network has missed its disability recruitment targets. And for what? A sleaze story worthy of the *National Enquirer*? Are you expecting a bouquet of flowers?"

Luke's lawyer grinned broadly and spat back:

"Orchids are bred to grow with great slowness. Todd doesn't deserve them any more than his bonus. I'll see you in court on the Bauer case next week."

As they drove off Ben said, "Opal Pearl—she's a diamond—made our case. Her pearls were your eyes. We owe her big. Because she was a temp, she cannot take the studio to the Labor Tribunal. Technically, it is the temp agency that employs her and yet what happened is clearly not their fault. But she came through for you."

"I know what Hermione will say about the Labor Tribunal."

"Told you so?"

"No, she'll say, 'Women to the rescue. Your story so far.'"

While they were driving along Sizewell, Ben said, "Kid, you did good. Why so silent?"

Luke told him he was losing his hearing.

"I don't know what to say to Hermione. First, I'm going to call Opal Pearl."

"You really like her."

"She's the most perfect girl I've ever met."

As a youngster, Marie Louise had never been able to go on any school trip because no teacher would accept responsibility for her. Now, as a yuppie professional with some disposable income, she determined to make up for lost time. And Italy was her first choice. After a night in his apartment on Central Park West, her brother, Todd would drive Marie Louise to Kennedy Airport for her overnight flight to Rome, the eternal city, at the start of a package tour of Italy, paid for by Todd and Gina.

Marie Louise was a compact packer. For her Italian tour, she took only a few girlie clothes in an expandable child's suitcase on wheels. For easy identification, in case it might get mixed up with others at bus loading bays and airport carousels, Gina had identified it with Marie Louise's hallmark polka dots.

At Kennedy Airport travelers and staff were aghast. None was more so than the Japanese student sitting next to Marie Louise on the overnight plane. After a few words of conversation, she discovered she would be Marie Louise's constant companion on the tour. She had, using her father's status as a UN diplomat, already angled for a front seat on the coach behind the courier nearest the great front picture window. Now she realized, to her evident chagrin, that she would have to share this optimum vantage point with its landscape panoramas, courier's special attention, and, every night, bedrooms and bathrooms, with this deformed parody of human entity.

Marie Louise smiled back at her discomfort with grim determination.

"It's not as if I'm Hannibal Lecter. Or am I?"

After the plane landed in Rome, the handler designated by the airport conducted Marie Louise in a wheelchair through immigration, baggage claim, and customs. At every process the worthy staff adopted a mask of courtesy through gritted teeth. None more so than waiting tour courier Mario in blue blazer, all camp smiles that hardened when his flinty eyes first focused on the dot of scrawny flesh at his knees.

A gaggle of English schoolgirls from a different plane milled around, giggling with anticipated delight. Marie Louise waited patiently for the crowd to disperse. Then, she noticed a stick with some leather on the floor that had probably come adrift from some suitcase. She bent down and picked it up.

"Riding crop?" she wondered.

Momentarily keeping his equilibrium to rally the rest of his American and Australian flock, tour guide Mario began.

"Signore e signori, benvenuti all citta eterna, benvenuti a Roma. Io sono la vostra guida turistica. Welcome to Rome, your eternal city. I am your courier."

He was an accomplished flaneur.

"Our coach is just outside. It's red. Il nostro pullman e nel parcheggio che si trova in fondo."

"Go through the last doors and turn to the right and there you will see it. Andate diritto fino all'ultima porta a destra, poi uscite e vedrete il parcheggio dall'altra parte della strada. Il nostro Pullman, e quello rosso. Sopra c'e sento, 'Viaggio Forcellini.'"

"Follow me and my little red flag."

The thirty-plus group proceeded, the women trailing

their bags on wheels, the older men clasping their bags under their arms, the younger ones hoisting them on their shoulders.

Marie Louise gasped. She realized she could not see between the ranks of moving people. Just how far would they have to go to the exit? The corridors were palatial in length if not décor.

Now without her wheelchair, Marie Louise was tottering along. She quickly sensed that her group was getting farther and farther ahead of her. Passengers from other airlines, other tours, further interrupted her limited perspective all jostling one another. Her stumpy little legs moved as fast as they could but not fast enough. Fatigue set in.

Suddenly, she thought to herself: "What would streetwise Della do?"

When a space cleared, she realized the group was getting smaller as it began to move out of sight. But it was not out of earshot from someone expert in street lingo. Marie Louise stopped dead in her tracks and stood quailing on tiptoes. Using her streetwise vocabulary and her perfected street accent learned from Della, she cried out, "Get back here you mother-fuckers!"

She was yelling with the full force of her tiny cramped lungs, shaking her voice along the airport corridor like the tiniest of fists. But it resonated.

"You dickheads, this is my vacation as much as yours."

Then, playing her disabled card for all it was worth, she went on hoarsely: "I paid my dues. I expect to be treated with consideration. Mario, get your fat ass back here and give a hand."

It seemed that the entire airport froze. All tongues were suddenly silenced. The entire world involuntarily revealed it understood the crudest English from all-American streets. Rooted to the core by Marie Louise's calling his name out to the wide world, Mario scuttled back shamefaced.

"Mille grazie signorina. Perdono il mio errore. I apologize sincerely for my oversight. I will help you. Momento, tutte le gente."

A trolley appeared from nowhere. Marie Louise was hoisted upon it atop her luggage and propelled along the walkway. Swinging the riding crop, she thought of herself as Doris Day as Calamity Jane whipping the Deadwood Stage to heel until she and Mario reached the assembled throng of anxious package tourists, newly apprehensive of Little Miss Dynamite in their midst.

On an Indian summer day in October, Luke was lying on his bed in his dusty, dusty room, listening to a treasured CD. When he lay down, it was as if he were trying to draw strength from the white bedside fan whirring away as its breeze obliterated the rest of the world.

Hermione called up to him. When Luke did not hear her, she came into his room.

"Luke, you need to take this call—it's from the publishers of the great and the good."

"Hi, kiddo," said that familiar voice, as if they had spoken only yesterday.

"It's Mickey Garnier. How're you doin? I'll get straight to the point. We want you back. You don't need to explain. We don't need your eyesight. This decade, editors focused on editing books; this coming decade, editors won't be editing books, they will utilize their contacts with agents. You've got the gift of the gab. It's the Irish in you. You will be an acquisitions editor. You won't need to look; far less to see; far less to read—just to acquire. What d'ya say?"

Before Luke could reply, Hermione touched his sleeve.

"You have another call, Luke dear, on the other line. It's Leo Guerra."

"Leo Guerra? The ex-police chief? What does he want? Shout at me? Turn back the clock? Undo the damage he caused?"

"I don't think so," Hermione whispered. "Don't get rattled. I think he's going to offer you a job. What will you do?"

Luke should not have been surprised. After all, he was Luke Reader, blind seer.

To Be Continued

ABOUT THE AUTHOR

After studies at Oxford and Yale, Sean Dennis Cashman combined careers as a professor of American history and a writer, principally for New York University Press and The Ford Foundation, and as a music and theater journalist in New Haven, Connecticut. His classic history for NYU Press, *America in the Gilded Age*, has remained a focal text on the period 1865–1901 since it was first published in 1984.

He is a member of the Howard League for Penal Reform and Action Aid and works as a volunteer for the BBC Philharmonic Orchestra.

SEAN DENNIS CASHMAN

AMERICA

FROM THE DEATH OF LINCOLN TO

IN THE

THE RISE OF THEODORE ROOSEVELT

GILDED

THIRD EDITION

AGE

REVIEWS

America in the Gilded Age: From the Death of Lincoln to the Rise of Theodore Roosevelt
New York University Press: first edition, 1984; second edition, 1988; third edition, 1993: 400 pages, 60 illustrations, hardback and paper

"The writing is clear, graceful and lively. An excellent collection of photographs enhances the attractiveness and persuasiveness of the written presentation."
The Historian

"A lively, often entertaining, and generally well-balanced treatment of the period between the end of the Civil War and the turn of the century . . . enlivened by the lavish use of illustrations, the selection of colorful, often amusing anecdotes and by the author's gift for the memorable phrase."
History

"The Gilded Age in American history has presented a myriad of problems to textbook authors . . . In this comprehensive survey Sean Dennis Cashman has integrated the period's complex issues, themes, problems, and responses into a lucid and perceptive examination of the era. This wide-ranging work is a fine synthesis of primary research and recent scholarship that emphasizes personalities of the age without slighting the overriding issues. Furthermore, the frequent use of anecdotes and occasional comparisons to recent historical events enhances readability and adds color to what many college students consider a colorless period . . . The anecdotal style and emphasis on personalities should delight students who read this work."
Journal of Economic History

"This book is a delight to read. It is loaded with interesting data that makes history consuming. There are many helpful illustrations, a complete index, and an engaging reading list. In all, this is the work of a competent historian who has made his subject both instructive and fun."
Kliatt Paperback Book Guide

AMERICA
ASCENDANT

From Theodore Roosevelt to FDR
in the Century of American Power, 1901-1945

SEAN DENNIS CASHMAN

America Ascendant: From Theodore Roosevelt to FDR in the Century of American Power, 1901–1945
New York University Press, 1998: 562 pages, 104 illustrations, hardback and paper

"There is no shortage of general histories of the United States. They come in all sizes (one, two, and multi-volumes), colors (social, economic, political complexion), and shapes (hardcover, softcover, electronic). Sean Dennis Cashman has come forward with a brilliant book in this competitive market, and he has done so with no gimmicks or flashy printing . . . an excellent synthesis of the history of the United States from Theodore Roosevelt's succession to the Presidency in 1901 to Franklin D. Roosevelt's death in 1945 or, actually, the end of the war in the Pacific . . . Race, ethnicity, and gender are discussed in every decade, particularly in terms of the degree to which changing status or circumstances presented what were perceived as threats to the existing social order . . . The reader receives a strong sense of the backward and forward movement of these groups in a society constantly in flux, shaped by and shaping the political tone of the day . . . The book ends . . . with the United States poised to assume world leadership in the second half of the twentieth century.

"Perhaps a greater achievement than the political/social/diplomatic history of the book is the discussion and commentary on several other aspects of life in early twentieth-century America that are often neglected. Those topics are the impact of technology and popular mass culture, both elusive subjects with which to deal in general terms . . . The importance of the automobile ripples through American society from the impact of Henry Ford's assembly-line manufacturing techniques to the social implications of widespread personal transportation to changes to the rural landscape through both mechanization and depopulation . . . Cashman also discusses the development of commercial airlines, explaining the steady improvements of airplane design, the organization of airline companies for both domestic and overseas travel . . . Cashman takes a serious look at both popular culture and high culture . . . how the invention and widespread accessibility of the record player and then the rapid spread of the radio created a whole new dimension of popular culture . . . the growth of the motion picture studios, the system of distribution through studio owned theatres, the emergence of 'stars,' and specific movies that had an impact on the public consciousness. High culture, particularly novels, plays, and poetry, is seriously examined, with a discussion of what key writers were attempting to do.

"*America Ascendant* is a very sound history of the United States in the early twentieth century, and it presents a very broad picture of the country . . . Cashman suggests that the United States had the energy to struggle with its problems to reshape itself in each generation, and to create a new social culture. The book reads well and has a compelling fascination."

Francis M. Carroll, co-author of the *Free and the Unfree*, in *Canadian Journal of History*, December 2000

263

www.ingramcontent.com/pod-product-compliance
Lightning Source LLC
Chambersburg PA
CBHW031937240626
47153CB00003B/772